A SHAMWELL TALES NOVEL

SPUN!

JL MERROW

RIPTIDE
PUBLISHING

This book is dedicated to Jofli Aloysius, a Most Excellent Bear.

It's tough for a natural hooker to give it up.
— Ian Chappell, former Australian cricketer

TABLE OF CONTENTS

CHAPTER ONE
THE END, PART ONE

David leaned on the balcony, gazing out over his boss Charles's unimaginatively landscaped garden, its edges softened by the relentless drizzle that had made a washout of the firm's annual garden party. He sighed. If the tops of the boxwood hedges had been clipped to resemble not bizarrely deformed peacocks and unappetising Turkey Twizzlers but instead the letters *e*, *n*, *n*, *u*, and *i*, they'd have summed up his mood to a redundant *t*.

He turned to glance tipsily at the man beside him—someone he'd never seen before, so it was probably safe to go for a touch of candour. "God, this party is dull. This house is dull. Life is dull, dull, dull." He raised his champagne flute to knock back the contents, and pouted to find he'd already done so.

"Let me," a deliciously cultured voice purred in his ear.

David blinked at the champagne bottle now hovering over his glass, courtesy of his unknown companion. "I thought we were on the cheap stuff?"

"Not if you happen to know where Charles keeps the decent bottles." The stand-in sommelier tapped his nose in an impressive display of coordination, and David made an effort to focus on him. "I'm Xav, by the way."

Xav—*my xaviour*, David's inner damsel gushed—was tall and lean, with artfully floppy grey hair and a pair of roguish green eyes that twinkled with promise. There was insouciance in his very stance.

Suddenly David's insides were fizzing, and it couldn't entirely be attributed to the bubbly. "David," he breathed. "But you can call me Davey. So how is it you know all of Charles's most intimate secrets?"

Xav leaned closer. "I could tell you, David . . ."

"But then you'd have to eat me?" David finished for him in hope.

"Oh, I'm planning on doing that in any event," Xav murmured. "But in fact it's frightfully banal. Charles is my brother-in-law."

David barely had time to reflect what a marvellous thing it was that siblings could be so completely unalike as Xav and Charles's wife, Traute, before Xav continued, "Now, I think that's enough chitchat, don't you?"

David found himself seized and kissed to within an inch of his sanity. After that, matters soon came to, well, a head, and David was on his knees, willingly sucking down Xav's sizeable manhood.

Then the curtains, which had at some point closed behind them, were flung open. There was a shrill cry of "*Xavier*!" followed by a hand which clapped David's shoulder with bruising force and yanked him away from his task.

Oops. David twisted and came face-to-face with his employer, who was visibly quivering with ire.

Charles's complexion, never precisely dewy, was now livid puce. "You disgusting little fairy. What the bloody hell do you think you're playing at?"

David wiped his mouth on the back of his hand, but before he could speak, Xav, who'd zipped up with impressive and, dare one say it, *practiced* speed, was striding past him towards a tall, elegantly trousered woman who bore a marked resemblance to Charles's wife.

"Marthe, darling, I'm so sorry. I think I may have had a little too much to drink. I don't know how this can have happened . . ." Xav waved a graceful—and dismissive—hand in David's direction.

Marthe's lip curled as she looked down her stately nose at David, then softened as she turned back to Xav. "Poor darling. I'll get you some coffee."

David blinked at them.

Ah. Not the wife's brother. The wife's sister's husband. Language, he felt rather strongly, really ought to be more precise about such things. He clambered to his feet. "Bit of a misunderstanding, there," he started with a nervous laugh.

Charles looked like a stroke was an imminent possibility. "Get out of my house," he said icily. "And don't bother coming in to work on Monday. You're fired. If I ever see you again, I'll set the bloody dogs on you."

David wove his unsteady way out of the room, to the accompaniment of shocked whispers, muttered censure, and Xav's protestations of undying love to his spouse.

On the whole, he'd liked the party better when it had been dull.

CHAPTER TWO
THE END, PART TWO

Rory took in Jenni's folded arms and narrowed eyes. He wasn't great on body language and all that guff, but he reckoned she might be mad at him again. "All right, love?" he asked warily.

"Let's see, shall we? Do I have a wedding to go to tomorrow? Yes, I do. Have I got my hat sorted, and the matching handbag and shoes? Yep, all present and correct. Have I got my frock, the one what you promised on your mother's *life* to pick up from the dry cleaner's tonight, cos there won't be time to go in tomorrow before we have to drive up to Sheffield?" She paused and tapped her foot while Rory's stomach did its best to make for safety in Australia. "Well, have I? Cos if it's in your pocket, all I can say is it's shrunk in the bleedin' wash."

Shit. Shit, shit, shit, and . . . shit. "I'm sorry, Jen. See, Barry called me up and said he was having major stress at work and could I meet him for a pint. And I was gonna get the dress, honest I was, but, um. I just forgot. Sorry." He tried to radiate sincere regret, but had a nasty suspicion he was just making that face his ex-wife Evie had always said looked like a constipated hamster.

Jen's expression softened, and for a moment there, Rory thought he was going to get away with it. Then she spoke. "Oh, love. It's not gonna work."

"You mean picking it up tomorrow?"

"No, I mean this. You. Me. Us."

Oh, buggering shit. "I'll make it up to you, I swear. I'll buy you a new dress. Like, a really posh one. And I'll . . . do all the dishes for a month. And the cooking." Rory wanted to cross his fingers, but that'd look well daft, so he crossed his toes instead, cos she couldn't see them inside his shoes.

Except he'd taken his shoes off when he came in, hadn't he? Oops.

"What, you? Cook? That's adding injury to insult, that is." Jenni smiled, but it was twisted. "It's not just the dress. It's all the other stuff too. What about that time we was supposed to be going out for the day with my Patrick and his Mark, and you ended up blowing me off when Barry got in a paddy over his wife's birthday present?"

"You said you didn't mind. You said it was all right, cos it wasn't like you'd be on your own."

"Well, of course I *said* that. I didn't want to make you feel bad about it. I mean, he is your best mate. And if it'd only been that one time . . . but it wasn't, was it? There's been meals out we booked and had to cancel, and all them nights I've ended up on the sofa on me lonesome when you promised me we'd have an evening in together. And I grant you, some of them times was cos you had your kids over unexpected, and I'd never grudge you that, but a lot of them wasn't. Rory, love, I need a bloke I can rely on. All I can rely on you to do is to drop everything and go running as soon as Barry crooks his little finger in your direction."

"But—"

"No. I've made up my mind." She unfolded her arms and stepped forward to give Rory a hug. Her familiar clean scent, a mix of coconut body butter and hospital disinfectant, flooded his nose one last time.

Funny how it'd never made his eyes water until now.

"You'll be fine, love," she went on. "It's not like when your ex left you for that bloke and everyone knew she'd been messing around on you. This is just us accepting it's not gonna work. And you don't need to worry I'll be doing you down to half the village like she did, neither. I'll tell everyone this was a mutual decision, yeah? That we realised we didn't have as much in common as we'd thought."

Rory nodded and forced a smile as they stepped apart. "Course. Um. What about tomorrow? You still want me to come?"

"What, as my plus one to a wedding the day after we split up? I'm not that much of a cow. No, I'll go on my own, and you can have your Saturday watching the sport with Barry like you always wanted anyway."

Well, there was that. Rory tried to console himself with the prospect of a lads' day of beer and telly as he made his lonely way back to his house on Pig Lane.

It didn't seem to be working very well.

CHAPTER THREE
THE BEGINNING

Three weeks after the Garden Party of Doom, David checked his reflection in the full-length mirror in Ryan and Samir's bedroom. Technically, the room was supposed to be off-limits to him while he camped out on their sofa under a spare blanket and a large amount of sufferance on Samir's part—honestly, David might have had a bit of a *tendresse* for Ryan back when Ryan and Samir were first getting coupled up, but that didn't mean he had designs on him *now*—but he felt sure they'd have agreed, had they been here, that this was an emergency.

After all, wasn't this about getting him out of their hair? Figuratively speaking, as both had, with encroaching baldness, embraced the fully shaven look. Their heads, seen over the back of the sofa, now resembled nothing so much as a couple of ethnically diverse hen's eggs snuggled up for warmth.

That comment hadn't gone down at *all* well. Hence, today's mission. And the mirror.

Not too bad, even if he did say so himself. His tailored shirt clung in all the right places—not, in David's considered opinion, that there were actually any *wrong* places for a little clinging to occur. It emphasised his trim waist and made him seem at least six inches taller, while its deep-purple colour set off his pale complexion and dark hair beautifully. His super-skinny black jeans added a casual note, and not incidentally clove lovingly to what had more than once been described as a pair of rather finely sculpted buttocks. Hmm. Should he add a belt? Perhaps the one with the large silver buckle that drew attention to certain other assets?

"What do you think, Gregory?" he mused aloud. "To flaunt, or not to flaunt, that is the question."

Gregory, being a teddy bear of very little voice, said nothing.

"I think *not*," David said decisively.

He frowned at Gregory, who was perched on Ryan and Samir's bed. This was perfectly allowable; the prohibition had only been regarding *David* laying a finger on their specially imported Tom of Finland duvet cover. He'd therefore felt nary a qualm in placing Gregory strategically on one bulging, denim-clad crotch. When you were a teddy bear, you had to take your thrills where you could find them.

"Don't look at me like that. There are, believe it or not, times when discretion really is the better part of valour. And I'm almost positive that turning up at the house of your ex-crush and his current boyfriend to beg a favour is one of them." Samir's lukewarm reception had, David felt uncomfortably sure, been merely a pale reflection of the antagonism he was likely to encounter from Patrick upon arriving at his and Mark's rural idyll.

Gregory's glassy-eyed stare seemed to show a certain cynicism.

"I said ex-crush, and I *meant* ex-crush. Ex, ex, *ex*. Oh, bugger it. Now you've made me think of Xavier. And look at you—you're not even ready to go yet." David retrieved Gregory from his place in 1970s gay heaven, and marched out of the bedroom, pausing at the door to check no trace of his penetration into Ryan and Samir's inner sanctum remained.

Then he took the tiny deerstalker from its temporary home on the living room mantelpiece and fastened it securely onto Gregory's head with the attached elastic. "There. You're a perfect little classic Holmes. Try not to have an identity crisis."

Now, to drive or not to drive? Hmm. Although it was a crying shame to leave Mrs. Merdle, his lovely sunset-orange MG GS— bought, with exquisite irony, mere weeks before he'd lost his job—languishing in her garage, David instinctively felt that turning up, metaphorical cap in hand, at the wheel of a brand-new car wouldn't be the best way to get results. Public transport it was, then. Not without some difficulty, he slid his Oyster card into his back pocket.

Still, David rather liked travelling by Underground. True, it was death to any kind of grooming—particularly the Northern Line, which always left him feeling as if he'd indulged in a bit of rough trade in an abandoned coal bunker and then spritzed lightly with eau de burnt diesel—but you saw such fascinating people on the Tube. And people always seemed so interested in *him*, particularly whenever he took Gregory along for the ride.

Today was no exception. By the time he'd made his way across town to St. Pancras, David had starred in three strangers' selfies, had four people compliment him on his teddy bear, and fended off a couple of queries as to where the *Sherlock* fan convention was taking place.

All in all, David was in a fabulous mood as he wandered through the station. St. Pancras was his favourite station too, with its high arched roof, its bright shopping arcade, and its street pianos. There was a music student—at least, he looked like a student, with his un-ironed shirt and vitamin-deprived pallor—pounding out something stolid and Russian-sounding on the piano just past Eurostar arrivals. A couple of Japanese tourists, or possibly his proud parents, were taking photos of him.

David smiled fondly and strolled on. There was a second piano farther down the main concourse, out of earshot of the first. On a whim, David set Gregory atop its scarred wooden frame and sat down to give a spirited, if slightly rusty, rendition of *Danse Macabre*, just to confuse people. When he glanced up at the end, quite a crowd had gathered, and the Japanese couple were now taking pictures of *him*.

So probably not maybe-a-music-student's parents. Either that or family relations were about to get a tad strained.

The journey out to Bishops Langley was boringly uneventful, although David *did* have an interesting philosophical discussion with a four-year-old as to whether grown-ups were allowed to have teddy bears.

"I'm so sorry about that," the mother said, fussing with her son's collar as David rose to get off the train. "I hope he wasn't bothering you too much."

"Oh, no." David beamed at the little family. "Future politician in the making." From the over-reliance on "My daddy says" in his arguments, he'd undoubtedly be a Tory, but one couldn't have everything.

A taxi took him the short distance from Bishops Langley to Shamwell, and before he knew it, David was knocking on Mark's door.

The first hint that things might not all go his way today came when the door opened to reveal, not Mark, but Patrick, his current lover. Or, as Patrick himself would no doubt put it, Mark's *lover*, period, but David was of the hope-springs-eternal persuasion when it came to attractive older men.

"Oh. It's you," Patrick said flatly.

The frosty welcome was, David felt, unfair. Patrick had been the one who'd got the guy, after all. Where was his magnanimity in victory? David beamed resolutely. "Can Mark come out to play?"

Patrick heaved a sigh. "*Mark?*" he yelled in the direction of the stairs.

There was the indistinct sound of Mark's voice.

"He'll be down in a minute. Coffee?"

"That would be lovely. The little moppet tells me you've moved in here now," David added, perhaps a tiny bit pointedly, as he followed his reluctant host into the living room. Patrick might have won in love, but David was still persona *tres* grata in Fen's life. He set Gregory down on the sofa and straightened his deerstalker.

"All going well?" he asked, scanning the room surreptitiously for signs of Patrick's invading presence. Was that a new throw on the armchair? There was definitely a new games console by the television. At least Patrick hadn't stooped to marking his territory with loved-up photos of him and Mark in blissful coupledom on the mantelpiece . . . Ah, there they were. On the bookshelf.

"Yeah. Fine." Patrick ran a hand over his hair, throwing a glance over to the stairs. "Fen's out with her boyfriend right now."

"That's a shame. That they're out, that is. Not about the boyfriend. Ollie seems like a charming young man, from what I've seen. And what Fen tells me in her frequent phone calls, of course. Still, we can have a cosy little threesome." David's cheeks were beginning to ache from all this determined smiling. Which was rather unfair seeing as Patrick wasn't even *trying*.

Patrick shook himself minutely. "I'll go put the kettle on."

David sighed and joined Gregory on the sofa. He steadfastly avoided looking at the bookshelf with its wanton flaunting of the fact that Mark was happier without him.

Mark's welcome, when he finally appeared, was infinitely better than his lover's had been. He was dressed in new-looking jeans and a shirt David wouldn't personally have worn had the alternative been a bondage harness and leather chaps at a meeting of the Westboro Baptist Church. Apparently Patrick had failed to exert a positive influence on Mark's clothing choices. David mourned for the lost opportunity to take the man in hand. So to speak.

"David, how are you?" Mark held out his arms to give David a much-needed hug. "I've been meaning to get in touch. I hear you're, ah, job hunting?"

David reluctantly pulled back from Mark's embrace and allowed his face to fall into tragic lines. "It's true. Charles and I have parted ways. Some things just *cannot* be endured. I was deaf to his pleading—"

Mark fixed him with a stern look. "Strange that. I happened to meet up with him for drinks the other day, and he told me he'd fired you for sexual misconduct."

"Sexual misconduct? I like that!" David puffed up his chest.

"So I've heard."

"That was *not* what it was like at all." David pouted, deflating. "How was I supposed to know the cock I was sucking belonged to another woman? It didn't have a ring on it. If you ask me, I'm the victim in all this."

"From what I've heard, you might have a case for unfair dismissal." Patrick, who'd appeared behind Mark, said it as though the words were being pulled from him along with his fingernails.

But he'd said it. Touched, David beamed at him. "I knew you liked me really."

"Yeah, don't push it."

"Are you interested in pursuing that?" Mark asked. "Do sit down, by the way."

They sat, David back on the sofa with Gregory, and Mark on the armchair with Patrick's throw. Patrick remained standing, rather pointedly, in David's opinion.

"I should probably say at once," Mark continued, "I feel something of a conflict of interest. While I certainly don't condone Charles's behaviour, I have tried to stay on friendly terms with him."

David put on a glum expression. Not only was it rather restful after all that manic smiling at Patrick, it also reflected his current mood much more closely. "Tell me honestly, do you think it'd be worth it? I suppose a payout might be nice, but what if it all goes horribly wrong and I end up owing thousands of pounds of legal costs? Or worse, having to go back to work for Charles? No, I think I'm going to have to take this one on the fine-boned yet masculine chin. I did wonder, though . . . Fen tells me you're starting a business?"

"Yes, that's right. Accountancy and tax services, but with a focus on small, local businesses and charitable organisations." Mark smiled, his eyes crinkling up rather winsomely at the corners. "Going back to my roots. You see, most local organisations are run by people without an accountancy background. You wouldn't believe how many people working for very worthy causes that would be eligible for lottery funding or other grants, don't apply for them. Apparently they find the paperwork too daunting. It's not simply a matter of filling in a form, you see. The organisation has to make sure their financial statements are in order and up-to-date as well."

David did *not* clap his hands together in glee, but it was a close-run thing. "That sounds like a lot of work for one man," he said slowly. "Don't forget, you wouldn't want to find business eating into your time with the little moppet again." He paused and gave Mark a significant look. "*Especially* now she's started going out with boys. You never can tell *what* might happen if you take your eye off the balls. So you know what you need?"

"Let me guess—" Patrick said dryly.

"A paperwork fairy!" David cut him off, beaming brightly at Mark in the hopes a hitherto latent talent for hypnosis would suddenly manifest itself in his hour of need. It always seemed to work in stories. "It'd be perfect—you'd have me for all the tedious drudgery, and you'd be able to concentrate on . . . on the nontedious, un-drudgey stuff." It was a weak finish, but David couldn't be expected to do his best work in the face of Patrick's unsubtle glare.

"Are you sure it would work for you?" Mark sounded doubtful. "I wouldn't be able to pay you anything like what you were getting in London. And then there's the travel out here to consider on top of that."

David took a deep breath. Crunch time. "As it turns out, London isn't actually an issue. You see, I'm a *teensy* bit short of somewhere to live. You know I was sharing the flat with Brian, the bisexual ballet dancer? Funny story, but he's fallen totally, *hopelessly* in love with one of Charles's daughters. The eldest one, thank God, or he'd have had to change his name to Brian the bye-bye-bollocks. He's even planning to get down on one knee to her, and *not* in the fun way. And apparently the whole prospect of parental approval—remember, ballet dancer—becomes a lot remoter if he's cohabiting *avec moi.*"

Mark frowned. "Wouldn't Charles be more worried about the bisexual thing? Than the ballet dancing, I mean."

"Please. Do you know how much the corps de ballet get paid? NHS nurses look upon them with pity. Homeless people accost them on the street and ply them with spare change and out-of-date sandwiches. Besides, give Bri-bri some credit. He's hardly going to be waving his bisexual *thing* in dear old Charles's face, no matter how fetching the colours on the flag."

"If he's that hard up, how's he going to manage the rent if you go?"

David shrugged. "Meh. Trust fund. Some people have all the luck."

Mark's frown deepened. It didn't enhance his appearance, making him rather resemble one of those overbred dogs with an excess-skin problem. Maybe David should suggest Botox? A teensy nip and tuck? Although possibly not at this *precise* moment. "Doesn't that render the whole low-pay question moot?" Mark asked at last.

David gave Gregory a helpless look. Gregory, being literally unable to help himself, returned it. "I know you're an accountant, but don't you think you're rather hung up on money?" He sighed. "In any case, the whole thing is moot as a moot hall. Whatever that is. Somewhere people gather to discuss pointless questions? He kicked me out three weeks ago, and I've been homeless ever since. Forced to wander the streets, begging for shelter—"

"Meaning what, exactly?" Patrick cut in, a little harshly for David's liking.

"*Meaning*, I've been camping out at a friend's." David sent him a hard stare. "It's horrible."

Patrick raised an eyebrow. "The welcome run out already?"

David suppressed a wince. Loyalty to Ryan and Samir—after all, they *had* helped him out in a pinch—and perhaps a smidge of embarrassed pride prevented him from letting Patrick know how close he'd come to the bone with that little riposte. "No. It's the sofa. Far too short and entirely too lumpy."

Patrick's expression didn't soften. "Have you tried checking for peas under the cushions, Princess?"

Mark coughed. "I'm sure we'd all agree it's not an ideal situation to be in. But what do you want from us?"

David crossed mental fingers and took a deep metaphorical breath. "*Well*, I was thinking, what with you having more spare rooms than you can shake a feather duster at, and the little moppet *et moi* getting on so famously, maybe I could come and stay with you for an, ah, indeterminate period? Just until I get back on my graceful and elegantly shod feet?"

David glanced at Patrick, and his heart sank. The forecast, it seemed, was for sudden squalls followed by a sharp drop in temperature. Violent storms were not ruled out.

Mark, who'd apparently also been taking note of Patrick's expression, turned back to David and coughed. "Ah . . ."

Time for the puppy-dog eyes. "*Pleeease*? They've told me I have to be out by the end of the month. You wouldn't make a teddy bear homeless, would you?" David waggled Gregory at them in illustration, then had to bend down to pick up a carelessly dropped meerschaum pipe.

When he looked up again, Mark's face was doing complex contortions reminiscent of someone with chronic constipation. "It's just, well, given the circumstances you and Patrick met under . . ."

"But nothing was going on between us! I mean, I'd have noticed. I was right there. In front of your crotch. Not a creature was stirring, not even a mouse. Although what a mouse might have been doing in there, I hate to think."

Patrick made a breathy noise. "So you wouldn't only be working together, you'd be living together too?"

"But not in the biblical sense," David stressed. "Would it help if I promise to avert my eyes every time Mark emerges from the bathroom in a skimpy towel, all hot and steamy? Or walks around in his boxers on laundry day? Or—"

"Mark, it's your house, your decision." Patrick turned on his heel and left the room.

Mark's gaze tracked him helplessly. "I'm sorry, David. I don't think it'd be a good idea. And it'd be confusing for Fen too—you know how, um, invested she got in the idea of you and me getting together a few months ago."

David's shoulders went all slumpy. "No, it's fine. I wouldn't want to be the cause of *another* broken home for the little moppet. Gregory and I will pack our bags and be on our way. There are plenty of hotels in London. And hostels for the homeless. And doorways, and railway bridges . . ."

"David, I'm sorry. I'd like to help, honestly I would. But don't you have any family?"

"There's Hen. My mother. But she lives out in darkest Kent, and I really think the commute up to Hertfordshire would be unmanageable." David frowned, although only slightly, so as not to cause wrinkles. He sometimes felt his looks were all he had going for him these days. "You know, when I abandoned you and the little moppet to the tender mercies of your young man, I'd been picturing them as significantly more tender. Is he always this much of a grump?"

"No, God, no. You've just caught him on a bad day." Mark's smile faltered as he caught David's searching gaze, and he went on hastily. "Patrick only found out this morning his mum's relationship has ended, and, well, he's a bit protective of her. Doesn't like her to be unhappy. She *said* it was a mutual agreement to split, but he thinks she's just putting on a brave face. And, you see, it was with a friend of ours, so it's awkward all round."

"Anyone I know?" David perked up minutely. The prospect of gossip could generally be counted upon to raise his spirits a tad, although today it was more of a micro-tad. Possibly even a pico-tad.

"I don't think so. Rory—he's one of the Spartans. A couple of years older than me." Mark's eyes widened. "Actually, there's a thought. He lives up on Pig Lane, and I'm pretty sure he's got a spare room. Maybe he'd be willing to have you as a lodger? I get the feeling he'd be glad of some extra money—he's divorced, with two children."

"Tell him how good I am with the little moppet," David urged.

"They don't live with him."

"Oh. Then tell him about my stunning good looks and winning personality?"

Mark laughed. "He's straight. Very straight."

"A minor detail. And subject to change without notice, I've always found."

"David, sex was what got you into this mess in the first place. I'd hold off on trying to seduce anyone else right now. Besides, I don't think Patrick would be happy."

"What wouldn't Patrick be happy about?" said the man himself, standing in the doorway with his arms folded, the epitome of a stern, macho patriarch.

David was starting to see a glimmer of what Mark liked about him.

Mark coughed. "Oh, ah, we were talking about the possibility of David living with Rory. As a lodger," he added a tad too quickly and with just a smidge too much emphasis.

Patrick blinked. Then he smiled what David liked to think of as an Evil Vizier smile, although it'd be equally at home on the face of a shark spying a lone swimmer who'd ventured out too far on a particularly choppy day when he also happened to be wearing swimming trunks made out of bacon. "Yeah, that'd be a solution. Why don't you have a word with him?"

David wondered if the smile of foreboding was meant for him, or for that faithless seducer of mothers, Rory.

CHAPTER FOUR

R ory frowned and took another gulp of beer while he tried to get his head round it. "So this bloke you want to bung in my spare room, he's your ex?"

They were in the Three Lions, which was a friendly, old-fashioned village pub, all warm colours and low, beamed ceilings. The sort of place you'd want to go and drink at even if it wasn't your local, and that gave you a happy, smug feeling if it was. They had regular quiz nights and a weekly meat raffle, and if Rory came in on his own, there was nearly always someone he knew propping up the bar or watching sport on the wide-screen telly.

Mark put down his pint and shook his head emphatically, foam still clinging to his upper lip. "No, no. My ex-PA. And future business partner. Or, well, employee, really."

"So he's not gay, then?" Rory wondered if this bloke was divorced too, like him and Mark, and hoped if he was, he wouldn't be the sort to go on about his ex all the time. Rory had used to go on about *his* ex all the time, Barry reckoned, and apparently it had got right on everyone's tits.

Mark got a funny look in his eye. "Would it be a problem for you if he was?"

"Nah, course not." Rory was offended Mark had asked, cos him and Mark were mates, and Mark was gay. And the same with Patrick, 'cept *he* kept saying he was bi, despite the fact Rory hadn't seen him snog a girl once since he'd started going out with Mark.

"Good. Because he is." Mark paused, as if he was gonna say something else about this gay PA bloke, but then he coughed and just said, "Same again?"

"My shout," Rory said, cos it was, and got up to get the drinks in.

He had some time to think about it while he was standing at the bar. Not that it was all that busy in the Three Lions tonight, it being a Tuesday and there not being any footie on, but Trev, the landlord, had gone off to change a barrel and Trixie was on her own pulling pints, so he had to wait his turn.

Would it be weird living with a gay bloke? Gay blokes liked . . . musicals and stuff, didn't they? That'd be okay. Long as he wasn't into *Les Mis*. When Rory took his kids to see the stage show, he'd cried so much it'd been well embarrassing, and the film had been even worse. But yeah, he could cope with musicals on the telly every now and then. Happy ones, like *Mamma Mia!* or *Billy Elliot*.

It wasn't like he'd ever tell Barry this, but sometimes, Rory reckoned you could watch a bit too much sport.

And there'd be the—what did they call it now?—*grooming* thing. Hair products in the bathroom and all that. Still, couldn't be that different to living with a woman, could it? And Rory had liked that, when him and Evie had still been together, or the nights he'd stayed over at Jen's. Which hadn't been that often, seeing as Patrick had been living there most of the time they'd been going out. Bit of a passion-killer, that'd been, having a mate looking at him sideways when he'd been trying to snuggle up with his girl. It'd been nice, though, having someone who'd smelled good and had given him an excuse to watch rom-coms on the telly. Gay blokes were into that sort of film too, weren't they?

Course, it probably wouldn't be *quite* the same.

For one thing, there'd be no cuddling up on the sofa under a blanket with a bottle of plonk and a big bag of cheesy Wotsits. Rory missed that. Although he didn't miss getting told off for getting orange fingerprints all over the blanket. Or the moaning when he wanted to watch *Jonathan Creek* or *Star Trek* instead of *Strictly Come Prancing* and *EastEnders*.

"Same again, love?" Trixie asked with a smile. She was great, Trixie was. A big, no-nonsense bleached blonde with a good set of biceps on her.

"Yeah, ta. Brock for me, and Ridgeway for me mate there."

"Where's your other half tonight?"

"What? Oh, you mean Barry?" Rory chuckled.

"That's the one. Thought you and him was joined at the hip."

"Nah, he's on babysitting duty Tuesdays. The missus goes out to Pilates."

Trixie gave him a look. "They his kids?"

"Well, yeah. Least, he hopes so." Rory laughed.

"Then you can't call it babysitting. Bet no one calls it babysitting when it's her stuck indoors while he's out on the piss with you."

"S'pose not. Mind you, Evie always calls it babysitting when she wants me to have our kids for a night."

"Yeah, but you don't live with 'em. How are they, anyhow? Your Lucy still enjoying her football?"

Rory gave her a proud smile. "Yeah, they just started back after the summer. She got man of the match last weekend. Uh, player of the match. They won five nil, and she scored two and got the assist for another of 'em." She hadn't given away a single penalty or got even a yellow card, neither, which was what he reckoned their coach had *really* been rewarding. But there was no need to mention that.

"Bless. That it, then?" Trixie placed the pint of Ridgeway on the bar.

"Cheers, love." Rory handed her a tenner. Easy come, easy go. Course, with this David bloke staying, he'd have a bit more coming in. Might be able to get Leo that telescope he had his little heart set on for Christmas.

Show him his old dad was still good for something and he didn't have to ask flippin' *Lewis* for all the fancy stuff.

Rory walked back to Mark, decision reached. "Right, then. When's this bloke of yours want to move in?"

Mark's eyebrows shot up. "Don't you want to meet him first? Make sure you'll get along?"

"Nah, that's fine. He's a mate of yours, in't he? We'll be golden."

Mark didn't say anything. Just took a long swig of beer.

Rory told Barry all about it when he came over for a beer the following evening.

Barry scratched his armpit thoughtfully, then gave his fingers a sniff. He made a face and wiped them on his trousers. "So he's a woofter, this bloke?"

"Pretty sure you're not s'posed to call 'em that these days." Rory frowned, leaning back on the sofa. He liked his sofa. It was one of those L-shaped ones that was all cushions, so you could get proper comfy on it. The kids loved it, mostly cos it was great for building dens and stuff. And for having cushion fights, which they never got to do at their mum's. Probably on account of it not being *her* place. It was that smarmy git Lewis's house, wasn't it? His place was down the posh end of the village, one of the new houses built three storeys high and packed in like sardines, and still managing to go for the best part of a million quid.

And yeah, maybe Lewis had married her, in that big, posh hotel with little Lucy all tricked up like a sugar-plum fairy as bridesmaid— she'd been so gorgeous Rory had nearly cried—but that still didn't make it *Evie's* place, did it?

Anyway, Rory's sofa was the best. So what if it took up most of the floor space in his tiny living room? You didn't have a living room so you could walk around in it, did you?

Barry rolled his eyes and put on a posh voice. "Oh, I *am* sorry. He's a *homosexual gentleman*. That better?"

"Yeah." There was still something off in Barry's tone, but Rory didn't want to argue with the bloke when he was just being, well, Barry. "And he's a mate of Mark's, so he's gotta be all right." Barry couldn't argue with that, could he?

"Ain't your Evie got something to say about it? I mean, you have the kids to stay every other weekend. Say he meets some bloke on Grindr and brings him back for the night, and they see all kinds of stuff they shouldn't?"

Rory frowned. Okay, he hadn't thought of that, but . . . "He's not gonna be shagging them in front of the telly, is he? I mean, I might've had Jenni round when they was here, but we'd never of done nothing when the kids were around."

"Yeah, but gay blokes are different, aren't they? Gotta be all in your face about it." Barry sniggered. "Better watch out he don't get in *your* face."

"Gonna be a bit hard to avoid, innit? Not like there's a lot of extra room in here." Rory waved at his living space, or lack of it, with a grin. He didn't quite hit his hand on the opposite wall, but it wasn't far off.

Barry groaned. "No, I meant, *in your face*. Like this, see?" He pursed his lips, blew out his cheeks and used his tongue to make one side bulge out even more.

Rory stared, wondering if he'd got something stuck in a tooth—then it clicked, and he laughed. "Nah, not gonna be none of that."

Barry wasn't laughing. "Bloody well hope not. Not that I grudge 'em their rights, nothing like that, but they're taking over the world, the gays with their pink pound and their homosexual agenda. Your house is the only place I feel safe these days."

Barry was a good mate, the best, but he didn't half talk a load of bollocks sometimes. Rory took in his Barry's appearance: beer gut spilling over his jeans, tragic fashion sense, food stains and all. He didn't look anything like the blokes on that gay porn channel Rory had clicked on by mistake when he'd been trying to find out how to make a daisy chain for Leo.

"Don't worry," he said seriously. "I don't reckon you're in any danger wherever you go."

"Yeah, you're right. I can look after meself. But ain't you worried he's gonna be ogling you in your undies? Trying to convert you to the cause?"

Rory hadn't thought about that, either, but now he had, he still couldn't see why Barry was so flippin' worried about it. He frowned. "Don't you have to be born like it?" There'd been a song about it on the radio and everything.

"Don't stop 'em trying, does it? You better watch out, mate. Establish some ground rules. No touching, no walking around starkers, and no offering to save water by having a bath together."

Rory was starting to think Barry must get all his ideas about what lodgers were like from those pornos he watched some nights while his missus was out and the kids were in bed. There was no point arguing with him when he went off on one like this, though. "I'm more into showers, me."

"That's even worse, mate. Just keep a tight grip on the soap at all times."

"You what?"

"You know. No bending over to pick it up?" Barry made a suggestive gesture with one arm.

Rory winced. "Ohhh. Nah, no worries. My shower's tiny. You'd never fit two grown blokes in there. And anyway, aren't gay blokes all into grooming and fitness and that?"

"So?"

Rory laughed. "I got dad bod, ain't I? No way all this is driving some poor bloke into uncontrollable lust."

Barry shook his head slowly. "Rather you than me, mate. Rather you than me."

Rory thought about it afterwards, though, his feet up on the coffee table after Barry had gone home to the missus. Barry had been well insistent about this gay-agenda thing. Rory hadn't wanted to admit he didn't even know what that was. He got his laptop out and did a quick search. Okay, that all looked well confusing.

Then he tried spelling *agenda* with it ending in an *a* not an *er*. Yeah, those results made more sense. There were even example gay agendas shown. Although a lot of them seemed to involve buying milk.

Rory closed his laptop. He couldn't see what all the fuss was about.

CHAPTER FIVE

avid drove slowly up the hill. Rory's house, or at any rate, the one corresponding to the address Mark had given David, was second from the end of a terrace on the right-hand side as one went up the delightfully named Pig Lane. Mark had explained it was called after the pub at its far end, the Pig and Poke. Which was all very well, but did they *have* to go with *Pig*? David would have been far happier at the prospect of living on Poke Lane.

As Shamwell streets went, Pig Lane was definitely on the low-budget end of the spectrum, with almost a council-estate aesthetic. The houses were small and huddled together, seeking safety in numbers. Their tiny front gardens were landscaped with less of a regard for horticulture and more for the storage of children's toys and surplus white goods. A Methodist church stood halfway up, high gables pointing heavenward and austere frontage suggesting sternly that other afterlife destinations were also an option should one fail to repent—of what, precisely, David wasn't sure, but he was fairly certain he'd done it.

David parked Mrs. Merdle by the side of the road. She stood out like a sore but impeccably bandaged thumb among all the weary Vauxhall estate cars, Ford vans, and ugly little Fiats. Finding a garage for her was going to be a priority. Safety for his newest darling was paramount, and moreover it would hardly be neighbourly to give all the other cars an inferiority complex. He unbuckled Gregory's seat belt, gave Mrs. Merdle a gentle pat to reassure her that Daddy would be back soon, then trotted up the short path to the front door.

The man who answered his jaunty knock was rather on the short side, at least compared to David's six foot one. A Watson to his Sherlock, or perhaps a Frodo to David's Gandalf. Although he looked more like a shaven-headed Merry or a Pippin, to be honest. And David himself wouldn't, of course, be seen dead with lank grey hair and a straggly beard. Hmm. He mulled it over. Maybe a Pippin to his Aragorn? The man in front of him *did* have rather lovely brown eyes beneath strong brows, the right brow a smidge fuller than the left. David's fingers itched to even the score, but his tweezers were still firmly shut in Mrs. Merdle's boot.

Pippin coughed. "Uh, you the bloke what wants the room? Mark's mate?"

David realised he'd been mulling a tad longer than was strictly polite. "*Mais bien sûr*. You must be Rory? I'm David, but you can call me Davey. This is Gregory." He held Gregory up and was pleased to see Rory break into a grin. Perhaps he was more of a Merry, after all.

"Nice to meet you. Both of you. Come on in. Um. Sorry about the mess. I tried tidying up, but I sort of ran out of places to put stuff."

David wiped his feet and kicked off his shoes for good measure. Rory, he'd noticed, was wearing slippers that proclaimed him a *Footy Mad Dad*. David resigned himself to Saturday nights spent in front of *Match of the Day*. Still, at least it'd give him a bargaining chip to claim the television on Sundays. He'd been rather enjoying that new BBC costume drama. Admittedly, the lead actor was a little young for David's usual tastes, being barely into his thirties, but he did look absolutely delicious with his shirt off. Especially in scenes that were most definitely Not In The Book.

The hall, which was large enough for two grown men and a teddy bear in the same way that the average elevator could hold thirteen people—i.e. only if they were extremely good friends, or at any rate comfortable with the prospect of becoming so by the end of the experience—led to the stairs. Off to the left was a door leading to the living room, which was where Rory directed David with a wave of his hand.

"This is it," Rory said, shrugging.

The living room had wooden flooring, over which had been laid a thick rug with the kind of neutral, abstract pattern that fairly screamed *I buy my taste at IKEA*. Most of it was covered by a large, squidgy L-shaped sofa in front of a wide-screen TV. A sturdy, low wooden table took care of the rest of the floor space and was placed, if David was any judge, at the optimum distance from the sofa for Rory to put his feet up while watching the telly.

As he strongly suspected it had a secondary duty of dining table, David might have to have words with Rory about that. Not to mention, optimum distance for Rory meant that if David tried putting his feet up, he'd be able to use his knees as earmuffs.

Later, however. For now, he smiled. "Oh, how charmingly bijou." *That* was the understatement of the century. If Rory turned out to own a cat, David would have to advise strenuously against any attempt to swing it. Even a mouse would be pushing it. On the plus side, however, the place was delightfully cosy. The sofa, in particular—David was sorely tempted to *flump* down on it and let himself be buried in an avalanche of cushions, but he resisted manfully. Unsolicited flumping, he'd found, could sometimes cause offence.

Rory rubbed a hand over his shaven head. The faint rasp of stubble lent him a dangerous air that seemed intriguingly at odds with his personality. "Uh, thanks? Evie had most of our old stuff when we split, cos of the kids, so I put all this together meself. You wanna see the kitchen next?"

"Lead on," David said politely.

The room Rory showed him clearly *was* a kitchen, seeing as it contained a stove, a sink, and various cupboards and countertops under which nestled a minuscule fridge, a slimline dishwasher, and a washing machine, the latter thankfully of normal size. If it hadn't been for those visible clues, however, David would have thought he was in a corridor, and not a particularly wide one at that. If he and Rory were ever both in here at once and wanted to pass one another, the ensuing scene would probably bear a strong resemblance to a scene from the *Kama Sutra*.

Rory made a face. "Yeah, I know, it's pretty small. But it all works."

"As the bishop said to the actor," David murmured distractedly. "Maybe we could establish some kind of one-way system?"

"Be a bit of a faff, wouldn't it?" Rory actually appeared to be considering it. "Nah, 's not gonna work. Not unless we was end of terrace, and we're not. You'd have to go out the door into the garden, hop over the fence and come round the side of next door. I don't reckon Mrs. Willis would like that. We'll just have to breathe in or something." He laughed. "Course, if you breathe in, you'll disappear. You sure you're gonna want to use the kitchen anyhow?"

David pouted. "I do *occasionally* put food in my mouth. I also swallow, although the two statements aren't necessarily connected." He was most likely imagining the *whoosh* of that innuendo sailing straight over Rory's stubbly head, but the bemused expression was real enough.

Yes, definitely a hobbit of some kind. David glanced down, but with the *Dad* slippers on, it was impossible to tell how hairy Rory's feet were. "Bedroom?" he suggested brightly.

"Oh, yeah, right. This way. So you're going into business with Mark?" Rory asked as he led David up a steep, narrow staircase at an energetic trot. With his longer legs, David matched the pace easily by the simple expedient of taking two stairs at a time.

"Mm. We always did work well together. Strictly professionally speaking, alas. But how about you? I don't think he mentioned what you do."

"Me? I'm a postie. It ain't a bad job, long as you don't mind the early mornings. Keeps the beer gut in line, anyhow, all that walking around." Rory chuckled as they reached the landing, and slapped his belly, which was just on the right side of cuddly as far as David was concerned—Rory rather reminded him of a favourite teddy bear with all the fur loved off. "Here we go. This'll be your room." He opened the first door to the left.

David looked. And blinked. The room, while it was at least larger than David had feared, had pink walls, pink curtains, and a pine-framed bed with a pink duvet cover. Wand-wielding fairies flitted across it with appropriately gay abandon. "You know," he said slowly, "you really didn't have to redecorate on my account."

"Uh, yeah, sorry about that. I let Lucy choose the colours and stuff, cos the idea was for her to have that room. I get the kids every other weekend, see." Rory shrugged. "But she reckons it's more fun camping out on the sofa with her brother anyhow, so you don't need to worry about her getting the hump. And I'll get that duvet cover out of your way. I only left it on cos the cat don't always wipe his paws when he comes in."

"Oh, you have a cat?"

"Yeah— Shit, you're not allergic are you?"

David shook his head.

"That's a relief. Uh, it's more like half a cat, though."

Hideous visions of a feline horribly maimed by venturing into traffic, or perhaps from a difference of opinion with the local catriarch, danced briefly, if regrettably clumsily, in David's head.

Rory went on, apparently oblivious: "I sort of share him with her next door. Mrs. Willis."

"Oh, thank God. Don't ask," David added quickly.

Rory's expression didn't get any less curious, but apparently his mum had done her job well as he didn't, in fact, ask. "Uh, yeah, he's only half-grown and he likes to play, but she can't do much cos of her arthritis. So when he gets bored, he nips round here. I'm not s'posed to feed him, so I'm hoping you'll keep stumm about the odd tin of tuna that goes his way."

"My lips are never loose," David assured him politely. "Now, if that's the tour, all right if I get my things?"

"Yeah? You're gonna go for it, then?" Rory appeared flatteringly pleased, which made a nice change from the all-too-obviously heartfelt *"Thank God"* Ryan and Samir had uttered in unison when David had announced he'd found somewhere to live.

"*Absolument.* Gregory loves it, don't you, Gregory?" David placed the teddy bear gently on the bed and straightened his deerstalker. "He's always been fond of fairies."

"That's great. Oh, haven't shown you the bathroom yet."

"Don't worry," David said gravely, halfway to the stairs. "I'm sure its location can't elude me for long."

Rory laughed. "Then let's get your stuff inside." He followed David downstairs, his footsteps oddly light for a man of his stocky build.

"Oh, there's no need—"

"Nah, don't be daft. I ain't gonna sit on my arse while you're humping stuff around."

"It's true I've always found humping to be more fun when done in company." David opened the front door.

"Did you hire a van or . . ." Rory's voice trailed off, and David turned to see why.

Rory was standing on the doormat staring, open-mouthed, at Mrs. Merdle. "Bloody hell. Is that yours?"

"Yes. Rory, meet Mrs. Merdle. She's a flighty young thing, but we mustn't hold her youth against her."

"She's *beautiful.*" Rory let out a sigh like a Dickensian orphan confronted with a baker's Christmas window display. "And blimey, you went for the top-of-the-range model, dintcha? The whatchamacallit—"

"The Exclusive," David butted in proudly.

"That's the one. Eighteen-inch alloy wheels, turbo-charged engine . . . you go for the automatic?"

"Manual. I always feel so much more in control with my hand on the stick."

Rory was nodding. Clearly he was a man of far greater taste and discernment than had at first appeared.

David smiled. "I'd offer to take you for a spin, but she's a little overloaded at the moment." He waved a hand at his poor car, a thoroughbred racehorse suffering the indignity of being used as a pack animal. Boxes and bags were faintly visible through the tinted windows, pretty much filling her interior, although David had done his best to pack only the essentials.

Never mind. She'd forgive him as soon as he found a suitably open road and let her loose. "And would one of these be yours?" David gestured to the two nearest cars parked, as every car on the street was, half on and half off the pavement. The first was a sleek if well-aged navy-blue Volkswagen; the next a rather tired-looking red Škoda Octavia with a scratched bumper and dented wing. David mentally crossed his fingers and hoped for the VW.

"Yeah, that's mine. The Škoda." Rory grinned, so presumably hadn't noticed David's wince. "Bet you're too young to remember all them Škoda jokes that used to go around."

"You mean, such as, 'How do you double the value of a Škoda?' 'Fill the tank.' 'What do you call a Škoda with a sunroof?' 'A skip.' Mm, no, never heard of them."

Rory laughed. "What about, 'Why does a Škoda have a heated rear window?' 'To keep everyone's hands warm when they're pushing it.' Nah, they ain't so bad, these cars. Just got 'emselves some bad press a few years back. And, well, it ain't like I got money to chuck about."

David felt a little guilty. Beggars couldn't be choosers, and it wasn't like conspicuous consumption was a virtue. Some people might even consider the reverse to be true. His mother, for instance, who was always telling him if he had to be shallow, he should at least try not to be too openly *proud* of it. Darling Hen. He'd been *this close* to giving up on the job hunting and moving back to Kent to be with her. As soon as he was settled at Rory's, Hen was getting an invitation over to see the place.

Rory coughed, recalling David to the need to actually *do* some settling in before issuing invitations. "Sorry, where were we?"

"Uh, getting them boxes inside?"

"A man with a plan." David opened the boot of the MG and started hoiking out boxes to lay them in Rory's arms.

For a fortysomething-year-old man who'd presumably spent his morning tramping several miles to deliver the mail, Rory proved surprisingly energetic at transferring David's worldly goods and chattels from car to house. David's estimation of his fitness went up markedly. He even started to think it might be interesting to find out what Rory looked like stripped of his worn tracksuit bottoms and paint-stained T-shirt . . .

Where the hell had *that* come from?

He was overwrought, David decided, sitting down on his new bed to give Gregory a restoring cuddle. Worn down by the weeks of insecurity both professional and personal. He had a type, and Rory was most definitely not it.

Too short, for one thing. David preferred a man he could look up to, and not only when he was on his knees. And Rory wasn't precisely what you'd call classically handsome in the Cary Grant/George Clooney mould. For a start, he'd taken the Ryan and Samir approach to grooming, and David liked to be able to run his fingers through his man's hair.

Although possibly that faint five-o'clock shadow he'd glimpsed on Rory's head would provide an intriguing texture—

No. Rory fell short of David's ideal in more ways than simply the strictly physical. He liked a man who knew his own mind. Who took charge, both in bed and out of it.

Who was, frankly, a bit of a bastard.

David was willing to admit he might have many illusions about himself, but at least he was fully cognisant of what he liked. And *nice*, which Rory had in absolute shovelfuls, bless him, was not it. Clearly, their relationship was forever doomed to remain platonic. Which was good, David told himself. He'd always had a nagging feeling he should have more straight friends.

He recalled mentioning that to Mark one time, back in the far-off days of yore when they'd both worked for Charles at Whyborne & Co. Mark had just told him he should stop sleeping with them, then. Possibly the man had been in something of a bad mood, possibly due to David having temporarily mislaid an essential file just before a client meeting, possibly because he'd left it in the stationery cupboard after an unexpected quickie with bi-curious Colin from IT . . . anyway, that wasn't important.

What *was* important was that David was going to have a new Straight Best Friend. "I think this is going to work out *wonderfully*," he whispered to Gregory, then hurried out of his room to finish unloading Mrs. Merdle.

Only to find Rory dusting off his hands after placing the last of the boxes on the landing, having brought in the lot while David was away with the fairies. "Right, that's all I could see. By the way, I was thinking, you want somewhere safe to keep Mrs. M, don't you? Cos it ain't too bad round here, but a car like that? You want to get her off road before some boy racer zooms down the hill and takes out her wing. So anyway, I got this mate what's got a garage—you want me to give him a call? I'll make sure he gives you mates' rates, no probs."

What had David just been saying? *Total* sweetie. "Rory, you're a prince among postmen."

Rory smiled, a hint of a blush on his little cheeks. "Nah 's okay. Gotta keep the lady safe."

Several hours later, David had driven Mrs. Merdle to her new home a mere ten minutes' walk away through the village. He'd also unpacked his footwear collection (now lined up along the hall downstairs next to Rory's sturdy walking boots), enlivened the bathroom with his Molton Brown toiletries (he'd used to buy Dior Homme, but the packaging was so dreadfully dull and drab, although not quite as appalling as Rory's Tesco Value Shower Gel) and shoehorned his most essential articles of clothing into the dainty pine wardrobe in his new room. He was feeling in dire need of a good flump.

He hesitated. Should he go downstairs and flump on the sofa? Or was discretion the better part of valour as far as first-day flumping was concerned?

Mark had given him a stern talking-to when he'd called to say Rory was up for a lodger. He'd said it without the slightest appreciation for a good innuendo, too.

"Remember," he'd said. "Rory isn't used to anyone quite so . . . flamboyant. You might want to tone it down a little in the interests of getting along."

"You mean you want me to be less, well, *me*?"

"Er . . . I wouldn't have put it quite like that."

"So basically, that's a *yes*." David supposed it was only to be expected. Mark had been married to a woman for years, hadn't he? He must be something of an expert at hiding his rainbow light under a bush.

"Just give him a chance to get used to you, that's all." Mark hesitated. "And don't forget if he mentions his ex, that's Patrick's mother he's talking about. His most recent ex, at any rate."

"Ooh, am I moving in with a serial heartbreaker?"

David had wondered, at the time, why Mark had snorted so strangely at that, but having met Rory in the flesh, it made a lot more sense. Rory was a dear, but he was hardly the stuff of which *hommes fatale* were made.

Still, David knew they were going to get along splendidly.

He decided to go and flump on the sofa forthwith.

When he got downstairs, however, David found the sofa sadly unavailable for flumping. Half of it was already occupied by Rory and the other half by a well-rounded man of around forty, manspreading so far David was surprised his stubby little legs didn't snap off at the hips. The interloper, who had bushy dark hair, beady eyes and alarmingly aggressive eyebrows, looked up as David entered the room, and glowered.

David resisted the urge to glare daggers back at him, and pasted on a sunny smile instead. "Room for a little one?"

Rory, who'd been peering intently at some team sport on the television—football, from the chanting and the overexcited commentary—glanced up and turned the sound down. "David! Didn't see you there. Come on, Barry, budge up. This is David, my new lodger. David, my mate Barry."

"*Enchanté*," David murmured politely, and held out his hand.

Barry took it warily with a muttered, "All right, mate?" He gave David's hand a shake so brief it barely counted as one, then dropped it like a used condom and scooted over so far on the sofa Rory had to shift position or be squashed.

David sat down primly, his face beginning to hurt from the fake smile. "So, how long have you two known each other?"

"Years," Barry blurted out. "We're like that, me and him." He held up two fingers pressed close together, then went red. "Uh, not in a gay way or nothing."

"Perish the thought," David said sincerely.

Rory laughed and nudged Barry in the ribs. "Oi, mate, you don't have to come over all *no homo* with David."

"Just keeping the record straight," Barry muttered.

"Among other things," David couldn't help murmuring back. "Are you a postman too, Barry? Do you go around in those fetching little shorts, delivering hopes and dreams to the masses? And tax bills too. Obviously. One has to take the rough trade with the—"

"No." Barry cut him off sharply. "Bookie."

"What a shame," David said charitably, because on the whole he thought the village had rather dodged a bullet, being spared the sight of those undoubtedly gorilla-like legs.

The brows, however, beetled. "You got a problem with bookies? You one of them antigambling bastards out to spoil everyone's fun?"

David blinked and reviewed what he'd said. Ah. "Au contraire. I've even been known to have the odd flutter myself. And not only of my eyelashes." He gave Barry a winning smile.

Barry neglected to return it. David's smile sloped off to find somewhere it was more welcome.

He had half a mind to follow it. Was it just him or had the temperature in the room dropped around thirty degrees since he'd come down?

CHAPTER SIX

Rory couldn't quite put his finger on it, but somehow he got the impression Barry and David hadn't exactly hit it off. For a start, David had sat there all funny, sort of upright and pressed together, not taking up half the space Barry had made for him. And Barry had been banging on about everything under the sun until David had come down, from the footie to the state of the country to his missus's latest diet, and then he'd clammed right up. He hadn't stayed long, neither, before muttering something about hitting the chippie on his way home and heading off.

Rory had been going to suggest they all go, cos with Barry there he hadn't been able to make a start on the cooking, and in any case, it was like Evie said when he'd called her to let her know he had a lodger: he didn't want to poison the bloke before he'd paid his first month's rent.

But maybe it was for the best. David didn't look like he ate a lot of fish and chips. Or much else, come to that. Not that he was, like, skin and bones or nothing. Just, well, long and lean, with cheekbones you could cut yourself on if you weren't careful. He managed to look elegant in jeans and a T-shirt. Refined. God knew what he was doing renting Rory's spare room.

And there Jenni had said he wouldn't know *elegant* if it jumped up and bit him on the bum.

If he'd said that to Barry, he'd have gone on about not letting *David* bite him on the bum. Rory laughed at the thought.

"Something funny? Do share." David even *sounded* a bit off.

"Nah, 's nothing. I was just thinking about Barry. Oi, you wanna eat together? I thought we could get a takeaway, if you want. The Chinese in the village ain't bad."

David smiled and finally stopped looking so uptight. "Or I could cook for you? A little thank-you for *literally* taking me in off the streets?"

Rory felt a bit awkward. "You ain't gotta do that. I mean, if anyone cooks it oughtta be me."

"Don't be silly. I love exercising my culinary muscles." David jumped up off the sofa. He looked about six miles tall now from where Rory was sitting. "Mind if I have a poke in your pantry?"

"Don't think I've got one of them. Feel free to fossick in the fridge, though." Rory grinned. Yeah, what was up with Barry anyway? This was going to work fine, him and David.

David raised an eyebrow. It was so *him* Rory had to stop himself laughing. "Or comb through the cupboards?"

"You can even delve in me drawers, mate." Rory was proud of himself for that one, especially when David laughed.

"Promises, promises. What would *Barry* say?"

"Barry? He don't do cooking. Not unless it's a barbecue." Rory frowned. "Listen, mate, don't mind him. Dunno what crawled up his arse today."

David opened his mouth like he was about to say something, then pressed his lips together, did a twirl like a ballet dancer, and headed for the kitchen.

"Gimme a shout when you know what's what and I'll come and help, yeah?" Rory called after him, then he leaned back in the sofa and flicked through the channels with the remote.

Cool. *Red Dwarf* was on. Rory put his feet up and settled down to watch. It was an old episode, one he'd seen at least half a dozen times before, and his eyelids were feeling heavy, so he let them have a bit of a rest. He could just listen for a while. It wasn't like he didn't know what was going to happen.

"A-*hem*!"

A throat was cleared loudly and theatrically right by Rory's earhole. He sat up straight, his eyes flying open.

"I wasn't asleep," he said reflexively, blinking at the sight of David standing over him with a couple of plates. "Oh—you done it all, then? I was gonna give you a hand."

"No problem," David said, putting the plates on the coffee table with a smile. "I prefer to work alone. It gives free rein to my creative genius. Now, in my defence, you didn't leave me a lot to work with. Still, barring one or two *teensy* glitches, I coped admirably."

Rory stared at the food. "It's, uh . . ."

"It's scromblet," David said firmly, handing him a knife and fork. "Ham and cheese scromblet, to be precise. On toast."

"Scromblet?"

"It was *supposed* to be omelette. It just somehow, through *no* fault of my own, turned out to have more than a passing resemblance to scrambled eggs. Hence the toast. For preservation of structural integrity, which I'm sure you'll agree was a rather brilliant piece of improvisation under pressure."

Rory had to laugh. "Blimey, mate, you're as bad as I am in the kitchen. Still, the toast ain't burned, so that's a plus."

David looked so shifty that Rory picked up a corner of one slice of toast to peer at the other side.

Yep. Charcoal.

"It depends on your views about the distinction between *burnt* and, say—"

"And just really well done?" Rory shook his head as he cut himself a bite of scromblet. "No worries, mate. Been there, done that, got a bit of a taste for it these days. Least *you* didn't set the smoke alarm off."

"Ah. Remind me to put the batteries back in later."

"Heh, how come I never think of taking 'em out? This ain't bad, by the way. Congrats, mate. You got the job."

"Chief cook and bottle washer?"

"Nah, you cook, I'll wash bottles. Or we can take turns. I do a great risotto surprise."

"Which is? Or would that spoil the surprise?"

Rory laughed. "Rice and whatever's going out of date in the fridge. With soy sauce, cos otherwise it just tastes like, well, rice."

"Ooh, remind me to give you my mushroom soup pasta recipe." David paused, a forkful of food halfway to his mouth. "Although actually, that's it. Mushroom soup and pasta."

"You know what?" Rory said, tickled. "You and me, we're gonna get along fine."

David looked so chuffed Rory was glad he'd said it.

Not long after they'd finished eating, the doorbell rang.

Rory ambled over to answer it, expecting to see Mrs. Willis from next door—she tended to pop round any time she needed a light bulb changing or a cupboard door fixing, or just a chat, cos the old dear got lonely, bless her. Not that she'd ever admit it.

He was a bit surprised to instead see a teenage Goth girl standing there, wearing all black clothes, with black hair and a silver stud in her nose. Not to mention a look on her face like something had curled up and died on the doormat.

Come to think of it, she looked more like she wished *Rory* would curl up and die on the doormat.

"Fen?" He knew her, of course, although they'd never spoken all that much so he had no clue why she was here or why she had the hump with him all of a sudden. Rory wasn't sure how to talk to teenagers. He hoped he'd manage to work it out by the time Lucy turned thirteen. Funny, though. Fen was Mark's daughter. If Rory and Jen had got married, and Mark and Patrick had too, she'd have been his . . . step-granddaughter? Grand-stepdaughter? Granddaughter twice removed?

Rory scratched his head, and realised he'd missed her answer. "Sorry?"

"I *said*, 'Is David in?' I brought him something." She held up a large biscuit tin, and hugged it protectively when he reached to take it.

"Oh. Right. Come on in. He's in the living room."

Fen wiped her feet on the doormat and stomped in, the zips, chains, and other bits on her seriously metal boots jingling. Rory would've liked to ask her to take them off, but wasn't sure she'd be too happy about it.

Anyway, they were probably safer on her feet than out here unsupervised, terrorising Rory's work boots and taking a bite out of David's Gucci loafers. Rory grinned to himself at the picture.

David jumped up when Rory led her into the living room.

"Fen! Darling. How lovely to see you. Oh my. Look at you. I *swear* you've grown another inch since I last saw you."

She giggled. "David, you saw me like four hours ago."

Huh. Rory hadn't known they knew each other that well. He could remember Fen mentioning a David, now he came to think about it, but he'd assumed that was just some boy in her class. "So *you're* Fen's David?" he blurted out.

They broke apart from a three-way hug—Fen, David, and the biscuit tin—to turn back to Rory.

Fen's lip curled. She might as well have come out and said, *God, what are you even* like?

At least David was still smiling at him. "*Mais bien sûr*. Insofar as I could ever be said to belong to a woman, my dear *petite crevette* is she."

Rory frowned. Why he was he calling her one of them posh ties blokes wore for their weddings?

David was still speaking. "After my mother, naturally. And Cher. And Una Stubbs, bless her. And Joanna Lumley . . ."

"Shut up." Fen was giggling again. "Here, I made you a housewarming cake."

"Darling, you shouldn't have. Okay, that's a lie: you *totally* should have. Mwah. You're an angel. In unfeasibly devilish footwear, and I see Lex has been giving you shopping tips. Can I open it now?"

"Yeah." Fen turned to glare in Rory's direction. "But don't give *him* any. He broke up with Granny O."

"Uh . . ." She meant Jenni. Jenni Owen. Rory started to say she'd broken up with him, but Jenni had said to tell everyone it was a mutual decision, hadn't she? "We broke up with each other."

"Yeah, *right*."

"And does she know you're calling her Granny O? She might not be too keen, seeing as she's only forty-four."

Fen folded her arms. "I don't think, actually, you've got any right to have an opinion on how she feels about anything anymore."

She turned her back on Rory with a combo teenage flounce and Goth jangle.

David made brief, awkward faces over the top of Fen's head, then took her arm. "Tell you what, let's take the cake into the kitchen, shall we?"

"Fine. Long as *he's* not coming."

"Don't worry. There wouldn't be room for all three of us in there. Now, do tell—if Patrick's mum is Granny O, does that make Patrick your Daddio?"

Fen giggled. "*No.* He's *Patrick.* Duh."

"Paddio?"

"Oh my God, I dare you to call him that!"

The giggles faded as she closed the door behind them.

Rory tried not to feel too left out.

The sinking feeling in his stomach told him he'd failed.

CHAPTER SEVEN

en was all girlish enthusiasm as she opened up her biscuit tin to show David the treasure within. "Do you like it? I made it myself, decorations and everything. It's chocolate, with butter cream filling."

David was touched. He wasn't particularly into cake, as a rule, but clearly a lot of effort had gone into this one. Fen had used fondant icing to top the cake with what was obviously intended to be a house, and underneath it, something he couldn't quite identify. "Oh, how lovely," he said, with a fair amount of girlish enthusiasm of his own. "Is that a carnation? Shouldn't it be green, not red, though? If you're attempting to go all Oscar Wilde on me, that is."

"Uh?" A flash of confusion across her pretty, studded face was instantly supplanted by condescension. "It's a fire. Duh. Cos it's, like, symbolic? You know? House? Warming?"

"Oh, *très* droll. I'm glad to hear it's not because you'd like poor Rory to burn in hell for jilting Patrick's mother." David fixed her with an avuncular look. "Aren't you being a teensy bit harsh on him?"

"No." She folded her arms. "It's really rough on her, you know? Like, she's never had a bloke that didn't treat her like sh—like, not very well. It's not *fair*."

David patted her black-clad arm. "There, there. Perhaps she's a strong, independent woman who doesn't need a man? Like me?"

"Course she doesn't need a man," Fen snapped. "But I think she wants one. Why would she have gone out with Rory if she didn't want a boyfriend?"

"Irresistible attraction overcoming her higher thought processes?"

"What, for him?"

David felt obscurely defensive on Rory's behalf. "He has a certain cuddly charm."

"Ew. And now she's all on her own again, cos Patrick's living with me and Dad."

"So? *Regarde moi.* I haven't had a steady man in years. Do I bewail my lot? Do I rage against the dying of the light? Do I moon around, lovesick, pining for Mr. Unattainable?"

"Well, yeah. Duh." She sent him a sly side-eye. "So what happened to make you get fired? It must be something good cos Dad won't tell me."

"And neither will I. Not until you're older. Much older. Thirty, perhaps. Or thirty-five. Forty, even. Mark would never forgive me if I destroyed the innocence of his precious child."

"I'm nearly sixteen. I do *know* about sex. I've had lessons on it."

"Not from young Ollie, I hope."

"Course not." Her smile was treacled with insincerity, but David was *almost* certain she was pulling his pigtails.

Probably best not to know. "So, cake?" he said brightly, and by trial and error managed to unearth a knife and two plates, feeling rather guilty about poor, left-out Rory. He made a mental note to cut the poor man a generous slice after Fen had left. Still, if they were going to abuse his hospitality, they might as well do it properly. "And you can tell me all about my new housemate," he added in a conspiratorial whisper.

Fen frowned as she took the knife from him and cut two extremely large slices of cake. Oh, to have the metabolism of a teenager. David said a quick prayer for his soon-to-be-departed waistline and tucked in.

"Don't know him all that well," Fen said with her mouth full. "I only ever met him with Granny O, and he always seemed a bit . . . I mean, I wondered why she was going out with him, cos she was always . . . not really *laughing* at him, it was just stuff she said . . . It was like he didn't always get the joke, you know?"

"Not the sharpest needle on the record, hm? Maybe he has other talents," David suggested idly, and licked butter cream from his finger. "Fortunately I'm above such petty things as intellectual snobbery."

Rather uncharitably, Fen snorted a cake crumb and went red in the face. He manfully forbore from slapping her on the back in the guise of helping her breathe.

"I get no respect," he said instead. "And nor does poor Rory, by all accounts. Even from your Granny O, which *might*, I'd suggest, be one reason for the split."

"*No*. They split up cos he chucked her right before they were supposed to be going to a wedding. That's a shit thing to do."

"Language, *ma petite crevette*. And I'll admit the evidence seems damning, but we don't know what goes on between two people in a relationship, do we? Lessons on sex notwithstanding."

"*S'pose*."

"Good. Now, how about we concentrate on enjoying this scrumptious cake? Did I mention the cake is scrumptious, by the way?"

"No. you didn't, actually. Some people would call that rude."

"I was merely lost for words adequate to describe its delectableness. Or do I mean delectability? Whatever, it's very good."

"Yeah, well, don't go wasting it on *him*."

"Would I?" David mentally crossed his fingers behind his back. "But I don't think we should lurk in the kitchen much longer. Some people would say *that* was rude."

"S'pose. I can't stay, anyway. Lex is coming round later to watch horror movies."

"Bless." As long as it wasn't to pierce or tattoo something. Lex, who was a young person a few years older than Fen, had encouraged her love of black and introduced her to heavy metal boots. David had nothing against Lex's enthusiasm for body art, but he couldn't help feeling that any permanent physical evidence of their influence on Fen might not be good for Mark's blood pressure.

All friendship aside, he'd hate to have to go hunting for another employer so soon.

"Thank you for making time in your busy Gothic schedule for little old me." David put the lid back on the cake tin.

"Oh—I haven't seen your room yet." Fen glanced at the kitchen clock, which had hands in the shape of humorous vegetables, and screwed up her face in obvious indecision.

"Next time," David promised. He probably ought to at least think about changing the duvet cover first. Fen wasn't fond of pink, and she had an aversion to fairies.

Present company excepted, of course.

Rory looked up hopefully as they trooped back into the living room. "So, uh, Fen, you seen much of Jenni lately? Sorry. I mean, your gran? I was wondering how she's getting on."

His wistful tone made David suspect Rory regretted the split. Still, if one couldn't do the time, one shouldn't go doing the crime, in his view.

Fen glared at Rory. "Last Sunday. She came round for dinner." The words *And some company, because her heart just got broken, you unfeeling bastard* went unsaid, but hung in the air nonetheless.

Rory winced visibly. "Yeah? She okay?"

"S'pose."

"Yeah? Smashing. School going all right, is it?"

"*S'pose.*"

"Uh, and that lad of yours—Ollie, was it? He all right?"

"Yeah." Her words were getting shorter as the, for want of a better word, conversation went on.

All this tension was *not* good for the digestion. David broke in hastily. "Fen, darling, before you go, please tell me you've reconsidered about the cosplay? Because I had this marvellous idea for us—me as the fourth Doctor, and you as Leila. It'll be fabulously retro. And Gregory could come as a jelly baby. Say you'll do it?"

Fen's kohl-rimmed eyes narrowed, and she pulled out her phone to tap at it furiously. "Oh. Oh, no *way*. Me in a fu—a leather vest and half a skirt? That's like one step up from Slave Leia. Come on, you *know* Dad would have a heart attack."

David pouted. For something he'd just made up on the spot, he'd been rather warming to the idea. "*He's* not coming." He caught Rory's expression of extreme bewilderment. "London Comic Con. Fen and I have tickets, but she's proving remarkably resistant to the idea of cosplay. Dressing up," he added for the benefit of the hard-of-geeking.

"That's because *some* of us don't like looking stupid. And that Leila thing is the stupidest idea you've had yet." Fen glared at David, which was a marked improvement on her sulking at Rory.

Rory was nodding. "Yeah, I heard people do that. Sounds like fun," he added a little sadly.

"Whatevs. I gotta go. Bye, David." She gave him a quick hug and swept out with a jangle, the front door slamming behind her.

David sent Rory a sympathetic glance. "Cake?"

Whatever he might think of Rory as a callous heartbreaker, David still had to live with the man, after all. And he did appear to be *very* chastened.

"Nah. Ta. I'm good." Rory gazed dolefully at his knees. "Gonna have an early night. Work tomorrow, yeah?"

"Poor you. Don't wake me."

CHAPTER EIGHT

Next morning, Rory's alarm clock went off with a bell like a . . . like a really loud thing, which was just as well cos he usually slept like the dead. He reached out blindly and managed to turn it off on the fourth or fifth attempt.

Then he yawned, stretched, and had a bit of a scratch. Four thirty a.m. Time to get up.

Whenever he told people he was a postie, nine out of ten would say it sounded like a great job, but they couldn't hack the early mornings. Rory didn't get that. It came down to what you were used to, didn't it? Working a night shift, now, that had to be hard— sleeping in the daytime and only coming out at night like a vampire or a teenager or something. But mornings were great. How many people got to see the sun come up all year round?

Rory was heading downstairs for breakfast when David stumbled out of his room, dressed in his kecks and a burgundy T-shirt with some kind of cartoon on it. Bloody hell, he had long legs. He looked like a cross between a newborn kitten and a baby giraffe. Rory greeted him cheerfully. "Morning, Dave. You really were brought by the stork, weren't you, mate?"

"What? And it's Dav*ey*. Or David. *Never* Dave." He stood there, swaying slightly, his eyes half-shut and his hair all mussed up from bed.

Rory gazed at him affectionately, and chuckled when he got a proper gander at the T-shirt. "Heh, you a My Little Pony fan, then?"

David glared at him from beneath his mop of tousled hair. "It's My Little Sherlock, actually. Can't you see the scarf?"

Rory peered at David's chest. "Oh yeah. That's pretty good, that is. They oughtta have done a deerstalker on him and all, mind." He grinned at David.

David didn't grin back. "He's *series one* Sherlock."

Maybe he wasn't a morning person? "Uh . . . what you doing up so early? Thought you didn't have to get round to Mark's until nine."

"Oh, no reason. None at all. Apart from the fact that somebody seemed to think it would be fun to assault my eardrums *with a pneumatic drill in the middle of the night.*"

"That's it!" Rory beamed. "I was trying to think what my alarm sounded like, and you got it in one. Uh. Did it disturb you?"

"No, no. Perish the thought. Who needs more than three hours of sleep anyway?"

Despite the airy tone, Rory wasn't totally convinced he meant it. David's face was all puffy, and there were big, dark circles under his eyes.

Might be best not to mention it, though. That sort of comment had never gone down well with Jenni or Evie. "Uh, why don't you go back to bed for a bit if you haven't got anything you need to be up for? I'll be heading out to work in a mo. Or, seeing as you're awake, feel free to join me for breakfast."

Rory probably imagined the way David's face went kind of greenish.

"*Tempting* though it is, I'll pass. You just . . . do what you do. I'll be in my bed. Wake me only in case of apocalypse, and preferably not then." He turned back into his room with a flash of powder-pink underpants.

"Right you are, then," Rory told the closing door, then ambled off to get into his morning routine. He whistled the *Postman Pat* theme song as he jogged down the stairs cos it was nice and cheerful and his kids had always loved the show.

He stopped when David called his name from above.

"Yeah, mate?" Rory yelled, one hand on the kitchen door.

"Just a teeny, tiny thing." He paused.

"Yeah?"

"If you don't stop whistling, I may have to kill you."

"Oh. Fair 'nuff."

Rory had been right. *Definitely* not a morning person. He made a mug of tea, then grabbed himself some toast and marmalade and sat down in front of the telly to eat. The sports news was boring, and he found himself thinking about David. Should he tell the bloke his kecks were a bit girly? Did he know? After all, he was gay. He most likely hadn't seen a lot of girls in their underwear. Maybe he thought everyone wore them? Nah, that didn't work, did it? He must have seen *loads* of blokes in their undies. He was probably, like, a connoisseur of blokes' undies.

Rory glanced down at his own boxer shorts and heaved a sigh of relief, his brief—heh—panic subsiding. They were the nice checked ones Jenni had bought him, not the worn-out sort-of-whitish ones from Tesco's clearance bin that'd made her laugh out loud and call him a cut-price Casanova when she'd seen them.

Rory sighed again. It'd been fun with Jenni, while it'd lasted. He missed that. Okay, not the foot-tapping and the digs about his cooking, no, he didn't miss those. If he was honest, he didn't miss the sex that much. It was having someone to have a laugh with. And they *had* laughed, him and Jenni, and it hadn't even always been at Rory.

Still, he had David living with him now, didn't he? And he seemed an all right bloke. Maybe they could have a laugh together.

Only not in the mornings.

Rory made sure he was extra quiet as he had a quick shower, bunged on his uniform shorts and shirt, and laced up his walking boots, which were the most expensive bit of kit he owned. When you walked about ten miles a day, every day, you needed to keep your feet happy.

Everything was bright, clean, and quiet as Rory set out to drive the short distance from Pig Lane to the delivery office in Bishops Langley where he'd collect his mail. Hardly anyone was on the roads. It was like the world—well, this little corner of it, anyhow—was all his.

Rory loved his job. As much fresh air and exercise as a man could want, walking around the best village in the world. And the lads at the delivery office were a good lot too, although some of them were lasses, of course.

The first couple of hours were always spent at the delivery office, sorting out his mail and putting it into round order, which was when he got to have a bit of a natter with the other posties and catch up on the gossip.

Collette was having a moan about the junk mail they had to deliver and how it was killing the planet, while Rob pointed out that if they got rid of that, then half of them would be out of a job. Same old, same old. Like a faded sweatshirt that'd worn thin, with frayed cuffs and paint splashes on the sleeves, that was still the comfiest thing to chuck on to watch the telly. Rory wondered what his new lodger would wear to watch telly. He couldn't imagine David in a worn-out sweatshirt. Maybe one of them velvety tracksuits he used to see women wearing with a sparkly logo and *Juicy* scrawled on the bum? He chuckled at the thought.

"You're looking chirpy today." Collette paused by Rory's desk, a cup of coffee in her hand. "What've you been up to?"

"Not what you're thinking. Chance'd be a fine thing."

"Still single, then, babe? Join the club."

"Got a new lodger, though."

"Oh? Bloke?"

Rory nodded. "His name's David. Young bloke, mid-twenties or so."

"Ooh, is he single?" Collette, who'd been thirty-nine for several years now, moved in closer and perched her bum on the edge of Rory's desk.

"Gay. Sorry."

"Bum. At least tell me he's ugly."

Rory laughed. "Sorry, love. You know the bloke what plays Sherlock on the telly? Bit like that, only younger."

She groaned. "Now you're just being mean. Sure he's not bi and in the mood for being a toy boy? Quite fancy myself as a cougar, and a girl needs something to warm her up on a cold winter's night."

"Bed socks," Rory told her. "And a hot water bottle. And don't forget your mug of Ovaltine before bed."

"Even my granny never drank Ovaltine. Oh well, I s'pose I'd better see if my sister's lad is still looking for a bloke. He's a good catch, you know—works in IT in the City. He's shy, that's all. Needs someone to bring him out of his shell. You did say this David of yours was single, didn't you?"

"Uh, I'll find out. Better get on with the sorting now, though." Rory put his head down, feeling a bit weird.

He'd only met David last night, and already he was supposed to be fixing him up on dates?

A bloke couldn't keep anything to himself these days.

CHAPTER NINE

The clock, David decided, was undoubtedly laughing at him as it took its slow, laborious time ticking round to a reasonable hour. After his rude awakening at four thirty, he'd completely failed to get back to sleep, and even caffeine, when he finally gave up the attempt and dragged himself downstairs, could only do so much.

At five to nine, David leaned heavily on Mark's front door, rang the bell, and closed his eyes. When the door opened, taking his support with it, he staggered and practically fell in the house, only saving himself by clutching Mark's broad, manly shoulder. David was rather proud of himself for that little manoeuvre—at least, until he opened his eyes and realised it was in fact Patrick he was clinging onto like a lovestruck barnacle.

He unclung rapidly. "Oops. Sorry. Is the master of the house in?"

Patrick glared at him through eyes so narrow he must only be able to see a tiny sliver of David and none of the best bits. Which was a crying shame, in David's admittedly not-so-humble opinion. "Mark's in the kitchen. Try and keep your hands off *him*, yeah? I'm going to work."

He stomped out noiselessly—David would never have been so ill-prepared as to be wearing trainers when there was stomping to be done—and shut the door behind him with a disappointingly soft click.

David's shoulders slumped. He might not *actually* be a threat to Patrick's relationship with Mark—he did have some morals—but it would be nice to be credited as one beyond a sarcastic warning, all the same. His ego was a fragile, delicate flower that needed careful nurture.

That was what David always told people, at any rate. He wasn't sure why they never seemed to believe him.

"Mark?" he called, walking into the kitchen in cautious hopes of finding his employer, although he wouldn't put it beyond Patrick to have misdirected him. "Your humble wage-slave is here."

Mark emerged from behind the kitchen table—he'd been delving into a cardboard box of . . . well, charitably speaking, accounting records, but mostly the box seemed to be filled with scribbled-on old envelopes and curled-up, fading shop receipts. "Morning, David. Fancy a coffee before we start?"

"I could kill for a coffee. Although you realise you're putting your reputation as Scrooge to my Cratchit in serious danger by being so nice."

Mark laughed. "Okay, I know the wages aren't high, but at least I'm paying you more than thruppence an hour. And I promise faithfully to let you have a full two days off for Christmas. How's it going at Rory's?"

David collapsed gracefully into a chair. "Fine, except he gets up *in the middle of the night.*"

"Hm. You do look a bit . . .tired."

"Tired? I have *dark circles. Moi*! If I went along to any of my usual haunts with a face like this, everyone would think I was dressing up early for Halloween."

"As a zombie?"

"As the ghost of a young man, cut down tragically in his prime by sleep deprivation."

"I'm not sure you can actually die of that."

"*I* can."

"Well, try not to expire too precipitously. Having gone to all the bother of setting up a payroll system, I'd hate to lose you before your first salary cheque."

"Ooh, that's right, I'm your very first employee." David perked up enough to flutter his eyelashes. "I feel so honoured to have been chosen to pop your cherry. So tell me, oh Captain my Captain, what are my tasks for today?"

"Did you read up on Lottery funding like I asked?"

"Of course."

"And the introduction to bookkeeping I recommended?"

"*Naturellement.*"

"And financial reporting requirements for charitable trusts?"

"*Mais bien sûr.*"

"Excellent. Then your first task is . . ." Mark dug in his pocket and pulled out a fiver with a flourish. "Go and get us a couple of coffees from the baker's. Mine's a latte."

David pouted.

Mark laughed. "And while you're gone I'll get these records into some sort of order so you're not going in totally blind. Oh, and I can recommend their chocolate croissants if you're feeling peckish."

"Ugh. Food, at this hour?" David shuddered and left.

Everything was better after coffee. Everything was *always* better after coffee. Mark actually let him do some real work, and David was quite enjoying himself by lunchtime, although it took a little getting used to the fact that the columns of figures in the financial statements Mark had given him were in pounds, not thousands thereof. He'd discovered Mark's filing system was shockingly badly organised, and was itching for Mark to pop out for a client meeting so he could get it all shipshape.

Hmm. Maybe one client meeting alone wouldn't cut it. "Any holiday coming up?" he asked artlessly.

Mark's eyes narrowed nonetheless. "Why? What are you planning?"

"*Moi*? I'm hurt by the very suggestion."

Mark continued to stare at him, suspicion seeping from every pore.

David gave in. "Fine. Just a minor overhaul of your filing."

"Touch my system and the teddy bear dies."

"You wouldn't dare." David hoped. "But it's so inefficient!"

"*Inefficient* would be me not being able to find anything, which is what would happen if you reorganised it."

"Idiosyncratic systems are all very charming and quirky, but what happens if you fall under a bus and nobody can ever find anything ever again?"

"For one thing, it wouldn't be my problem anymore." Mark put on smug-face, something he did a little too well.

David gave him a stern glare.

Mark's shoulders slumped. "Fine, fine. *When* you're not busy on client work. And no getting bored and leaving it half done."

"Would I?" David narrowed his eyes at Mark's nod. "That was supposed to be rhetorical. When did I ever give you cause for dissatisfaction in our previous incarnation as master and slave?"

"I wish you wouldn't describe it that way. And all right, that was unfair. I've never known you to be, ah, flighty in a professional context."

"Or any context. I'm a model of constancy and reliability."

"Tell that to Colin from IT."

"Oh, *that*. He's hardly one to talk. There's barely a heart among the female staff of Whyborne & Co. that remained untouched by young Colin."

"Strange—he told me something similar about you. Although the word *female* wasn't used. Or the word *heart*, for that matter."

David's own heart clenched painfully. He'd thought he and Colin had parted on good terms, or at least not back-stabby ones. "You seem to think of me as some kind of sex-crazed office Lothario. I'm surprised you even let me in your house, let alone gave me a job."

Mark was looking a little pink. "I'm sorry. I shouldn't have repeated that. Ahem. Shall we get back to work?"

"With pleasure," David huffed, and did.

CHAPTER TEN

Rory generally finished up work around half past one, but it was a bit later today cos of 33 Farm View's cat. It'd gone for him—again—when he put his hand through the letterbox to get the post past the stiff brushes they'd fitted to keep the draughts out. So not only had he had to stop and put a couple of plasters on—he kept a few in his van cos you couldn't go bleeding on other people's mail—he'd also had to fill in the accident book when he got back to the delivery office.

Number 33 would be getting a stern letter soon. Rory didn't mind so much on his own account, cos Muffy was only defending her territory and he was up-to-date on his tetanus shots, but it wasn't fair on the lads and lasses who covered his round when he had the day off. They weren't expecting it. Dogs, now, you got some warning, what with the barking and all. Cats, the first thing you knew about it was when your hand came back shredded.

By the time he got home it was nearly three o'clock, cos he'd nipped into the shops and got some groceries he could probably manage to put together for a halfway decent pasta dish. He felt a lot more confident about cooking for David after last night's scromblet. There was a lot to be said for a bloke with standards as low as his own.

Rory shoved the food in the fridge, changed out of his uniform, and settled on the sofa with his feet up and his head down for a nap. He was just drifting off when David popped into his head. Would David think it was weird if he got home from work to find Rory snoring on the sofa?

Maybe Rory should set the alarm on his phone. Make sure he was up before five. He patted his pocket, then realised he'd left his phone in his uniform shorts. Upstairs.

Ah well, that settled it. David would have to deal. Rory snuggled back down into the cushions and was away with the fairies in seconds.

As it happened, he woke up at half past four, a good half hour before he was expecting David. Actually, Rory wasn't sure when he was expecting the bloke home. Maybe Mark would take David for a drink after they'd finished up, to celebrate his first day at work? After all, it was Friday. Which had struck Rory as a funny day to start a new job, but David had shrugged and said at least it wouldn't be too long until the weekend, in case he hated it.

Rory frowned. He hoped David didn't hate working for Mark. Course, he'd done it before, but it had to be a bit different, doing small village-y stuff without even a proper office, compared to that high-flying City firm with big posh offices on the Thames him and Mark had been at before.

If David didn't want to keep on with his new job, he might have to move again. Shamwell was great, but it didn't have a lot of job opportunities. Certainly not the sort of thing David must be used to.

Come to that, there wasn't a lot of stuff to do outside of work for a young bloke like him either. Not like there was in London, with the theatres and the clubs and that. Still, they weren't that far away here—not much more than half an hour on the train, barring signalling failures, staff shortages, and the wrong kind of leaves on the track. In fact, there were plenty of people who lived around here and commuted in every day for work. Evie's new bloke, Lewis, was one of them.

Rory nodded to himself, relieved. Yeah, David would be all right.

Normally Rory used his afternoons to do odd bits of housework, but he'd had a blitz on the place before David moved in. He wouldn't have wanted to come over as a slob. Gay blokes noticed that kind of stuff, didn't they?

It was times like this Rory really missed his kids. They'd be home from school by now—they'd started back last week after the summer holidays—full of news about who'd hit who at playtime (Lucy) and what amazing thing Mr. Enemy had said or done today (Leo). That had been another perk of being a postie—he'd always been home from work to see them when they got out of school. Some of their classmates hardly saw their dads except at weekends.

Lewis hardly saw the kids except at weekends. Which was good, cos he wasn't their dad. Rory was. Except now Rory only got to have them staying every other week, Friday night to Sunday teatime. It didn't seem right. He'd loved walking them home from school, stopping at the swings and popping into the baker's shop to buy them doughnuts or gingerbread men and making them promise not to tell their mum. Not that it ever helped. Evie had always seemed to just *know*, somehow, even if he'd remembered to wipe their sticky little faces and fingers before he'd taken them home.

She had a bit of a thing about sugar, Evie did. Well, she had a bit of a thing about a lot of stuff, to tell the truth, and Rory hadn't always been that good at remembering exactly what was on the banned list that week.

Still, only another week to go, and he'd have the kids over for a whole weekend again. Rory smiled to himself. It was going to be brilliant. David was going to love them.

David got in soon after five, so he must have come straight from Mark's place, which was only a couple of minutes' walk away. Rory heard the scratching of a key—he probably should've mentioned the lock was a bit sticky—then David's posh voice calling out, "Honey, I'm home."

Rory grinned, and ambled out into the hall to meet him. "How'd it go?"

David shrugged. "*Comme ci, comme ca.* I've never spent a day working with someone on their kitchen table before. Doing *other* things, yes, but not work." He yawned. "How come you're so bright eyed and bushy tailed?"

"Had a kip on the sofa when I got in. No chance I'd make it through the Spartans tonight if I hadn't."

"Oh yes, Mark mentioned there was a meeting." David flashed a sudden smile. It was weird, the way his face changed so quick. Like he was more alive than other people. Rory felt a boost just looking at him, as if David was giving off waves of energy. "Did you know I helped him with his makeup when he had his induction?"

"He was wearing makeup? I never noticed."

"Only on his body. Those finely contoured abs? All down to *moi*." David waved a hand in a flourish at himself. It was smug and cute at the same time, like when Leo or Lucy did something they were really chuffed about and wanted him to know.

"Yeah? He was well popular with the ladies that night. And the blokes too, I s'pose. Patrick, anyhow. You done a good job there."

"Happy days. That is, until the boyfriend burst in as I was putting on the finishing touches and jumped to the wrong conclusion." His mouth turned down, and Rory couldn't help laughing.

"So you're on the outs with Patrick and all? Heh, join the club."

David unwound his scarf and hung it on the banister. He wandered into the kitchen, stood in the middle of the floor frowning for a mo, then grabbed the kettle. "Oh, yes, you're the ruthless heart breaker who toyed with his mother's tender emotions and tossed her aside like a rag doll, aren't you?"

Rory winced. "It wasn't like that, all right?"

David seemed to have forgotten what to do with the kettle, so Rory, who'd been watching from the hall, walked the couple of paces into the kitchen and took it from him. He filled it and set it on to boil. "Cuppa?"

"Mm, please. But what was it like, then?"

"Look, don't tell no one, cos she told everyone it was a mutual decision and I ain't going around calling her a liar, but she dumped *me*."

"Really? How noble of you then, taking all the blame like that."

"Nah, it was still my fault really."

"Ooh, what did you do?" David gave him the side-eye. "Was it sleep deprivation?"

"It's . . . complicated." Rory got busy getting out mugs and tea bags cos, yeah, confessing his romantic failings? Not actually his all-time favourite occupation. "There was lots of things."

"Like?"

Rory had to laugh. "Nosy sod, ain't you? Well, for starters, she reckoned I spent too much time with Barry."

"Let me guess, they didn't get on?"

There was a bit of a funny tone in David's voice when he said that. Kind of flat. Rory shot him a glance, but couldn't tell anything from David's expression. Then the kettle boiled, and David sprang into action, grabbing the mugs and pouring on water.

Rory scratched his head. "Not really. Dunno what it was, mind. I mean, he's a good mate, Barry is. Dunno what I'd have done without him, back when me and Evie first broke up." Okay, that was enough of all that. David was going to think Rory was a right saddo if he kept harping on about *both* his exes. "Milk?"

"Please. And half a sugar."

"Didn't reckon you were the sort to take sugar."

"I'm not. Hence the half. I'll just go and get changed."

"Yeah, that suit's way too nice to go spilling your tea on." It was, too. Probably designer or something, and that midnight-blue shirt fit like it'd been tailored. Rory frowned. "So, like, Mark, yeah? Does he wear a suit and all when he's working from home?"

"More of a dressed-down Friday ensemble. But it is his house. If a client loomed on the horizon, he could always get me to stall them while he nipped upstairs to change." David pursed his lips. "Why, do you think it's a bit much?"

"Dunno, mate. You're looking at a bloke who wears shorts to work. Nah, I don't think so. Never hurts to dress for success, does it?" Rory glanced down at his own beer-fest T-shirt and jogging bottoms, which somehow seemed a whole lot slobbier than when he'd put them on. He wasn't dressed for success, was he? He wasn't dressed for failure, for that matter. He was dressed for not even getting his arse in gear to make the attempt.

Maybe he'd change into jeans and a proper shirt before he went out tonight.

David was smiling. "Excellent point. I shall go and slip into something more comfortable. Back in two shakes."

Rory had taken the tea through to the living room, put his feet up, and switched on the telly by the time David got back downstairs.

He'd changed into a tight, plain T-shirt and some soft jogging-bottom-type trousers that looked exactly like the ones Evie had used to wear to her exercise classes—Pilates and yogalates and God knew what else, only about ten times as expensive. On a bloke, they were a bit, um, revealing. Rory didn't know where to look.

"You hungry?" he said, jumping back up to his feet as David sat down next to him.

"God, yes. Look at me. I'm skin and bone." David patted his flat stomach with a pout. "I wouldn't go so far as to eat a horse, but maybe a small Shetland pony."

"Yeah? Well, there's a woman keeps some of them in the fields behind the church, but I don't reckon she'd be too chuffed if you nabbed one for a barbecue. My turn to cook, anyhow. Just don't expect, like, Gordon Blew, and we're golden. You all right with chicken pasta?"

"Oh, you know me. I'll put anything in my mouth."

"You say that now, mate, but you ain't seen my cooking yet."

Rory's mum had given him a quick lesson in not killing himself with food or the lack of it before he'd left home, but she'd always cooked traditional English meals of meat and two veg. He'd been in his early twenties before he'd realised there were other ways to cook a vegetable than boiling it into soggy submission. Ever since then, he'd liked to experiment when he got the chance, but Evie hadn't wanted him in her kitchen. She'd said he made a mess and put things away wrong, and he never made stuff how she'd have done it. Which was fair enough, really, but now he was on his own—well, with David, these days—he could play about a bit.

The pasta turned out all right, if Rory said so himself. He'd forgotten to buy onions, so he added extra garlic and threw in some chilli powder for fun, and he had half a packet of pepperoni going out of date in the fridge so he bunged that in too, mixing it all up with a load of passata cos you had to have a few vegetables, didn't you? And he'd even bought a bag of salad to have on the side, so it was dead posh. At any rate, David tucked in all right, although he did drink a shed-load of water with it.

"Less chilli next time?" Rory asked as he laid his fork down on his empty plate and leaned back on the sofa.

"It is a touch on the fiery side. Very tasty, though," David said encouragingly. He chased a bit of pasta across the plate with his fork, but he was just playing with it. Rory made a mental note to give him smaller portions from now on. He always forgot not everyone liked their food as much as he did.

David put the fork down decisively. "But that's my limit. Oh, I've been meaning to ask, do you have plans for the weekend? Plans, in particular, that might involve small people colonising the sofa?"

"Nah. I had the kids last weekend. I only get them once a fortnight."

"Then would you mind if I invited my mother to stay? Only for the one night, and of course I'll be the one on the sofa. You'll love Hen. Everybody does."

"Yeah, that'd be great. Uh, so's you know, I'm working tomorrow morning. I do the Saturdays I'm not looking after the kids, and then I get the Monday off after. They've been great about being flexible like that."

"Ah, well. Forewarned is forearmed. I have earplugs. And earmuffs. And I almost certainly won't smother to death if I sleep with my head under a pillow."

Rory felt a bit awkward. "Um, if it's gonna disturb you, I could try using my phone alarm instead of the clock. It's just, it doesn't always wake me up."

"No, no. I'm sure I'll get used to it. After all, you were married long enough to produce spawn. It must be possible to become desensitised to extreme noise. Unless that really was one of the reasons for the divorce?"

"Nah. Least, if it was, Evie never said. She met a bloke she liked better than she liked me, that's all." Rory shrugged at David's shocked face. "'S okay. I mean, it wasn't, but it was a while back now. Spilt milk under the bridge. So, uh, yeah, your mum? She lives on her own, does she?"

David nodded. "Armand—my father—passed away when I was a wee thing."

"Oh, mate, that's rough."

"Rougher on Hen. I hardly remember him, to be honest. She always says he used to make her laugh." David seemed sad for a moment, then he brightened up. "And now that's my job. I'll show you a picture of her."

He scrolled through his phone for a mo, with a few muttered comments—*no, no, not that one... ye gods, you don't want to see* that—then held it out to Rory.

Rory blinked. He'd been bracing himself to see someone around his own age or a year or two older—David could only be, what, twenty-four or twenty-five—but David's mum was, well, *old*. Not that she was a bent old granny, mind. She had shoulder-length, wavy grey hair with a pure white streak at the front, and wrinkles around the corners of her big brown eyes and her full, smiling mouth.

She was also, in an older-woman, Helen Mirren sort of way, absolutely stunning. "Blimey, did she used to be a model or something?" Rory asked without thinking.

David looked dead chuffed. "Psychologist, actually. She's written several books."

"Wow." Smart *and* gorgeous. Rory peered at David, trying to see the resemblance. "Hey, you got her eyes. And the cheekbones." Funny, that. He'd been half joking when he'd talked to Collette earlier, but David really was pretty fit.

And he was a nice bloke. How come he was single?

If he was single. Rory still hadn't asked, had he? "Um, are you seeing anyone? A ... a bloke, I mean?"

David's eyes went wide. "Rory, darling, I'm flattered, truly I am, but you should know I consider myself married to my teddy bear. Although maybe Gregory would consider a threesome—"

"What? No! I wasn't— I'm not—" Rory stuttered, his clothes suddenly too tight and his face so hot he could have cooked a scromblet on his head.

David burst out laughing. "Oh em *gee*, your face!"

"You git." Rory laughed as well. Mostly from relief. He had nothing against David shagging whoever he wanted to, but Rory and blokes? Not a thing. He wouldn't know where to start.

Which he didn't want to, anyway.

Start, that was.

"Admit it," David was saying. "You *asked* for that one."

"I— What? *No*, I just made a friendly enquiry. It's not like you haven't heard all about my sorry lack of a love life. So have you got a . . . a boyfriend, or not?" Rory wasn't prying. He simply wanted to know if he was likely to walk in and find David snogging some bloke on the sofa.

Not that there was anything wrong with that. It was just . . . a bloke liked a bit of warning, that was all.

"Sadly, I'm as single as you are." David pouted.

Thank God. Relief washed over Rory, and then he felt bad about it, cos he'd thought he was okay with the whole gay thing.

Then again, he was probably simply relieved he wasn't the only bloke round here without a partner. Sometimes it felt like the whole world was coupled up. Yeah, that must be it. "No one who measures up to your exacting standards, is there?"

"Or down to them, more likely. Based on my recent romantic history, at any rate." David slumped, sliding along the sofa cushions so far his knees knocked on the coffee table.

"Yeah? Never mind, mate. We can be sad lonely old tossers together. Uh-uh," Rory added quickly, wagging a finger at David, who'd perked up a bit. "No taking that literally, neither." Heh. He was already getting better at spotting these moments coming.

"You spoil all my fun," David said, but he was smiling up at Rory from his nest of sofa cushions. It was a smile Rory couldn't help returning, but it made him feel funny too. Like, sort of sad? Only he wasn't sure why.

"Nah, you don't have to worry," he said, cos the silence was getting awkward. "You're young, you are. Plenty of time for you to find someone decent."

"Everyone always says that." David was pouting again. "It completely misses the point. Armand didn't meet Hen until he was sixty-one, and look where that got him. A mere five years blissful togetherness and that was it, gone. I want someone *now*. Before I'm too old or too dead to enjoy it."

"Whoa, your dad was in his sixties?"

David's eyes narrowed. "*And*?"

Uh-oh. "Uh, so he was pretty young to die." Rory was proud of the save.

"Ironically for a Frenchman, heart disease. And before you say Greenlake doesn't sound very French, he was a Dupin. Hen doesn't think women should get married."

But it was all right for blokes? Rory couldn't quite get his head round that one.

"Nobody knew he had a weak heart—even he didn't, Hen said," David went on. "The first symptom was also the last, if you get my drift." He sat up suddenly. "But, God, it's Friday night, why are we being so morbid? We should be living it up, enjoying the single life—"

"Shit!" Rory slapped his head. "I oughtta be at Spartans by now. Sorry, mate—gotta run." He stood up, casting a worried glance at their dirty plates.

David made shooing motions. "Go, go—I'll wash up. We can't have you being late. There would probably be a ritual flogging, and it's murder getting blood out of a T-shirt."

"You're a champ, mate," Rory said in relief, and left.

CHAPTER ELEVEN

David watched Rory dash out of the house a little sadly.

Which was silly, really, as it wasn't like he hadn't spent plenty of evenings in on his own back in London. What with Brian being a dancer, their flat-share had been more like a time-share, with one coming in from work as the other went out. It wasn't even like he had nothing to do—from the amount of homework he'd been given, he was beginning to seriously suspect Mark had missed his vocation as a teacher.

Oh well. He loaded the plates into the minuscule dishwasher and washed up the pans, then flumped back down on the sofa and rang his mother. She answered almost immediately, and David could picture her sitting in her favourite armchair with her book, her phone having rested on the arm in readiness for a call. "Hello, darling. I was just thinking of you."

"Liar. I bet your mind was firmly focused on the latest Booker Prize contender. But I forgive you. How are you, Henny-Penny?"

"Oh, good, good. And you? How's the new place?"

"Remember that doll's house I had when I was a wee thing? The one that used to be Great Bron's, but she never played with it so it was as if it was brand new, and all the little dollies still had their own hair and everything?"

"Of course. I think it's in the attic somewhere. You know I haven't lost hope you'll make me a granny one day."

"That day, alas, is not this day. What were we talking about that for? Oh, yes. Rory's house is about that size."

Hen laughed. "Oh dear. I hope you're getting on all right with this Rory."

"He's a total sweetie. Straight, but one can't have everything. Divorced, with two children, Lucy and Leo. And his wife left him for a Lewis, presumably because Rory wasn't fitting in with the family *L* motif."

"Oh, what's her name?"

"Evie. The hypocrite."

"And how old are the children?"

"School age. But still winsome. He has a photo of them on the mantelpiece. And the kitchen windowsill. And on the wall on the upstairs landing."

"Poor man. Not in the downstairs loo?"

"There isn't one."

"Then we'll have to hope that neither of you is ill. Have you met the children yet?"

"No—they're only here every other weekend. And oh! That was what I was calling about. Can you come and visit? Tomorrow?"

"I would love to, but I'm afraid it's far too short notice. I'm seeing Auntie Bron tomorrow. I hear she has a new girlfriend."

"Ooh, do tell."

"Her name is Sarah, she's seventy-eight, and she moved into the care home a few weeks ago. That's all I know. Oh, except that she still has all her own teeth—"

"That's not necessarily an advantage."

"Don't interrupt, darling. I'm sure I taught you better than that. And *apparently* she used to have a piercing in her . . ."

David waited a moment or two, but no more was forthcoming. "Well, go on, where?"

"Auntie Bron wouldn't say on the phone. She left it as a dramatic pause."

"Bless her. Give her my love, won't you? And if you can't come this weekend, how about in a fortnight?"

"Let me see—I just need to check my calendar."

David drummed his fingers on the coffee table while he waited. Then he got bored and drummed his toes. They turned out to be significantly less drummy so he went back to fingers, then whole hands. He was so caught up in the rhythm that he almost missed Hen coming back on the line.

"Darling?"

"I'm here. And queer."

"And dear."

David smiled at the fondness in her voice, then panicked mildly as he realised it was his turn. "And . . . austere?"

"More like insincere. Now, don't make me be severe."

"Why do you always win at word games?"

"Because, as you know, I'm without peer." Hen laughed. "But you're off your game tonight. Something troubling you?"

"It's nothing."

"Really?"

"Oh, Rory was talking about . . . things."

"Things?"

"About his ex-wife. And his ex-girlfriend. Hen, do relationships ever work out? And stay worked out, I mean?"

"Of course they do. But you have to be prepared to work for it. Make compromises. Adjust your expectations, perhaps." Hen put a certain amount of emphasis on the last phrase.

"You mean marry the coachman instead of Prince Charming. And learn to grin and bear the tendency to gnaw on the furniture and the addiction to cheese."

"Ah, but if you loved the coachman, you'd find all that charming in itself. Just because he's only a coachman doesn't mean he can't sweep you off your feet. And if you think about it, a pampered prince and a poor girl who's been abused and treated as a slave all her life are bound to bring rather different expectations to their marriage. Maybe Cinderella would have been happier, in the long run, with a coachman."

"You're forgetting the very real attraction of tiaras and palaces."

"All that glitters, darling . . . Anyway, the answer to your question is yes."

"What question was that?"

"Do try to keep up. Yes, I can come up to Hertfordshire in a fortnight. As long as it's all right with your . . . Rory."

"He isn't *my* Rory."

"I hardly know what to call him. Landlord, I suppose, as he's renting you a room. Does he own the property, or is he renting himself?"

"Renting, I think."

"Housemate, then." Hen said it firmly.

David wasn't so sure. His name wasn't on the lease. *Any* lease. Rory had simply named a price which seemed eminently reasonable—for which, read: insanely cheap—and asked for cash at the end of the month. The arrangement was wholly informal, and David had a sneaking suspicion it might not even be all that legal.

It was undoubtedly best to say as little as possible about it and hope no one would notice.

"Anyway, he can't wait to meet you," he went on swiftly, if not entirely truthfully. But if Rory knew how wonderful Hen was, he would be dying to meet her, so it was true in all essentials. Just not *literally*.

"And I him. Now, is there anything you want me to bring up from home?"

"Well, an extra room or two would be nice. Say the front room from downstairs—you hardly ever use that."

Hen laughed again. "I'll see you in a fortnight. Now, do try and behave yourself in the meantime."

"*And* you. Love you."

"Love you too, darling."

David hung up.

David had been through as much of Mark's Recommended Reading List as he could stand and was sitting cross-legged on the sofa in his T-shirt and yoga pants playing a game on the PlayStation when Rory finally rolled in through the front door. David glanced at the clock to find it rather later than he would have expected, given the whole early-morning-start thing.

Rory more or less wafted into the living room on a cloud of beery fumes. "Hey! David! You're still up." He beamed, and sat down heavily on the sofa. "Oops."

"I see the meeting took its toll," David said drily, leaving his little avatar to bob helplessly on the screen and turning to Rory.

"Nah, Barry needed to talk so me and him had a pint after."

A pint of what? Whiskey? "What was the emergency?"

Rory frowned. "Uh . . . Not sure. Something about the wife maybe?" He yawned. "Not sure we actually got round to it, whatever it was, but he seemed to have cheered up anyhow by the time they called last orders. You had a good evening?"

"Mm. I spoke to Hen. She can't make it this weekend, but she's coming over in two weeks—is that okay?"

"Yeah, no problem." Rory yawned again, this time so widely his jaw clicked loudly.

David tutted. "You should be careful doing that. I had a friend who dislocated his jaw once and he said it was *awful*. Hideously uncomfortable, and everyone just laughed at him. Of course, in *his* case it wasn't yawning that caused it . . . Shouldn't you go to bed? Don't you have to be up for work in an hour or so?" He shuddered.

"Yeah. 'N a minute." Rory shut his eyes and almost immediately began snoring softly.

David closed down the PlayStation, switched off the television, and sighed. Should he wake Rory up and get him to bed? Or would it be easier to bring the bed to Rory?

And how on earth had the man managed when he'd been living on his own? Then again, that alarm clock of his probably woke people living several streets away.

David had an idea. He lifted Rory's feet up onto the sofa so he was lying flat, then pillowed his head on one of the squashy, oversized cushions.

Satisfied Rory was still dead to the world, he nipped upstairs to fetch the instrument of early-morning torture, brought it back down, and shoved it under Rory's makeshift pillow.

David gazed at Rory with a fond smile. There. Humanitarian duty done. Hmm. Should he bring down the duvet?

No, it was a warm night, the chills of autumn having not yet fully taken hold. David settled for taking the throw that was over the back of the sofa and tucking it loosely around Rory's boozy form. After a moment's thought, he brought a pint glass of water from the kitchen and, while he was at it, the washing-up bowl, and placed them strategically where they could do the most good.

Now he could go to bed.

CHAPTER TWELVE

Whoa.

Rory sat bolt upright in bed, his teeth still feeling weird from where the ringing of his alarm clock had got in somehow and made them vibrate . . . Wait a minute.

He wasn't in bed, and he couldn't even see his alarm clock which, shit, was still going strong. David was going to give him that grumpy look again if he didn't turn it off. Although it didn't seem quite as loud as usual . . .

Shit. Was it upstairs doing its nut while he was down here? Rory jumped up, put one foot on the edge of something hard and plasticky that tipped up and nearly had him face-planting on the coffee table, fought free of some blankety thing his legs were all tangled up in, and swore again as something heavy hit him on the *other* foot.

Oh. *There* was the clock. On the floor, next to his throbbing toe. And the washing-up bowl. What was *that* doing there? Rory collapsed back onto the sofa and grabbed the clock to turn it off.

Lovely, lovely silence. Rory breathed a sigh of relief and took a swig from the handy pint glass of water on the coffee table. He must have put it there last night before he fell asleep. Funny, that. He wasn't usually this organised. He had to have been well out of it last night to have done that and not remember it this morning.

But then there was the alarm clock. And the washing-up bowl. Rory couldn't for the life of him think why he'd have put that there. It wasn't like he'd been feeling queasy or anything. He hadn't actually had that many pints last night—Barry had laughed at him for being a lightweight. It'd been the tiredness that'd done him in. By the time he'd walked home he'd barely had the energy to talk to David . . .

David. He must have been the one who'd done it all.

Huh. That was nice of him. After all, he'd only known Rory for a couple of days.

Rory hoped he hadn't just paid the bloke back by waking him up again. Shit, he had to have, didn't he? What with the alarm going off for ages and then him clattering about dropping stuff. Still, David hadn't come down to complain yet. Might be best to keep quiet from now on and hope.

Rory got to his feet a bit more carefully this time, put the throw back on the sofa, and took the glass and the bowl into the kitchen. Then he tiptoed upstairs as softly as he could and paused on the landing.

David still hadn't appeared. Had he managed to sleep through the racket? He had to be in the house, didn't he? Despite all the faffing around, it was still only quarter to five, so he had to be in bed. Unless he'd gone out after Rory had got back last night, or got abducted by aliens, or . . . Rory hesitated, then carefully opened David's bedroom door a crack.

There was David, snuggled up in the pink fairy duvet with his teddy bear, a pair of Hello Kitty earmuffs on his head. *Lucy would like some of those,* Rory thought idly. David's hair was rumpled, and he was smiling in his sleep.

Aw. Rory gazed at him for a second, soppy smile on his face, then realised what he was doing and shut the door hastily. Yeah, that'd be pretty near the top of the "Ways to creep out your lodger" list.

But anyway, David was all right so Rory could go to work.

He had a quick shower and chucked last night's clothes in the laundry bin. They smelled a bit beery, probably cos Barry got really expansive with the hand gestures when he'd had a few and last night he'd forgotten he was holding his pint glass half the time. Rory felt a lot better once he was clean and dressed in his uniform, and he whistled as he drove to the delivery office.

Best job in the world.

Rory's good mood lasted all through sorting his mail and getting halfway through his round, but when he got to 14, The Rise, the hair on the back of his neck started to prickle. The local free paper, which came round on Thursday afternoon, was still sticking out of the letterbox wrapped round a wodge of junk mail flyers. And old Mrs. Young was always very particular about taking stuff in, which Rory reckoned was more down to her not getting a lot of proper post than anything else. He hadn't had a delivery for her yesterday, or he'd have noticed then.

Repeated knocks on the door, first at normal volume and then as loudly as he could manage, didn't get a reply, so Rory crouched down, pushed the paper through the letterbox, and peered inside. "Mrs. Young? You all right in there?"

Nothing. Or was there? Rory wasn't sure if he'd heard some kind of scratching noise, or only imagined it. He called once more, and this time was almost certain he heard it in reply.

He had a peek in the living room window, but there was nobody there.

Shit. Rory sat back on his heels and considered his options. Best to try the neighbours first. Number 16 was away—he'd had to leave a note about a parcel, and the place had had that abandoned look, with windows all shut and curtains left half drawn—but number 12 was a young working couple with no kids—lots of activity holiday brochures and lifestyle magazines—so hopefully they'd be in.

He jogged down the path and up next door's, and knocked.

It was a good old while before the door was opened by a young woman in her dressing gown. "Morning," she said, and yawned.

"Morning. I'm a bit worried about Mrs. Young next door. Number 14."

"Oh, is that her name? What's happened?"

"Not sure, to tell you the truth. She ain't away, is she?"

"Not that I know of. But we're both at work all day, so . . ." She shrugged.

And, yeah, they could have missed her getting picked up, and God knew it was peak season for old age pensioners going on coach tours and stuff, but Rory still didn't like it. Mrs. Young, far as he knew, didn't do that sort of thing. And if she did, she'd arrange for someone to come round and look after the post and the papers, not leave them sticking out of the letterbox as a signal to burglars to come on in and make themselves at home. And then there was that noise—if it *had* been a noise. "You seen her around since Thursday?"

"Since Thursday? I don't know . . . I don't think so." She yawned again. "Sorry."

"Don't suppose you got a key? I'm worried she might have had a fall and can't get up."

"No. Sorry. We don't really know her."

Course they didn't. They'd only been living next door to the old dear for about a year now. "Right. In that case, you got a stepladder?"

"Why?"

"So I can hop over the side gate and have a butcher's in the back windows."

"Oh. Are you allowed to do that?"

"You let me worry about it, love."

She huffed. "Okay, wait there and I'll get the key to the garage." She disappeared inside.

Rory stood there on the doormat until he heard the garage door clattering up and then he headed over to where the woman, still in her dressing gown and fluffy slippers, was lugging the ladder out to him.

"Cheers." Rory hopped over to Mrs. Young's side with it—the fence between the houses was low at the front—and held it up to the tall gate that closed off the path between her front and back gardens. No lock, luckily: it just had a bolt near the top, which was easy enough to lean over and undo from a few steps up the ladder. He moved the ladder aside and walked on through.

The first window he came to was from the living room, which stretched the length of the house, and he already knew that was empty. Rory jogged on to the next room, the kitchen, and had a shufti in the window.

That was where he saw her. Lying on the floor, her face so sunken it looked like a skull wrapped in wrinkled parchment. Rory took a step back in shock before he realised she was moving, thank God, one hand scrabbling at the lino. "Mrs. Young?" he called, hoping his voice would carry through the window.

She shifted again, this time more energetically, and he could see her mouth moving. "It's all right," he yelled. "I'm gonna get help."

Rory had his phone out before he'd finished speaking, and called 999. "I'm gonna break a window and get in," he told them after he'd given them all the details. "She don't look so good. Just tell 'em not to arrest me when they get here."

It was a blooming good thing she was too old-fashioned to have double glazing. Rory pulled off his boot and used it to break the pane in the kitchen door. Once he'd cleared the broken glass from the edges, it was easy enough to unbolt the door and turn the key in the lock, and then he was in.

Mrs. Young was in a right old state. He didn't dare try to get her off the floor, in case she'd broken something. She couldn't speak—probably hadn't had a drink in near on two days—so after he'd nipped upstairs to grab a blanket off her bed to wrap the poor old dear in, he fetched a cup of water and helped her take sips until the police and the ambulance arrived.

They were great—thanked him for calling them, like anyone else wouldn't have done it.

Rory was about to head off, when he remembered he ought to take the stepladder back to number 12, reminded by seeing the couple standing on their doorstep watching all the kerfuffle with wide eyes and guilty faces. The woman in her dressing gown had been joined by her bloke, in jeans and a T-shirt but no socks. "Cheers for the loan," Rory called out, leaning the ladder up against the garage wall.

"Is she going to be okay?" the bloke asked.

"Hope so." Whether she'd ever be coming back to live in number 14 was another matter. That'd been how it went with his gran—one fall too many and she'd gone straight from hospital to nursing home.

"We didn't know she was so frail," the woman said, pulling her dressing gown tighter around her middle.

"She's in safe hands now," Rory said, cos what else could he say?

Then he got back on with his deliveries.

He couldn't help thinking what a narrow escape the poor old dear had had, though. If Rory hadn't been working this Saturday, what was the chance whoever covered his round would've known to be worried? She could've been on that floor till Monday.

He didn't reckon she'd have still been moving by then.

Rory was that rattled by it all he didn't even stop to change out of his uniform after he got home before knocking on Mrs. Willis's front door. He wasn't able to relax until he heard the familiar *swish* of her slippers as she shuffled up the hallway.

"All right, Mrs. Willis?" he asked, as she opened the door and peered up at him from under her tight grey curls—well, more white than grey, these days. Funny to think she'd probably been as tall as him before she got old.

"Yes?" She looked him up and down. "Are you here to deliver something?"

"Nah, just wanted to check you're okay. If you need anything, I'm off for the weekend now. I see you've got your posh frock on— you got a hot date?" She was wearing a black and white dress with a zigzag print Rory was pretty sure was new. He wasn't one for noticing women's clothes all that much, but it was the kind of pattern he'd remember. It made his eyes go funny.

"I should think not. I like to be smart. Unlike everyone else these days, it seems."

"It's lovely, Mrs. Willis. You'll be turning all the blokes' heads in the village, you will."

She sniffed. "Not *all* the men, if I'm any judge. I see you moved your young man in the other day."

"What, David? Yeah, he's the new lodger."

"I didn't realise people still called it that." She didn't seem to approve of lodgers, but then Mrs. Willis didn't approve of a lot, bless her.

"No? S'pose you could call him my housemate."

She *humph*ed at him. "I only saw him through the window, but it was *quite* clear that young man was light in the loafers. I'm surprised at you, though—a family man."

She didn't mean . . . Did she? "Nah, my loafers ain't light." Rory found himself lifting up a boot to show the old lady and put it down in a hurry, feeling like a prize muppet.

"Oh, I'm sure it's none of my business. Times change. I'm not saying it's for the worse, but I'm not saying it's for the better, either."

Rory swallowed. "Right. Fine. So, you're okay, then? Don't need nothing?"

"No, thank you, I don't need anything." There was a bit of an emphasis on the *any*, to remind him that she'd been an English teacher in her day and didn't hold with bad grammar. Then she closed the door, leaving Rory standing like a lemon on the doormat. Bloody hell, that'd floored him and no mistake. He hadn't even thought to ask about Mr. Willis, which he'd been meaning to cos he hadn't seen him around lately.

Was this what everyone was going to think? That him and David were, well, *living together*, not just living together?

Rory wasn't sure how he felt about that. He paused, his hand on Mrs. Willis's front gate. Maybe he should go back and tell her he wasn't gay?

Except, did it really matter if she thought that? Making a fuss about people thinking he was gay would feel like he was saying it was *bad*, which was disloyal to Mark and Patrick and Mr. Emeny at the school and Mr. Emeny's bloke too, who Rory had never met socially but felt a vague sort of connected-ness to through the kids and the village and that.

And, to be honest, it was kind of flattering if people actually believed someone as young and good-looking as David would be with a boring old fart like him . . .

Rory gulped.

David was going to go spare when he found out.

CHAPTER THIRTEEN

David's return from the Land of Nod was blissfully peaceful on
Saturday morning. He luxuriated in that state of being half-asleep
but still awake enough to enjoy it until a nasty thought struck.

What if he hadn't set Rory's alarm properly?

Oh God, it was almost eleven o'clock. Rory would be *hours*
late for work. David sprang out of bed with the speed of a gazelle.
Also the coordination—provided said gazelle were a newborn that'd
been plugged into the mains. He hurtled downstairs . . . only to sigh
in relief and flump down on the sofa when he found it reassuringly
unoccupied.

Now all potential emergencies were out of the way, brunch seemed
to be called for. If he'd been in London, he'd have called someone and
suggested they meet at a café somewhere. He *could* still do that, of
course—London wasn't *that* far away from here—but catching trains
or taking Mrs. Merdle for a run in the weekend traffic seemed to
defeat the whole point of a relaxed Saturday morning. Brunch was
something you strolled to, not consulted timetables or braved the
M25 for. But who did he know in Shamwell apart from Rory and
Mark, whom he'd be seeing five mornings a week in any case?
And Patrick, of course, but David had an instinctive feeling that
brunching with Patrick would involve paying close attention to
ensure the eggs didn't come garnished with a sprig of hemlock and the
mushrooms weren't genus Amanita.

There was only one person he could call. David grabbed his phone
and scrolled through his contacts with a practised finger.

Fen answered on the third ring. "'S up?"

"Me. I am. Are you?"

"Almost. Why?"

"I need you to come to brunch with me." David thought about it. "Although only if you can make it in the next half an hour. I might actually expire from hunger if you make me wait until you've put your full face on."

"God, you're worse than *Dad*. Fine. Are we going to the café by the bridge?"

"Is there much choice?"

"*Duh*. There's like *millions* of cafés in the village. At least two. But that's the best one for chocolate croissants."

"The bridge it is, then. Eleven thirty. Don't be late."

"Whatevs."

In fact she made it to the café in a very respectable forty minutes. David, who'd arrived twenty minutes ago to bag a table, glanced up from his borrowed copy of the *Daily Fail*, and beamed at her black-clad figure. "Darling! How ravishing. Is this the new incognito look?"

Fen had her hoody up and was wearing large, dark sunglasses, which she pulled down her nose so he could see her roll her kohl-free eyes. They seemed shockingly small, young, and innocent. "No. This is the look of someone who got dragged out of bed way too early and didn't have time to put on her makeup. So what's the emergency? What's Rory done?"

David frowned. "Nothing. There's no emergency. Can't I want to see you just for the sake of it?"

"Yeah, but you saw me like two days ago."

She had a point, David realised. Usually they only saw each other once a month, although their phone calls were every week or so. "And isn't it nice that, now we're living so close, we can see each other more frequently?"

Fen gave him a withering stare over the top of her sunglasses. "Do we need to get you some friends your own age round here?"

David frowned. "You sound like someone's mother. Note I didn't say *my* mother. Hen is above such things as ageism."

"That's cos she's old. I mean, no offense, but you told me she's in her sixties. That's bus-pass age. That's old enough to get a cup of tea and a cake in here for half price on a Wednesday. Are we ever going to order? I thought you were hungry."

"So impatient. Fine. What is it? Chocolate croissant and . . .?"

"Hot chocolate."

"You do realise that just because sugar highs are legal doesn't mean they're good for you?" Having seen her face, David didn't wait for a reply, going straight up to the counter to order his skinny latte and egg on wholemeal toast, and her exercise in dental caries.

When he got back to the table, she was flicking through his discarded paper. "You'll rot your brain as well as your teeth," he warned, sitting back down.

"*You* were reading it."

"I'm past helping. And I read it with a critical eye."

"Yeah? Which one's that?"

"This one." David shut one eye tight and leered at her with the other, making her giggle.

Then he sighed.

She didn't appear to have noticed, so he sighed again, adding a bit of shoulder slumping for good measure.

Fen folded the paper up noisily. "What?"

"It's hard, isn't it? Moving to a new place. Carving out a new social circle."

She nodded. "Yeah. I hated it here at first. But then I got to know people at school, and Lex in theatre class, and . . . Are you missing your mates?"

"A little. Oh, thank you." Their order had arrived. David took a grateful sip of his latte as Fen set to dismantling her croissant.

"I was surprised you moved here," she said, a large blob of chocolate filling poised in front of her mouth. "I thought you loved living in London."

David cut a precise square of toast. "I did, but . . . I don't know. I can't help thinking they never really took me seriously."

"Who?"

"*Anyone.* Take Bri-Bri. Cast me out on the street without so much as a 'So long and thanks for all the fish.' And Ryan and Samir—they let me stay, yes, but it was quite clear it was under sufferance. And they were the ones suffering. Oh, I don't know. Ignore me. Lack of food is making me maudlin." He popped the eggy toast in his mouth and chewed thoughtfully.

"That's not true. Dad takes you seriously." She blushed. "Mostly. Well, he said you were good at what you do. In the office, I mean, before you say anything rude. I heard him say that when he was arguing with Patrick about you working for him."

David winced. "Here I go, strewing domestic discord in my wake like blood-soaked confetti. And it's sweet of you to say it, but I'd take that with a bushel or two of salt. What else was he going to say to his lover in defence of his hiring me—'Oh, I know, darling, but he has an arse like a peach and his cheekbones are to die for'? I can't see that going over well with the little rottweiler."

Fen giggled, then frowned as she peeled a strip off her croissant and gestured at him with it. "Language. You should be nicer to Patrick. He's all right." She stuffed the strip of croissant in her mouth, chewed hastily, and went on, "And ew. You made me think of Dad saying 'arse like a peach.' That's so gross."

"Meh. You have to learn sometime that parents are people too. People who have *needs*, and *desires* . . ."

"Shut up! Jeez. It's bad enough walking in on him and Patrick snogging on the sofa. If I barf, you're clearing it up. And saying sorry to the café people."

"Thank you so much for that word picture. It's really enhanced my enjoyment of my scrambled eggs."

"You started it. What were we even talking about, anyway?"

"My need and desire for a fresh start."

"Yeah? Okay, that's cool. So what you need to do is meet people. You've got to join the Sham-Drams. I bet you'd be brilliant at acting—you're a total drama queen. Oh, I know. You could do what Dad did and join the Spartans."

"Because Patrick would be so overjoyed to have me muscle in on that too?"

"Um. Maybe not, then. And, anyhow, you need to meet *new* people. And they're all old in the Spartans. Patrick's, like, the youngest there."

"Isn't he my age?"

"Maybe. You seem younger, though. Half the time I forget you're not my age. Patrick seems more like Dad's age."

"You say that like it's a bad thing."

"That's cos I'm not weird like you and I don't only fancy blokes twice my age."

"There's a lot to be said for a mature gentleman. For a start, there's a greater proportion of them who *are* gentlemen." David couldn't help thinking wistfully of Xav. He'd been so charming . . . Right up until the moment he'd been revealed as an adulterer.

Still, nobody was perfect.

"What does that even *mean*? Like, they hold doors open for you and stuff?"

"You wouldn't understand. You're a child of the modern age."

"What, and you're not?"

"I'm a classic. I never go out of style." David sipped his coffee. "But I suppose we'll have to agree to disagree about my serial gerontophilia."

"When you say it like that, it sounds like something you ought to see a doctor about." Fen's phone rang. She pulled it out of her pocket and scowled as she accepted the call. "Yeah?"

There was a pause. "I'm at the café. *No*, with David." Pause. "*Daa*-aad. I'm like thirty seconds down the road." Pause. "You were upstairs. With *Patrick*." Pause. "Well, I wasn't gonna—"

Pause.

Glower.

"*Fine*." She turned off her phone and shoved it back in her pocket so hard David heard a stitch go. "I've got to go home."

David winced. "Forgot to mention you were going out?"

"It's so *stupid*. I'm nearly sixteen. Dads are stupid." She froze. "Um. Sorry."

"Don't worry about it. Go, go. Before I lose *another* job for being a bad influence." David made shooing motions.

After she'd gone, he finished off his rapidly cooling egg on toast, and thought.

She was right. He needed to meet people. Find some new friends who wouldn't be so fickle as the old ones. But how?

Time to draft a plan of action. The new David Greenlake wouldn't idle his time away in cafés and bars. Well, not as soon as he'd finished his latte. The new David would be a mover. A shaker. A joiner.

He drained his mug with a decisive slurp and swept out of the café, pausing only to pick up one of every local leaflet displayed in the jaunty little rack by the door.

Yes. David Greenlake was going to make his mark on this village.

CHAPTER FOURTEEN

Rory returned from work rather later than David had expected, less like two-ish and more verging on three-ish. Fortified by his brunch, David had been busily researching local organisations on his laptop. The Sham-Drams did indeed seem promising, but he wasn't so sure about the Campaign to Bring Back Hare Coursing. For a start, David hadn't the faintest idea how one actually coursed a hare, and whether the hare enjoyed it or not. Perhaps he should ring up the chairman, a Mr. Onslow, and ask.

There was something of the startled rabbit in Rory's big brown eyes when he walked into the living room. "Listen, uh, about Mrs. Willis next door . . . It looks like she's got the wrong end of the stick about you and me."

"Oh, do tell."

"Uh, she thinks we're . . . you know." Rory blushed pillar-box red.

David beamed. "Oh, how sweet! Did you tell her it's all strictly platonic?"

"Yeah, but she didn't believe me. Uh, aren't you hacked off about it?"

"Why should I be?" David shrugged. True, Rory wasn't the dapper, urbane man-about-town David usually went for, but neither was he the kind of other half you'd want to hide in the attic whenever company came over.

"Uh . . . no reason. Cup of tea? I'll go get me kit off first."

Rory disappeared upstairs before David had a chance to respond to that little conversational gem, which was a crying shame.

He'd just turned back to his laptop when there was a banging at the front door. It was, to be honest, fairly unlikely that Rory had *actually* meant he'd be coming downstairs naked, but nevertheless it would probably be best not to leave answering it to him.

David jumped up and opened the door to greet the visitor, whoever it might be, with a beaming smile, but had to adjust the angle of the beam significantly downwards. Two small children stood on the doorstep. They were easily recognisable from the photos Rory kept around the house, if noticeably less well scrubbed. The larger—Lucy, he remembered—had long brown hair in plaits that were coming undone and a smudge on her nose, a grimy button island adrift amid a sea of freckles. She fixed him with a dark, suspicious eye. "You're Daddy's lodger."

"Guilty as charged. But you can call me Davey." He frowned. "Is your mother around?"

"She's gone to Gran's."

Lucy had a rucksack on her back, and the boy—Leo, a smaller, neater version of his sister with shorter, fairer hair and spectacles perched on his equally grubby nose—was clutching what looked like a large, cuddly Cthulhu.

"Where's Daddy?" Lucy demanded.

"Upstairs." David turned to find that was no longer true and waved them on inside so he could make helpless gestures at their father over their heads.

Rory, standing at the bottom of the stairs and thankfully decently clad, shot him a puzzled glance, and smiled at his offspring. "'Ello, then. What are you lot doing round here? Did your mum bring you?"

Lucy heaved her rucksack off her back and dumped it on her father's slipper-clad feet. "Daddy, we've come to live with you. We don't want to live with *him* anymore. I've brought our toothbrushes and pyjamas and my football kit, and Leo's got Mr. Squiddy."

"Lucy, love, you know I'm always glad to see you, but we talked about this, yeah?" Rory, bless him, had screwed up his face as if he had a headache coming on. "You can't just up and leave the house every time Lewis does something you don't like."

"But, Daddy, Mummy told Leo he could play on the Xbox as soon as he did all his homework, and he did it *all*, and then Lewis wouldn't let him."

Rory sat on the stairs and patted his son's face, which, David now noticed with a pang, had clear tear tracks running down it. "Did you and him have another row?"

Leo nodded.

"You gotta give him a chance, yeah? I'm sure he's doing the best he can."

"But it's not *fair*," Lucy butted in. "He had some stupid programme he was watching on the telly, and he wouldn't even *listen*, and he called Leo an ungrateful little brat."

There was a ringing silence for a moment.

Then Rory got to his feet, a storm gathering on his brow. "Where's your mum?"

"Gone to Gran's," David put in, eager to show he'd covered that one.

"Yeah?" The storm clouds vanished in a fog of concern. "Luce, is your gran poorly again? I dunno why Evie doesn't *tell* me these things . . . I'm gonna give Lewis a call. He's probably going spare, wondering where you are."

David held his tongue about his own doubts on that score. He'd have thought, if that was the case, surely Lewis would have been in touch with Rory by now—wasn't his house the obvious port of call? Especially if, as Rory's words seemed to suggest, this had happened before.

"Can we play on the PlayStation?"

"Course you can. But, oi, none of the eighteen-plus games, yeah? They're just for me and my mate David." Rory blinked and turned to David for the first time since the underage invasion. "I ain't introduced you yet, have I? David, this is my kids, Lucy and Leo. Kids, this is David. You be nice to him, all right?"

"We met him when he opened the door." Lucy tossed her head, dark pigtails flying, as if to say, *Dads, what are they like?*

"Yeah, but that's not like being introduced, is it?"

"Why not?"

"Uh . . ." Rory looked a bit floored.

David stepped forward. "Because if someone you trust introduces you, you can be certain the new person is the sort of person you want to get to know." He held out his hand. It was never too early to teach the value of a firm handshake.

Lucy stared.

Rory cleared his throat. "When you meet someone, you gotta shake hands, yeah? Like this." He grasped David's hand with exactly the right degree of pressure.

Warm, reassuringly strong hands, David couldn't help but notice. Softer than he'd expected. Nice.

"That's silly," Lucy said. "What if they've got a cold, or if they've been to the toilet and didn't wash their hands? You might catch something."

"But then, what is life without risk?" David realised he was still holding on to Rory's hand, and its owner was starting to look as though he might want it back. He released his grasp hurriedly. "Nevertheless, I think we can waive the formalities on this occasion."

"You talk posh," Lucy said. "Come on, Leo."

Leo, bless his little heart, stepped forward and held out his hand to David. It was his left hand, his right occupied with holding tightly to the fluffy spaghetti monster, but David took it with the gravity with which it was offered. And did his best to resist the urge to wipe his palm on his trousers immediately afterwards. "*Enchanté*," he murmured.

"That's French for 'All right, mate?'" Rory explained helpfully. "Now, you go and set up the PlayStation, yeah? I got a couple of phone calls to make."

"He's a man of few words, isn't he, your son," David commented after they'd scurried off to the living room. "And by few, I mean none."

Rory smiled faintly. "Yeah, he's always been shy. Lets Lucy do the talking for him. I'm hoping school's gonna change that—he's only been there a year. He loves it, mind. 'Specially Mr. Emeny. Leo can't wait to be in his class next year. He's the one who's getting married to the pest-control bloke."

"Ooh, first gay wedding in the village?"

Rory's brow furrowed. "Dunno. I mean, Mark says Sean's bi like Patrick, so does it still count as a gay wedding? Anyhow, I gotta call Evie. And Lewis," he added with a sigh.

David took the hint and left him to it.

He headed into the living room, where he found Lucy already hooked up to the PlayStation and driving dangerously fast around a virtual racetrack. Leo was watching avidly, possibly the only little brother in the history of the world who would do so instead of trying to wrest the controller out of his sister's grasp. "You know, I'm almost certain we've got some two-player games," David said mildly.

"Leo's getting his turn in a minute." Lucy didn't take her eyes off the screen for a nanosecond.

David sat down next to Leo. "So you did all your homework by midafternoon on Saturday? That's very impressive. Although to be honest at your age setting any homework at all seems a tad draconian. That means 'mean.' What kind of homework was it?"

"Colouring," Lucy said shortly. "And he had to collect leaves for the display. He got really good ones too—all red and gold. That was your fault."

She'd crashed.

"Sorry. But you didn't *have* to answer for your brother," David reminded her as she handed over the controller.

She ignored him. Unless you counted the eye roll and the sotto voce *tsk*, which on the whole David was inclined not to. "Leo, you ready?"

Leo nodded, fierce concentration on his little face, and then proceeded to be rather adept at the racing game, given his age. Perhaps five-year-olds were evolving greater hand-eye coordination in this digital era? Doubly dextrous thumbs?

When Leo finally ran out of lives, David was surprised and touched to be mutely offered the controller.

He waved it away. "No, no. I can play this any time, and there's a good chance you two are about to be dragged back home by the scruffs of your necks."

Lucy made a rude noise. "Mummy won't be home for hours, and *he* won't want us back."

"The wicked stepfather?" David guessed, then realised his error at Lucy's gleeful expression. "Um, perhaps it would be better if you forgot I said that."

"Said what?" Rory had apparently finished his phone calls.

"Um, nothing. Nothing at all. Far be it from me to cast aspersions on the man who stole your wife from you."

"You can cast as many nasturtiums as you like, mate," Rory muttered, joining them on the sofa. "Don't mind me. Whose turn is it?"

"Yours, Daddy," Lucy said firmly. "David didn't want a go."

"Yeah?" Rory grinned. "Right then, sit back and watch the old man show you how it's done."

When the doorbell rang, David hopped up to answer it, and found himself looking into a rather grumpy male face. "Lewis?"

Mr. Grumpy-face nodded. "You're the lodger?"

"For my sins. Or maybe Rory's, come to think of it." That glower was making him nervous.

Lewis managed to convey with a tilt of his blocky chin that he didn't give a monkey's whose sins were being punished in this particular instance.

Given that they'd each been married to the same woman, David had expected to see the odd superficial similarity between Lewis and Rory. In fact Lewis was about as unlike Rory as it was possible to get without being, say, *David*. He was David's height but more heavily built, with the beginnings of a belly from too many hours spent at a desk after expense-account lunches. His full head of dark-brown hair stood up bullishly above a low forehead and thick eyebrows that were currently drawn together above a smidgeon too much nose. Nevertheless, Lewis somehow managed to be greater than the sum of his parts. Not David's type, perhaps, but there was a certain arrogant attractiveness about the man.

Lewis huffed impatiently. "Where are the little so-and-sos?"

"This way." David was about to wave him into the living room when Rory emerged, making the narrow hallway rather too crowded for comfort.

"Lewis," Rory said in a tone that could almost be called antagonistic, if that hadn't been absurd. Admittedly David's experience of the man was limited, but he'd imagined Rory would be nice to *everyone*.

Lewis nodded in reply, a quick, sharp bob of the head. "I can't believe she's pulled this again. I didn't even hear them leave the house. I sent them up to their rooms—"

"Why?" Rory interrupted, squaring up to Lewis, the visual effect something akin to a pug attempting to face down a German shepherd dog. The weird thing was, David wasn't entirely sure his money would be on the German shepherd, and moreover, to his eye there was a distinct hint of Afghan hound in the larger dog's makeup. Come to think of it, the pug might well be a pit bull cross in disguise . . . Caught in the middle, he attempted to sidle away, but there were no sides to sidle *to*. He smiled helplessly at Lewis.

"Discipline," Lewis said shortly. "Something that appears to have been sadly lacking in their early lives."

"He said you called him a brat," Rory growled past David's shoulder. And was that a whiff of danger in his breath? David's shiver was quite involuntary.

Lewis rolled his eyes. "Oh, for God's sake! Yes, I lost my temper. It happens. There's no need to overreact. Anyone would think I'd hit the boy."

"You lay one finger on my kids—"

"And this is just what I mean! Overreacting again. No wonder the children get so overdramatic about things." Lewis folded his arms, fortunately realising in time that he'd need to take a step back on the doormat or elbow David in the ribs.

"They're *kids*, for Christ's sake. You can't make promises and then not deliver." Rory stepped up closer to Lewis. David breathed in and pressed his back to the wall. "And you don't go calling them names when they get upset about it, you got that?"

Lewis just stood there with his arms folded. His face wore the sort of patronising smile politicians always gave while letting their opponent speak, suggesting they knew far better and were only holding back from interrupting because they were far too well bred. There was even a hint of a headshake.

Rory didn't seem to notice. Never mind. David could, and did, seethe on his behalf.

"Fine," Lewis said, when Rory ran out of steam. "I suppose you'll be wanting them to stay here until Evie gets back?"

David had to admire Lewis's base cunning—he'd managed to divest himself of a clearly unwanted burden while making it appear as though he were making a huge concession.

Rory nodded curtly. "Too right. I'll give her another bell and tell her what's what."

"Fine," Lewis said again, before turning on his heel and walking out of the house.

David sagged in relief. That had all been a lot more exciting than he'd really been prepared for.

"Sorry you got caught in the middle there, mate," Rory said, clapping him on the shoulder.

David jumped. "*Literally*. Is it just me or is he not a very nice man?" He shivered again, but he wasn't sure it was down to the loathsome Lewis. Rory's hitherto unsuspected steely core might have had something to do with it.

Rory rubbed his face. "Yeah, but . . . I know what I said earlier, but don't say that around the kids, will you? It'd only cause more problems. They're like little tape recorders—everything you say will be taken down and used in evidence against you."

"Voice of experience?"

"Just a bit. Evie went spare last time I slagged him off in front of them and they repeated it back to him. Not that he didn't deserve it, mind. But she says that ain't the point and it only makes it harder for 'em. She's probably right." Rory sighed heavily. "He's not *all* bad. Takes them out, buys them stuff. Got a house that's much nicer than this place, and all."

His shoulders slumped, the transition back to mournful teddy bear now complete. David felt an unwonted urge to punch Lewis on his annoyingly large nose. "Meh. Houses. Tots don't care about that sort of thing. *I* never did."

"What was the house you grew up in like?"

David flushed. "Um. It was called The Grange. The Greenlake ancestral home, if three generations counts as ancestral. But it wasn't *enormous*. Half the rooms didn't even have proper heating, so we never used them . . . Hen sold it, anyway, when I was ten. She's got a little country cottage now." *About twice the size of your house*, he thought guiltily and definitely didn't say.

"Don't take this the wrong way, mate, but if your family's got money, what are you doing slumming it in a shoebox with me?"

"I'm twenty-four years old. Hen hasn't given me pocket money for some considerable time." David shrugged. "And anyway, this isn't a shoebox. It's a compact, modern residence."

"What, and battery hens live in spacious, well-equipped apartments?"

"If you're expecting me to lay eggs, you have a long wait ahead of you. But it's perfectly adequate. And very handy for work. Almost to a fault. Now, what do children eat?"

"Uh . . . pizza, given half a chance, but other than that, normal food, really. Except Leo only eats carrots if they're raw, and Lucy won't touch 'em unless they're cooked. Why?"

"It's my turn to cook, isn't it? I thought I'd better pop to the shops to make sure we've got some wholesome food in for the little mites."

"Nah, I can't ask you to cook for my kids."

"That's all right. You didn't. I offered." David only had half his mind on his answer. The other half was feverishly scanning through his mental recipe book to try to find something, anything, that wouldn't provoke an eye roll from Lucy.

He came up a total blank. Should he call Hen?

No, she was visiting Auntie Bron. He'd just have to wing it.

CHAPTER FIFTEEN

Rory sat back in the sofa while Lucy and Leo battled it out on the PlayStation, and wondered what had happened today. More ups and downs than a flipping seesaw. Having the kids over, that was an up and a half, that was, and God knows he'd needed it after finding Mrs. Young in such a state. Although as ups and downs went, that'd been sort of teetering in the middle, cos what if it'd been Rory's week to have Saturday off, and he hadn't found her till Monday? That would have been *way* worse.

Lewis, now, he was always a down. Fair dues, Rory probably would've hated him anyway, what with the bastard stealing his family and all, but Lewis didn't have to be such a git about the kids. Rory realised he was clenching his fists, and forced them to relax. It was what it was, and he had to deal with it. Sensibly. Maturely.

Not by smashing Lewis's stupid bleached-white teeth down his throat.

And then Rory had to laugh at himself, cos seriously, when had he ever done the whole physical-violence thing? Not since he'd been three years old and hit his big sister for taking his toy train, and she'd hit him back so hard—with his own flipping train—he'd needed three stitches. The scar still showed, faintly, and in the days when he'd grown his hair out, it'd been a little V-shaped bald patch.

But what about Mrs. Willis and her making assumptions, eh? That was . . . Rory wasn't sure how he felt about that. It wasn't *bad*, maybe, but it wasn't *right*, either. As in, *not strictly accurate*, not as in *shouldn't be allowed* . . . He was getting a headache just thinking about it.

David had taken it so well, though. That'd been a surprise. Maybe it shouldn't have been, though, cos he was a good bloke, David was. And he'd been great with the kids, and now he was going to cook for them . . . If Mrs. Willis was to pop in and see *that* going on, she'd have 'em married by sundown. Weird to think that was possible these days. But good. Definitely. People ought to be able to get married to whoever they wanted to. As long as the other person was happy about it too, that was. Probably not if they weren't.

Rory stiffened as an idea hit him. If David didn't mind people thinking him and Rory were a couple, did that mean he actually wanted them to *be* a couple? Was he going to start coming on to Rory, just like Barry had warned him? Rory had thought Barry was barking, and not up the right tree, neither, but maybe there was something in it after all?

Maybe he ought to set David straight. Heh. Pun not intended. Like, tell the bloke he was too old to be bi-curious.

Although it was hard *not* to be curious, sometimes . . .

"Daddy," Lucy interrupted his thoughts, putting down her controller as Leo slipped off the sofa and scurried away. Loo break, probably, from the pained expression on his little face. "Why is David sleeping in my bedroom? I had a look when I went upstairs, and his things are all over and there's a teddy on the bed that isn't mine."

"Uh, well, sorry, love, but you weren't using it—"

"Yes, but why isn't he sleeping with you?"

Rory stared at her.

"Lewis sleeps in Mummy's room with her. We're not supposed to go in there, and one time Leo forgot and he said Mummy didn't have her nightie on and they were *really* cross with him. So why doesn't David sleep with you, now he's living with you?"

"Uh . . . Love, there's living together, and there's *living together*. I mean, me and David, we don't . . . cuddle, like mummies and daddies do."

"Why not?"

"We're just mates, see?" When had the room got so hot? "Like Daddy and Uncle Barry."

"Oh. I know Uncle Barry isn't really my uncle. Mummy said." She frowned. "Do I have to call David *Uncle David*?"

"Do you want to?" Rory crossed his fingers, cos while he was beyond glad they were off the sleeping-together subject, he wasn't sure how David would take *that*.

"No. It's silly."

Thank God for small mercies. "Call him David, then. He won't mind. Right, that's reminded me, I gotta ring your Uncle Barry."

"Barry," Lucy corrected him, picking up the controller as Leo scrambled back onto the sofa.

"Uh, yeah. Whatevs." Rory stood up, grabbed his phone and wandered over to the window to make the call.

Barry answered on the first ring. "Rory, my man! Hope you're all set for a night of boozing, cos I'm gonna drink you under the table."

"Uh, yeah, about that. Bad news, mate—I'm not gonna make it tonight."

"Ah, no, mate. Don't do this to me. I been counting on you."

Guilt tightened Rory's chest. "Sorry. Can't be helped, though. I've got the kids round. Evie's mum's ill, so—"

"So she dumped 'em on you? What about that useless git she married? Too posh to babysit, is he?"

"You know him and them don't get on great. And it weren't Evie's fault. Lucy done it all. Packed their little bags and marched on down here. What was I gonna do?"

"You know what your trouble is, mate? Too flippin' soft by half. If they'd of been mine, I'd have dragged 'em straight back up there. And given that stepdad of theirs a piece of my mind and all." Barry laughed. "What do you bet he put 'em up to it? Slipped Luce a fiver and sent 'em packing so he could go and play golf or whatever posh gits do at the weekend."

"Nah, it wasn't like that, mate."

"Yeah, whatevs. Listen, that lodger of yours, he in tonight? Or is he putting on his sparkly disco suit and painting his nails for a night on the town?"

"Uh . . . he ain't said nothing about going out."

"So put him to use, then. Get the kids in bed early and he can mind 'em, can't he? You can be down the pub by nine, easy. What do you reckon? Am I a genius or am I a bloody genius?"

"Sorry. Evie's picking 'em up on her way back from her mum's, but she don't know when. I'm waiting for her to call. I'm gonna have to give it a miss tonight."

"Ah, mate, mate . . ."

"Sorry. Gotta go. We'll do another night, yeah?" Rory hung up before Barry could come up with any more genius ideas.

He didn't get it, Barry didn't. He had his kids with him all the time.

CHAPTER SIXTEEN

Fortunately for David, when he got to the village Tesco he found a harassed-looking woman perusing the shelves while fending off childish demands for crisps, sweeties, and for some reason, green olives and smoked salmon. Her two tots were, as near as David could judge, approximately the same size as Rory's little angels. A bit of surreptitious stalking was clearly in order. Utilising all his cunning and skills of concealment, David followed the family around the shop, noting where they paused. Pizza, yes, tick; garlic bread—he hadn't thought of that—and apples, yes, good to get some fruit inside them.

He almost had a full menu in his head when the woman turned on her heel and brandished her shopping basket menacingly in his direction. "Excuse me, do you want to tell me what your problem is? Because if you don't stop following me and my kids around, I'm calling security."

Ah. Apparently more work on being unobtrusive was called for. David flashed her a sunny and only slightly panicked smile. "Sorry! Honestly, I'm only interested in the contents of your basket."

"What, did I take the last veggie pizza or something?" She clutched her basket closer to her impressive chest, as if worried he might try to wrest it from her grasp.

"No, no. I'm fairly sure we're all carnivorous anyway. I was simply trying to pick up tips. I've never cooked for children before."

Her brow cleared. "Oh—how old are they, then?"

"Lucy is seven, and Leo's five." David was proud of himself for remembering.

"Ohhh. You're Lucy's dad's lodger. I've heard about you." She was smiling now, all thoughts of summoning burly men to lay their meaty hands on him apparently forgotten.

David reminded himself firmly that that was *not* a pity. "You have? I only moved in two days ago."

"Oh, word gets around. My Eloise is in Lucy's class at school, aren't you, love?"

David beamed. "Oh, how lovely. Are you friends?"

Eloise shook her curly head. "She's scary."

"Oh, thank God." David sagged in admittedly exaggerated relief. "I thought it was only me she terrified. So what do scary girls eat? Apart from their father's lodgers?"

Eloise giggled, and her mother favoured David with an indulgent smile. "Best thing is if you let them help you make it. If you've got time, which we haven't tonight because Amber's got ballet. Don't buy a pizza, get a pizza base—you can use pitta bread if the shop's out—and let them pick their own toppings and put them on. Works for mine, anyhow."

"You're a lifesaver. Thank you." David bade them a fond farewell and then hurried round the shop picking up an assortment of items that could conceivably be put on pizza. He hesitated over the pineapple—would Rory thank him for encouraging the children in such an excruciating lapse of taste?—but went with it in the end, reckoning tasty beat tasteful any day when you were seven.

If David was brutally honest with himself, it tended to win at twenty-four as well, at least when no food snobs were watching.

He'd barely got home with the ingredients when the doorbell rang. Putting the bag down in the kitchen, he turned on his heel and went to answer the door.

Standing outside was a little old lady, her back bent and her hair a mass of white curls.

Bless. "Oh, hello. Can I help you?" he cooed.

She gave him a thorough examination, and didn't appear to be overly pleased with her findings. "I'm looking for Mr. Willis. Is he round here?"

"Oh—would you be *Mrs.* Willis? From next door? I'm David. But you can call me Davey." He held out a hand.

She ignored it. "I haven't seen him since breakfast, and it's time for his tea. Is he here?" Her beady eyes narrowed, and David took an involuntary step back. "Has Rory been giving him food again?"

"I . . . ah, I don't think so. I've been home most of the day." He was fairly sure he'd have noticed any geriatric freeloaders hanging around. Even a small one. The house really wasn't that large. "Does he do this often? Disappear for hours at a time?"

She *humph*ed. "Always wandering off. He'll get himself into trouble one day."

This didn't sound good. Also, what with Rory's children and now Mr. Willis, David was beginning to wonder if half the village population was going walkabout without telling their loved ones. Maybe it was something in the water? "Should we call the police?"

Mrs. Willis stared at him as if he'd gone mad. "And what would they do? Well, I suppose he'll come home when he's hungry."

She turned and stomped back to her own front door, which she banged shut behind her.

David frowned. How old was she? Seventies? Eighties? A hundred? If her husband was a similar age, it didn't strike him as a good idea to leave the poor old man wandering around, possibly in a state of confusion.

He stuck his head in the living room, where Rory and the kids were playing Hungry Hippos. "Rory?"

"Yeah, mate? Oi, you wanna come and join us? I'm getting thrashed here."

"Um. In a minute. That was Mrs. Willis from next door."

"Yeah? What was she after?"

"*Mr.* Willis. She hasn't seen him all day."

Rory shrugged. "He'll come back when he's hungry."

"That's what she said. But it'll be getting dark soon. Don't you think we should call the police?"

"Bit overkill, innit?"

David was rather disappointed by this callous rejoinder. He'd thought better of Rory. "I'm not sure we should leave a vulnerable old man to his rambles—"

"You what?"

"A vulnerable old man?" David said slowly, wondering where Rory had misplaced his marbles. Had the hippos eaten them? "Mr. Willis?"

Lucy burst out into squeals of laughter. Apparently *callous* was a heritable trait.

Then Rory started to laugh too. As David watched with outrage and a growing sense of the surreal, even little Leo clapped his hands to his mouth, his shoulders shaking.

Rory recovered first. "Sorry, mate. Shouldn't laugh. But flippin' heck, your *face*. Mr. Willis—"

Lucy yanked at her father's arm. "I'll tell him, Daddy. Let me tell him!"

David folded his arms and waited.

She giggled again. "Mr. Willis isn't a *person*, silly. He's a *cat*."

Arms still folded, David dropped onto the sofa with an audible flump. "Well, I don't see how I should have been expected to have known *that*." He turned to glare out of the window.

"Sorry," Rory said, not sounding all that apologetic to David's mind. "His name's Tom, really, but when she told me that was what her husband was called . . . well, I started calling him Mr. Willis for a joke, and the old girl seemed to like it."

There was another laugh. When David looked, Rory was very busily pretending it hadn't been him.

David felt somewhat mollified later. The homemade pizzas were a singular success. Apparently the children didn't get much chance to help out in the kitchen at their mother's, and they took to the task of creating their own dinner with gusto. Possibly a little too much gusto in the case of the special pizza they made for Rory, whom Lucy barred from the kitchen and told to go and play on the PlayStation. He ended up with *every* topping on his pizza.

Seemingly fatherhood had given him a cast-iron stomach, though, as he ate it with every appearance of enjoyment.

After dinner they settled down to watch DVDs, which brought on a brief but intense squabble between Lucy and her father over whether it was Leo's turn to choose the film. She gave in with extremely bad grace, only to have Leo mutely point to the DVD of *Frozen*, the one she'd wanted all along.

Rory seemed inclined to let it go, but David gave both children a Hard Stare. "Gregory," he said sternly, waggling the bear at them—he was dressed today in his Inspector Clouseau outfit, with mini trench coat and a natty brown herringbone hat, so looked suitably official— "isn't entirely convinced that's the film Leo wants to see. What do *you* think, Lucy?"

Lucy held out for a long moment—then managed a whole-body *huff*. "All *right*. Leo?"

Leo beamed and proved that no good deed went unpunished by grabbing *Up*. David, who hadn't seen the film before, was in floods of tears after the opening sequence, and he noticed Rory having a bit of a manly sniffle too.

"It's not so bad when you've seen it a few times," Rory muttered, passing David the box of tissues.

"*Shush*," snapped an unrepentantly dry-eyed Lucy.

Rory's phone rang near the end of the film, and he nipped out of the room to answer it. He was gone only a few minutes, which was just as well as Lucy insisted on pausing the film—"Because Daddy can't *miss* any of it."

David raised a questioning eyebrow at his return, but Lucy started up the film again, so he had to wait until the closing credits to find out who'd called.

Rory cleared his throat. "Right, you lot, that was your mum on the phone, and she'll be round to pick you up in ten minutes or so."

"Oh. Can't we stay here?"

"No, sweet pea. Sorry. Your mum wants you back."

"Daddy, are you taking me to football tomorrow?"

"Yeah, course, love."

David frowned. "I thought this wasn't officially your weekend?"

"I always take her to football. Evie's not really into it."

"She wanted me to do *ballet*." Lucy mimed being sick with a realism that suggested not all of the performing arts were beneath her. "She made me do it for a *whole year* before I was allowed to give it up. She never made *Leo* do ballet."

David smiled in fond reminiscence. "I did ballet when I was a wee thing. I was the only boy in the class. I had to leave in the end, though. Too much sexism. You'd think it'd be less of a problem, nowadays."

Rory laughed. "Let me guess—they wouldn't let you wear a tutu?"

"It was *so unfair*. I was far prettier in pink than half the girls there."

"Why don't you wear pink now, then? You're a grown-up. You can do what you want." Lucy sounded like such freedom was her personal Holy Grail.

David patted her on the head. "Bless your innocence." He snatched back his hand when she quite literally snarled at him.

Rory laughed, the traitor. "He's got a point, Luce. See, I'd like to have you two living with me all the time, but I can't, can I?"

"It's so stupid. Why did Mummy have to marry *him*? Why couldn't she stay with you?"

"The heart wants what it wants, I'm afraid," David answered for Rory, sensing this might be something of a sore point for him.

"Hearts are stupid."

"Can't argue with you there, *ma choupinette*."

"What's a . . . what you called me?"

"It's a term of great affection," David assured her gravely. "Not in any way related to a cabbage."

"You're funny," she said, her tone making it clear that she had yet to make up her mind if that was a good thing or not. David decided to take her uncertainty as a positive sign.

The doorbell rang. Rory got to his feet. "Right, you two, get your stuff."

"You said ten minutes!"

"I said *or so*."

"That's not fair."

"That's life, love. Leo, you got Mr. Squiddy? Come on, then."

"*Au revoir, mes enfants*," David bid them sadly as they trooped after their father in a sullen little procession. He heard a female voice, by turns angry and defensive depending, perhaps, on whether its owner was talking to the children or to Rory.

What must it be like to send your children back to live with someone neither you nor they got on with? It seemed vastly unfair on all concerned.

Eventually the door closed and Rory returned, his step heavy. "Know what I fancy right now?" he asked as he slumped, rather than flumped, down on the sofa.

"An undetectable method of murdering wicked stepfathers?"

Rory managed a weak smile. "Don't tempt me. Nah, I'll settle for a beer and a *Doctor Who* marathon. You up for that?"

"Is the Pope homophobic? Which Doctor?"

"You choose. I got the lot—well, all the modern ones, anyhow."

"Hm. Normally I'd go with Nine, but I think in the circumstances Ten or Eleven is called for. And I'm always ready for a bit of David Tennant—not that I'm saying which bit, of course."

"How about them ones with the Master?"

"You, sir, are a man of taste and discernment. The Master it is." David threw himself down by the DVD stack and selected the relevant discs.

They spent a surprisingly congenial evening, given the drama of earlier. But after the end of the series they were watching, Rory turned to David, an oddly solemn expression on his face. "You know when you were talking, earlier? About when you were little and you did ballet and wanted to wear a dress?"

"Mm?"

"Didn't you, you know, get teased by the other lads?"

David hesitated. "Well, maybe a bit. But you get used to it. And Hen could put the fear of God into any head teacher who let bullying go on." He shivered, a phantom pain in his ribs and the taste of dirt suddenly strong in his mouth. "Cup of tea and a biccy before bed? I'll put the kettle on."

CHAPTER SEVENTEEN

What with all the kerfuffle on Saturday, Rory felt he deserved a lie-in on Sunday morning, and didn't get up until gone six. He'd still had breakfast, had a shower, and done two loads of laundry by the time David emerged from his bedroom, yawning.

"All right, mate?"

"Peachy." David yawned again and stretched, his T-shirt riding up over his flat belly. It was hairless—was that natural, or did he wax? Rory had heard gay blokes were into that sort of thing, which only went to prove no one ought to call them sissies. Jenni had dared Rory to try one of her wax strips once, on what she'd called his mankini line, and it'd hurt like buggery.

He realised he was staring and looked away hurriedly. Wouldn't want David to think he was checking him out. "You got much planned for today?"

"Mm, no. If by *much* you mean *anything at all.* Unless you count communing with the sofa and lying in wait for Mr. Willis the half-a-cat, who I'm only half convinced actually exists. You?"

"Oh, he's real. Wait till he decides he likes you and brings you a present. Nothing realer than a dead vole stuffed in the toe of your slipper, trust me. And no, not till after lunch—Lucy's got her football match."

"Oh, yes, the father-daughter bonding experience." David paused. "I never really *got* football. What's so important about kicking a ball between two posts anyway?"

Rory had to think about that one. "It ain't about the ball. It's, like, proving you're better than the other team. Working with your mates. Helping each other out."

"Like competitive choral singing?"

"Yeah . . . but more like dancing, see? Cos the footwork's important too. And the whole physical thing, right? When you're bombing along to the other team's goal, passing the ball to your mate just before the defenders can get in a tackle . . . it's a . . ."

"Rush?"

"Yeah, that." Rory smiled. "So what were you into at school? Sports, I mean."

"Athletics. And I never minded a game of cricket."

"Yeah? You oughtta think about joining the village team, then. Patrick's a member. Broke his ankle playing a while back, though— put his foot down a rabbit hole. Nasty."

"You're not exactly selling it to me here, on either count. But I'll think about it. There's something quite attractive about the idea of being a modern-day Raffles. Only without the breaking and entering, of course."

"Uh . . . a what now?"

"Raffles. You *must* have heard of him. He even had a TV series, back in the seventies. Hen has it on DVD. I used to dream of white tie and tails, cricket flannels, and a faithful Bunny of my very own."

"A bunny?"

"Not an actual rabbit. The sidekick. The Watson to his Sherlock. Raffles, who was known as the gentleman thief, was a sort of Sherlock gone to the dark side. Like Moriarty, but without the delusions of grandeur. And, well, the delusions. The author even admitted as much—he and Conan Doyle were close, although not in a Raffles/Bunny way."

"They were, like, a couple? The characters, I mean." Rory hadn't thought you were allowed to do that in those days.

"Not *completely* explicitly. But the subtext simply screams it out to the point of becoming the text."

"Huh. And how's the cricket come in to it?"

"For the best pickings, thievery wise, you want to go for the best people, don't you? And by best I mean richest, obviously. Raffles did it by being an excellent cricketer and getting invited to country estates to help the local cricket team thrash their rivals in a grudge match, which there were apparently an endless succession of in those days.

It saved him a lot of the breaking and entering part of, well, breaking and entering. But you really ought to watch the series. I'll get Hen to bring the DVDs when she visits."

"Yeah? Okay, sounds great." Rory was always up for a bit of good telly. "Anyway, I was thinking beans on toast for lunch—wanna join me?"

"Mm, love to. Just let me put my face on first."

Rory laughed. "Nothing wrong with the one you're wearing right now, mate."

"Ugh. I have stubble. It *itches.*" He grimaced, which made Rory laugh even more.

"Go on, then, princess. Make yourself pretty, and I'll get started in the kitchen."

"Less of the 'princess.' Patrick called me that."

"Duchess?"

"Makes me sound like a dowager."

"Uh, countess?"

"Too prone to being misheard."

"You're out of luck, then. That's all I got."

"I'll get you a copy of Debrett's for Christmas."

"You do that, mate." Still smiling, Rory ambled downstairs. He didn't have a clue what David was on about half the time, but who cared when he was this much fun?

Rory had a bad feeling about Lucy's football match from the moment he picked her up at Evie's, just after lunch. She slammed the front door behind her without shouting good-bye, and Leo's pale face at the window almost broke Rory's heart.

"Hey, maybe we oughtta take Leo along too, like we do when it's my weekend?" Rory asked as she tugged him down the drive by the hand. "Let him watch you play, help cheer you on and stuff."

"I asked Mummy. She said they're going to have *quality time* with him while I'm out."

Jesus. Poor little sod. "Uh, that'll be nice?" Rory winced at how unconvincing it sounded even to him. He glanced at the house, but Leo had disappeared and all he saw was Lewis's unfriendly mug, obviously watching to make sure Rory pissed off like he was supposed to.

"*No*. They're going and try to make him *talk* to them, and he won't, and then everyone's going to be in a bad mood when I get back."

She was probably right. Rory hated feeling this helpless, but Evie was only doing what she thought was best for Leo. Maybe it *was* what was best for him. It wasn't like Rory had a degree in kiddie psychology or anything. And, well, it couldn't be normal for a kid not to talk to his mum and his stepdad. "He must talk to them sometimes, yeah?" he asked, looking back again.

"We've got to *go*, Daddy. I'll be *late*. I'll miss the warm-up, and Greg'll be cross, and he might not put me on at the start of the match."

"All right, all right. Keep your shin pads on." Rory got in the car, made sure Lucy was strapped in, and set off.

The match was a disaster. Lucy's team started a player down (three of 'em had colds and another had broken his leg, although not while playing football, at least as far as Rory knew) and the opposing team, who *could* have dropped down to ten players to give them a sporting chance, didn't. Because obviously, winning the game was far more important than the feelings of a bunch of seven-year-old kids.

They were already two goals behind when the ref gave a penalty against them and a yellow card for one of the forwards, Moh, who was the smallest lad on the pitch, for a so-called dirty tackle that Rory could see hadn't so much as touched the kid on the other team. Which was something *nobody* should do to kids, with their fierce sense of fairness.

Rory wasn't even surprised when five minutes later Lucy barrelled into the kid who'd taken the dive and flattened the little so-and-so for real this time. Or when she got a red card shoved in her face for it. Or, for that matter, when she refused to leave the pitch and just stood there bad-mouthing the ref until Rory stepped in and bodily carried her off.

"Love, you can't do that," he told her gently, wiping the tears that'd come as soon as he'd got her off the pitch.

"But it wasn't *fair*."

"I know. But sometimes life ain't fair. And you gotta deal with it without getting physical, yeah? It ain't helped, getting riled up, now has it? All it's got is your team down to nine players." And probably facing a fine, but Rory didn't have the heart to mention that now.

Or the letter he'd have to write to the league excusing Lucy's conduct—again—and hope the coach backed her up and she didn't get chucked out this time.

"But they *cheated*. And . . . and . . . if I hadn't done something they'd have got away with it."

"Love, they got away with it anyway. Fighting's not the answer."

Lucy squirmed in his arms, her little face red and tearstained. "How do you know? *You* never fight!"

She meant argy-bargy. Squaring up to a bloke, taking it outside, the works. Not fighting for his marriage or for custody of her and Leo. Rory knew that.

Which didn't stop it hitting him where it hurt.

CHAPTER EIGHTEEN

Rory hadn't been gone long when the doorbell rang.

David, who'd been idly sketching ideas for a new outfit for Gregory—it was way past time he had a superhero costume—went to answer it. "Hello?"

Standing on the doorstep were a woman in her thirties and a round-faced boy of ten or so, both of them smartly dressed in Marks and Spencer's finest. David perked up. He hadn't had any Jehovah's Witnesses to chat to in *ages*.

It was the woman who spoke. "Oh, hello, are you Rory Deamer? The postman?"

Perhaps not the God Squad after all, unless they'd taken to targeted attacks. "No, I'm David Greenlake, the postman's lodger. Are we playing Happy Families?"

She sent him a familiar look—half-baffled, half-amused. "I'm Sarah Meadway. Susan Young's daughter."

"We *are* playing Happy Families." David smiled at the boy by her side. "Would this be Master Bun, the baker's son?"

Although if he was, he was a poor advertisement for his parent's wares, with his doughy, undercooked complexion.

The boy favoured David with the sort of sidelong, narrow-eyed stare usually reserved for the mentally challenged. "No. I'm Todd."

"Todd Cod, the fisherman's son?" David asked hopefully. Now he came to think about it, there was definitely a hint of fish belly in that complexion.

George's mother made a firm effort to wrestle back control of the conversation. "We wanted to thank Mr. Deamer for what he did for my mother. Is he in?"

"I'm afraid he's at a football match." David wondered what services Rory might have rendered to the presumably elderly Susan Young. The mind positively boggled.

"Oh, that's a shame. Would you pass on our thanks, please? And please give him this." She handed him a gift bag containing a bottle of some sort. "It's only a token. We really are very grateful—I hate to think what would have happened if he hadn't gone round yesterday. I mean, I call her every Sunday night, but . . ."

She gave David a significant look. He nodded wisely, as if he had the first clue what, exactly, it signified.

"And please tell him she's doing well in hospital. We're not sure when she'll be out, or if she'll be going back to the house . . ." She made a helpless gesture. "It's all rather up in the air for now. But please do thank him for us."

"Of course."

After they'd taken their leave and he'd shut the door, David took a sneaky peek into the gift bag. It held a bottle of Lagavulin that was older than Fen.

David's estimation of whatever aid Rory had rendered to Mrs. Young went up several notches, along with his eyebrows.

When Rory returned home, sans Lucy, he seemed a little abraded around the edges.

"How was the football?" David asked with forced brightness.

Rory slumped down onto the sofa. "God, don't ask. Lucy got sent off, and when I got her back to Evie's, Leo was crying his little heart out cos flippin' Lewis lost his temper with him again."

David stared, an uneasy hollow in his stomach. "He didn't . . .?"

"What, hit him? Nah, nothing like that. Just words." Rory sighed heavily, looking wearier than David had ever seen him.

David knew only too well how deeply words could pierce a boy, and he had a fair idea that Rory knew it too. Would a hug be received in the spirit in which it was intended? He wasn't sure—and by the time he'd considered it, the moment was past.

It was safer in any case to go for a manly pat on the shoulder. "Never mind. Here's something that'll cheer you up. Hopefully. Do you like single-malt whisky?"

"Why, you got some?"

"No, but you have. Dropped off with fervent, if cryptic, thanks by someone who described herself as Susan Young's daughter." David gestured at the gift bag which he'd left on the coffee table as a gaudy conversation piece.

Rory's eyes lit up but not, apparently, at the prospect of alcohol. He didn't even glance in the bag. "Yeah? Did she say how the old girl's doing?"

"Fine, she said, although that could mean many things. She didn't go into detail, but it sounded reassuring. So what's all this about?"

"Ah, 's nothing, really. The old dear had a fall and couldn't get up, so I got an ambulance for her."

"I don't believe for one moment that's all you did. That's barely worth a half bottle of Teacher's. There must be more to it than that."

"Nah." Rory ducked his head, a blush spreading over it. "I only had to borrow a ladder and nip round the back. Well, I had to break a window to get in. Poor old girl was in a right state. She'd been there a couple of nights."

It was all making sense now. "And, presumably, you were the one to notice there was potentially something wrong in the first place?"

"Yeah, but . . . You do a round long enough, you get to know people's habits. And she never leaves post sticking out the letterbox. Likes the place to be tidy, see? So I thought I'd better check up on her. And there she was."

"Waiting for her gallant saviour. Why didn't you tell me about your heroic exploits yesterday?"

Rory rubbed his head with a faint rasping sound as his calluses caught on the stubble. "Didn't think about it."

"Because saving lives is all in a day's work for you?"

"Nah, well . . . I didn't do nothing. I just found her. It's the doctors what do all the work."

Rory's speech, David had noted, had a tendency to get more ungrammatical in direct relation to how uncomfortable or emotional he was feeling at a given moment. It was rather adorable.

"Whatever you say, I think this calls for a toast to the hero of the hour. Whisky? Or tea?"

"Seeing as the lady took the trouble to bring this over, we might as well crack it open—you're gonna join me, aren't you?" Rory finally delved into the gift bag and brought out the bottle of Lagavulin. "Whoa, nice."

"Sure you still want to share now you've seen what it is? No, don't get up—I'll fetch the glasses."

David managed to locate some plain glass tumblers on only the second try—he was getting the hang of Rory's kitchen. "Now, normally I'd say the more fingers the better, but just a small one for me or I'll be away with the fairies."

Rory poured them each a modest amount, then held up his glass. "Right, here's to Mrs. Young's health."

"And to her dashing saviour," David added firmly.

Rory blushed, muttered "Shut up," and drank.

Bless.

They were two snifters in and had reluctantly decided against a third when David's phone rang.

It was Fen.

David picked up with a smile, already rising from the sofa so as not to disturb Rory's television watching. "*Bonsoir, ma petite crevette.* To what do I owe the pleasure? You spoke to me like, one day ago. Do we need to get you some more friends—"

"Shut up and listen," Fen said by way of friendly greeting. "This is *important*. You've got to help me."

"Of course, darling. Just let me slip into something more suitable for burying bodies. The combination of blood and mud can wreak havoc on delicate fabrics." He started upstairs.

Fen giggled. "There's no bodies. Well, not dead ones."

"Sorry. I draw the line at burying people alive." Reaching his room, David flung himself down on the bed. Gregory tumbled from his perch on the pillow to nuzzle companionably at his ear.

"*Listen.* We've got to get Granny O a new boyfriend."

"We have?"

"*Duh*. So she'll stop being sad about Rory. *And* I know there's someone she fancies."

"Ooh, do tell. Anyone I'm acquainted with?"

"Do you actually know *anyone* in the village apart from me, Dad, Patrick and Rory?"

"It's early days. I'm working on it."

"Anyway, his name's Si, and he's a roofer." She paused, clearly trying to evoke a sense of drama.

David pounced. "Is that some new way of saying he's a hottie? *Oh, him, he's a total* roofer?"

Fen made a strange, strangled noise. The audible equivalent of an eye roll? "He mends roofs. Rooves? I dunno. But yeah, she was talking about him on Sunday. One of her neighbours had him round to sort out her roof, and she said he was really good-looking."

"Probably taken, then. All the best ones always are, alas."

"No, he's not, cos I asked Dad and Patrick later and they know him from Spartans and they said he had a girlfriend back in Wales and he moved here to forget her. And then Dad made this stupid joke about him choosing Shamwell because there's not a lot of sheep farms around here, which is just *so racist*." She paused for breath.

"Let me guess, you told him this?"

"Well, duh. And then he got annoyed, and I never got to ask him and Patrick if they'd help me fix up Granny O with Si-the-roofer. Although they'd probably just have been useless anyway. Dad's always all, *You can't force these things*—"

"So who else have you tried to play Yente to?"

"Uh?"

"Yente? Bit of a busybody, not in the first flush of youth, fond of fiddlers in high places?"

"What are you even on?"

"Musical theatre, darling. Which reminds me, we need to continue your education. How about a trip to—"

"Look, this is *important*. We need to get Granny O and Si together."

David was impressed. Usually the mere mention of a trip to the West End would have all other thoughts scurrying from Fen's mind like rats from the Titanic. "Fine, then. How do you propose we do it?"

"You need to tell Dad you can see some loose tiles on our house."

"Why can't you do that?"

"I can't lie to Dad!"

"But it's fine to tell me to? You know, some people feel morals shouldn't bear too close a resemblance to cheap knicker elastic."

"What*ever*. I *mean*, you'll be way more convincing."

"Hm. I feel I've spotted a fatal flaw in your cunning plan. Won't he simply look up at the tiles himself and see that they're not, in fact, loose?"

"No." She sounded smug. "He's, like, really sensitive about needing glasses now. So he won't even check with Patrick. Cos he doesn't want Patrick to think he's *old*."

"Fine. I don't see how it helps, though. What if he calls a different roofer?"

"He won't. And not just cos he's a Spartan, Dad's got this big thing about employing local people. Which is good," she added earnestly. "Like, for the planet as well as the village, because they don't have to travel as far."

"That still doesn't explain how your Granny O comes into it. And by the way, you might not want to call her that in front of the object of her affection. Not that I'm an expert, but I believe the term *granny* doesn't immediately conjure up lascivious images in the mind of the average straight man. Certain Premier League footballers excluded, of course."

"You'll have to tell me when he's coming round so I can get her to come over at the same time."

"And what if it happens to be while you're at school?"

"I can take a sickie. That'd be even better, cos I could say I need her to look after me."

"So lying to your school and your grandmother would be fine?"

"Meh. She's not my *real* granny."

"And what about poor Rory's crushed feelings, when he discovers I'm plotting to find his ex another man?"

"Like he cares. He dumped her. *Ages* ago. Anyway, why would you tell him? *Duh*."

Duh, indeed. And, to be honest, Rory hadn't seemed all that upset about the breakup. More fatalistic. Certainly not as if he was hoping for a reconciliation. So it would probably be okay to fall in with Fen's plan.

Might be best not to mention it to Rory, though.

David went back downstairs with thoughtful tread. He couldn't help feeling this could all go horribly wrong. Mostly, for him.

"Everything all right?" Rory asked as David sat back down on the sofa.

"For a given value thereof, yes. Now, what did I miss?"

Rory frowned. "Not sure. Lot of moody shots of grey skies. And the victim's wife had a row with someone. Or it might have been the detective's wife. I get them two confused. And then she killed herself. I think. I'm hoping they're gonna— Oh."

Sombre music played, and the credits rolled. "That was the final episode, wasn't it?" David asked.

"Yeah. Huh. You know, I'm not sure I'm really into this Scandi noir stuff."

"Mm. Well, we gave it a good shot." David shrugged, then beamed. "PlayStation?"

"You're on, mate."

CHAPTER NINETEEN

David's opportunity to put Fen's cunning plan into operation didn't arise until Tuesday, when Mark offered to take him out for a pub lunch to celebrate their largest client having paid his bill without quibbling.

"Won't your *soi-disant* better half object?"

Mark laughed. "If he's fine with you working with me, I hardly think he'll object to us spending an hour together in public."

David wasn't so sure. Spending time together while working was very different from socialising. Especially in a place with easy access to alcohol. And what if people who saw them misconstrued matters, and assumed Mark was cheating on Patrick? Villages were hotbeds of gossip. It was one of the reasons David felt so at home here.

On the other hand, a free lunch was a free lunch. "I'll just go and freshen up, and then I'll be with you," he said.

Turning round to view the roof on exiting would have been too obvious, so David had to wait until they returned from the Tickled Trout, the heavier by a large plate of fish and chips (Mark) and a chicken Caesar salad (David).

As they neared the house, David scrunched up his eyes and squinted at the gables. "Have you got someone coming to see about those tiles?" he asked casually.

"What tiles?"

"Those loose ones, up there. Look, you can see where they're a bit wonky."

Mark shaded his eyes from the nonexistent sun and peered in the direction David was pointing. "Where exactly?"

"There, about four feet along. You see?" David crossed his fingers Fen was right about Mark's pride. "You really ought to get that fixed before the winter. It would only take a strong wind to bring them down, and then you'll have the rain in. Not to mention lawsuits, if they should happen to fall on someone and maim them for life."

"I— Yes. I'll give Si a call. He's one of the Spartans," Mark explained needlessly as he pulled out his phone. "Rather handy, knowing people personally when you need a— Si? Hello, it's Mark. I was wondering if you could come over and take a look at some loose tiles for me. No hurry, but— Oh, that'll be brilliant. Thanks. I'll see you later."

He hung up with a smile.

David had a moment's qualm. "Don't tell me he's dropping everything to come straight over. For a start, if a roofer drops everything, there could be unpleasant consequences . . ."

"No, no. He's got a job in the village, though, so he's going to pop over around six. It'll still be light enough then, fortunately. Right, we'd better get some work done." He sprang up the steps to his front door, a job well delegated.

David followed more slowly, occupied as he was with texting Fen a quick, *Si 6pm over to u.*

The timing couldn't have been better—everyone would be home from work or school—and now it was all down to Fen to get her Granny O to come over and be smitten with Si's no doubt rugged charms. It was just a shame David wouldn't be there to witness the flowering of true love.

Then again, he *also* wouldn't be there to witness Si realising there was absolutely nothing wrong with the roof tiles.

The next morning, Mark greeted David, not unexpectedly, with the news that Si had given the roof a clean bill of health.

Fen had apparently been too busy for a phone conversation last night, but she had texted him with, *IT WORKED!!!!*

"Really?" David said, peering intently at an honest-to-God, old-fashioned hand-written ledger he strongly felt should be in the British Museum, not forming the accounting records of any business in this day and age. "Oh well. It's always good to have these things confirmed, isn't it? I suppose it must have been something else we saw. A bird, perhaps. Do you think it could have been that? You saw it too, so it must have been *something*."

Mark coughed. "Yes. Must have been. Still, it wasn't a totally wasted trip for him. Jenni popped over while he was here, and apparently she's been having trouble with her gutters, so he went straight over to hers to sort that out."

"Oh, how serendipitous." David waited until his next bathroom break to smirk victoriously at himself in the mirror.

That night, though, he had a despairing call from Fen. "I don't think it worked after all."

"What didn't?"

"Getting Granny O and Si together. *Duh.* I went up to see her after school, and she didn't say *anything* about him, even when I *asked*. Just said her gutters were fine now."

"What exactly did she say? Was it along the lines of 'He gave my gutters a proper seeing to'?"

"No, because she's not *you*. She said he reckoned they looked more like window boxes than gutters."

David frowned. "You don't think she actually *did* need them clearing out? I assumed she was simply carpe-ing the diem. And the Si, for that matter."

"Me too." She was silent a moment. "Maybe he doesn't fancy her."

"Well, one can't force these things. As your father would say. What's he like, anyway, this Si the roofer?"

"Dad always calls him a mountain man. But that might be cos he's Welsh."

"What does he look like?"

"Um, big? Really tall—at least as tall as you. And like twice as wide over the shoulders." She sounded approving. "With a big black beard, though. Why would anyone want to kiss someone with a beard?"

"To exfoliate while they osculate?"

"While they *what*?"

"Kiss. Snog. Make out. Mack on. Indulge in a friendly game of tonsil hockey. If you're unfamiliar with the concept, I'm sure Ollie will be only too happy to demonstrate."

"You use *way* too many words, you know that? So do you like blokes with beards?"

"I prefer a man who's clean-shaven, as a rule. The more groomed look." David couldn't help thinking of Rory who, bless him, had taken shaving to the logical conclusion. He wondered what it would be like to shave a man's head. Under the right circumstances, rather erotic, he was sure—

"Are you still there?"

"Oh, sorry. What did I miss?"

"I *said*, 'I've got to go.' Patrick's doing pancakes for supper."

"But it's September."

"I know, right? He's so cool sometimes. Bye!"

David pouted. Not only had he been abandoned for fried food, now he was hungry. He decided to wander back downstairs.

Rory was still on the sofa, frowning at the TV listings. "Do you think we oughtta get satellite? Cos there is literally nothing on."

"Do you know how to make pancakes?"

"Uh, eggs, milk, and flour, innit? But it's September. Pancake Day's in March. Or February. One of them two."

"I feel like being a rebel. I don't suppose you know how *much* flour, milk, and eggs are needed? And what exactly one does with them?"

"Uh, you beat 'em up, and then you fry 'em. Wanna have a go? I'll warn you now, I'm a bit crap at the tossing bit."

David beamed. "Nothing ventured, nothing gained."

"Right, then. You get the eggs out, I'll see if we got any flour." Rory jumped up from the sofa.

After a brief discussion as to whether self-raising was suitable for pancakes (academic, as it was all they had, and even that was edging out of date) they sloshed some milk into a jug, made a guess at how many eggs would be needed (Rory was all for adding three, but David countered that surely any more than one would give them an omelette, or most likely a scromblet, with extra padding, so they compromised on two) and whipped everything up together.

David looked on with bated breath as Rory poured the batter into the heated frying pan, sizzling with a generous pat of butter. It spread out satisfactorily, bubbled a bit and then actually started to look undeniably pancake-like.

"Oh em gee, it's working," he whispered, awestruck.

Rory grinned. "Yeah, not bad for a first attempt, eh? Course, I've seen Evie do it a few times. The kids always used to want to watch her make them on Pancake Day. Sometimes she even let me have a go at tossing them."

"Do it," David encouraged.

"Hold your horses, gotta wait till it's done on one side . . . Right. Here we go, and if you end up wearing it, don't say I didn't warn you." He shook the pan a few times, the fledgling pancake moving gently in its nest—then with a sharp motion, tossed it into the air. It took flight for only a couple of seconds, performed a perfect somersault and landed almost exactly dead centre in the pan.

"Res*ult*. How about that, then?" Rory beamed at David, who couldn't help returning it.

"Rory Deamer, you have been hiding your culinary light under a bushel. We'll have you winning *MasterChef* yet."

Rory blushed and ducked his head. Bless. "Wanna grab a plate? We can bung this one under the grill to keep warm, and I'll get going on the next one. You see what you can find to put on 'em. Don't think we got any lemon juice, but there's syrup in the cupboard."

They ate their succession of sweet, syrupy pancakes standing up in the kitchen. Not all of them ended up as successful as the first—some decided to fold themselves in half when tossed, like an Olympic diver but without the graceful exit—but David had no complaints. He was still rather in awe of Rory's unexpected mastery of the frying pan, and said so.

"Didn't your mum used to let you help on Pancake Day?" Rory asked, spooning some syrup out of the tin. He twiddled the spoon until all the drips were caught and then drizzled it on his pancake. "I thought you and her were pretty close."

"Hen doesn't believe in pancakes. Too unhealthy. And Pancake Day itself is nothing more than a relic of an outmoded set of dietary restrictions." David dug into his forbidden fruit with only moderately guilty gusto.

"It is?"

"Mm. Apparently medieval Christians were required to give up eggs and milk for Lent. Hence using them all up on Shrove Tuesday."

Rory frowned. "So what did farmers do with them while no one was eating them? Chuck 'em away? Or did all the cows and chickens have to keep their legs crossed till Easter?"

"You know, I never thought of that." David licked a syrupy finger. "Maybe they were allowed to make the milk into cheese? Not sure about the eggs. How long do eggs keep for, anyway?"

"Keep 'em long enough, they turn into chickens. If the cock's been doing his job."

"I suppose it's one way to find out if your cock is shooting blanks. So to speak."

Rory chuckled. "Yeah. You gonna eat that last one?"

"If I eat any more now, I'll be fasting for forty days and nights to make up for it. It's all yours." David paused. "So do you have family close by?"

"Nah. I grew up local, but Mum and Dad moved down to Sussex when they retired. Got a little place near the sea."

"Handy for the Brighton gay scene."

"Yeah, I don't reckon that was what they were thinking about when they chose it. The other half of their semi's got a gay family in it." Rory's brow furrowed. "Uh, you know what I mean. Dunno about the kids, but the dads are definitely gay. They're married and everything. Mum babysits their kids sometimes."

"Missing the grandchildren?"

"Yeah, maybe. They visit, but it's a long way to come in the car. Especially in summer when the traffic's a mare."

"Must have been hard, not having them nearby when the marriage ended."

"Yeah. Wasn't an easy time." Rory gave David a heartbreakingly twisted smile. "Could've done with a few more of my mum's roast dinners around then."

David couldn't stand the pain writ large on Rory's face. "Ooh, I know," he said with forced brightness. "That's what we should do at the weekend—roast dinner with all the trimmings. Children like roast dinners, don't they?"

"My two do. If you're sure we can pull it off."

"Meh. All you have to do is shove a lump of meat in the oven and leave it there for a few hours. How hard can it be?"

"Yeah, and the trimmings? I dunno, veg, roast spuds, and stuffing or whatever?"

"That's why God gave us Waitrose, and preprepared everything. So when are we going shopping?"

Rory shrugged. "Tomorrow after work? I ain't got anything planned. Been trying to get an evening out with Barry to make up for missing Saturday, but he reckons his missus has got something on every night this week and she won't let him off of babysitting the kids."

Oh. David hadn't known about Saturday. "Did you have big plans? Painting the town in the colour of your choosing? You know, I could have looked after the children," he made himself add, because the sudden stab of jealousy that pierced him was clearly some kind of anomaly caused by too little sleep. He'd undoubtedly be over it in the morning. Even if he couldn't for the life of him see what Rory saw in the Neanderthal, which was his new pet name for Barry.

"Nah, we was only going down the pub. But I can do the shopping after work. No need for you to use up your evening. You ain't had a night out since you got here."

David gave him a sidelong look. "It's been less than a week. I don't think I'm in any danger of becoming a hermit just yet. If I grow a beard down to my ankles and start sitting on poles instead of dancing on them, that'll be the time to worry. Anyway, shopping is far more fun in company."

"Right, then. Tomorrow, after tea. My turn to cook, innit?"

"But you did the pancakes."

"You helped. Tell you what—takeaway?"

"It's a date." David beamed.

And wondered why the words felt hollow, somehow.

CHAPTER TWENTY

Thursday night, after a quick meal of chow mein and crispy pancake rolls from the village Chinese takeaway, most of which Rory ended up eating, he got his introduction to shopping in Waitrose. He goggled around in wonder at all the men and women in business suits, half of them trailing kids obviously picked up from daycare on the way over. "Posh here, innit?"

"Welcome to the Mecca of the middle classes. But you get a different crowd here during the day. Older, as a rule, and more casually dressed. The mummies tend to wear Boden or Joules, or Jack Wills if they're trying to cling onto their youth."

"What about the dads?" Rory asked, amused.

"Unfortunately the sample size is rarely statistically significant. The middle classes are nothing if not conservative." David met Rory's baffled gaze. "Meaning, you don't get many stay-at-home dads here."

"You see plenty of 'em at Asda, where I usually shop." Rory hoped he wasn't going to have to sell a kidney or something to pay for all this. He eyed the nearest shelf, which had a lot of the shop's own brand stuff on it. "Waitrose Essential artichoke hearts? Since when are them things *essential*?"

David gave him a worrying smile. "Wait till you see the ostrich eggs."

"Oi, I've seen ostrich eggs. They had some at the farmers' market in the village. Dunno what people use 'em for, mind. Unless they're making pancakes for the whole street."

"Ooh, I didn't know there was a farmer's market around here. What do you buy there?"

Rory's face got a bit hot. "Nothing. I only went along to have a laugh and try the cheese samples."

"Philistine. Next time, we're going armed with carrier bags. We can bypass the muddy veg and emu steaks and head straight for the artisanal quiches. When's it on? Third Sunday in the month?"

"Uh, yeah. How'd you know?"

"Farmers' markets are always on the third Sunday in the month. I think there's a law. Now, onwards and veg-wards!" David strode off in the direction of the greengrocer's bit.

Rory followed, but was stopped halfway there by a familiar voice. "Oi oi, what's all this, then?"

Startled, Rory spun. "Barry! Mate, good to see you. Here with the missus?"

Barry looked like he'd been sucking on some of that ice with slices of lemon Rory could see in the freezer behind him. "No, but I see *you* are."

"What? Oh." Rory flushed and forced a laugh. "Yeah. Nice one, mate. We're just getting stuff in for the weekend—you know, kids coming over."

Barry huffed. "Sounds cosy."

"Yeah, David seems to get on really well with the kids." Rory wondered where David had wandered off to, then spotted him by the broccoli. Uh-oh. Better get over there quick. Leo and broccoli . . . not exactly a match made in heaven. "Sorry, mate, gotta go. See you around, yeah?"

"Huh, I never knew Barry shopped here," Rory said when he got over to where David was frowning at two heads of broccoli. "And you wanna walk away from that stuff, if you know what's good for you."

"The children won't eat it?"

"Oh, they'll *eat* it. Least, they did last time I tried it. Let's just say it didn't *stay* eaten." It'd been a bugger to get out of the sofa cushions in the middle of the night.

David put the broccoli down as if it'd burned him. "Carrots?"

"Safer," Rory agreed. "Long as we remember to keep some raw for Leo. Right, I reckon a bit of cauli and some spuds . . . Do you know how you roast potatoes?"

"Like this." David picked up a foil tray full of ready-prepared spuds.

Rory winced a bit at the price, but fair enough, this was why they'd come here. He took the tray and dropped it in the trolley. "I'm chopping me own carrots, mind."

"I do like a man who knows how to handle a carrot," David said absently. "Ooh, look, they've got sprouts already."

"They can keep 'em. Don't tell me you actually like them?"

"Does anyone? But it does make you feel that Christmas is coming." David smiled like a five-year-old.

Rory couldn't hold back a sigh. Great. Another year of missing his kids opening their stockings on Christmas morning. With the choice of staying in the village on his own so he could see them on Boxing Day, or going to visit his mum and dad down in Sussex and having Mum moan on about how she never saw her grandkids anymore. And David would go back to *his* mum's, no question, so Rory wouldn't even have him around . . .

"How do you feel about pre-floretted cauliflower? Or shall we be adventurous and get a whole one? We can do the vegetables well in advance, so they shouldn't get in the way of tending to the roast. If it needs tending, of course. I don't know how high-maintenance chickens usually are, do you? Rory?"

Rory blinked and realised David was standing very close, staring at him with a too-bright smile. "Uh, yeah, we can get a whole one. Sorry. Miles away."

"*Pas de problème.* Okay, you choose." David grabbed a cauli in each hand and held them up at chest height like a couple of comedy boobs. He jiggled them about. "They both feel quite firm, but I think this one has a more pleasing heft to it."

Rory had to laugh. "Right boob it is."

"An excellent choice." David tossed it over.

Rory caught it and put it in the trolley while David bunged the other back on the shelf. "What's next?"

David pursed his lips. "Well, I do like a good bit of stuffing . . ."

"So I've heard. Where do you reckon they hide that?"

"Not a clue. Maybe we should start with the chicken? Logically the stuffing should be somewhere nearby."

They followed the signs to where the meat was arranged in vast white fridge units.

And stopped.

"Have you ever bought a whole chicken before?" Rory asked at last.

"No." Like Rory, David was staring, wide-eyed, at what appeared to be an entire farmyard's worth of plucked, trussed birds.

Who'd have thought there'd be so many to choose from? "Me neither. Evie never used to bother with a roast on Sunday—said she was too knackered after a week of running round after the kids. Did you know they come in different sizes?"

"Um. Well, I suppose it's only logical." David cocked his head. "After all, *people* come in different sizes. Look at us."

"I dunno. I reckon we probably weigh pretty much the same. You got the extra inches"—Rory gestured with his hands—"but I got the . . . What do you call it when you're not all skin and bones?"

"Girth? And let me guess, that's what *she* said?" David smirked.

Rory groaned. "Shut up and tell me if we want free-range, organic, or . . . what's them yellow ones? Corn fed."

"Was it *radioactive* corn?" David shuddered. "And are the categories all mutually exclusive? Because organic *sounds* better—would you want to eat an inorganic chicken?—but surely free-range is kinder to the poor little chooks."

Rory glanced at the prices. "Bloody hell, they want an arm and a leg for them poor little organic chooks. Free-range'll do. How big, d'you reckon?"

"Not a clue. Hold on a mo. Possibly a mo and a huff." David turned to an old lady at the next fridge who seemed to be deliberating between breasts and thighs. "Excuse me, I was wondering if you could help us? We're trying to buy a chicken for a Sunday roast, and we're frankly bewildered. How big a bird do you think we'd need?"

She blinked up at him. "Oh, well, how many people will you be cooking for?"

"Four. Rory, yours truly, and the two little ones." David smiled.

"Oh, I always buy the Duchy Organic, but that's just for the two of us. If you're feeding a family, you might want to go for something more economical. I'd try a large own-brand one, if I were you. That should give you a nice dinner, and enough left over for curry the next day, if you're careful." She eyed Rory. "Mind you, with two men in the family it may not go so far."

Rory laughed. "Nah, David eats like a girl, anyhow. Couple of forkfuls and he's done."

"I'll have you know my eating habits are *extremely manly*, thank you." David sniffed and gave him a mock glare.

The old lady dimpled. "So lovely to see a happy couple. These May-December romances can work really well, can't they?" She put the chicken thighs in her basket and ambled off.

David cocked his head as he stared after her. "Do you think it's an old-lady thing? This . . . assuming we're a couple?"

Rory coughed. "Uh. Yeah. Probably."

No *way* was he going to tell David that Barry had called him *the missus*.

CHAPTER TWENTY-ONE

Rory hoped the weekend was going to turn out okay. David probably didn't realise how much it was going to change things, having the kids camped out on the sofa all weekend. It'd put a bit of a crimp on their evenings, what with the kids turning the lights out at nine. They wouldn't be able to watch the telly or play on the PlayStation in the living room. Well, him and David wouldn't be able to, at any rate, and so far the kids had been good about not watching stuff when they weren't supposed to.

Rory had tiptoed downstairs a few times to check on previous occasions, and they'd always been fast asleep. Well, except for that time he'd heard Lucy reading her brother a story by the light of a torch, which had been so cute he'd got all misty-eyed and nearly tripped over his own feet creeping back upstairs.

"If they get a bit much, you tell me, and I'll have a word," he said on Friday night as he was shoving his shoes on, ready to go and pick the kids up. "And no one's gonna be offended if you slope off to your bedroom to get away from the chaos. I'll make sure they know that's out-of-bounds."

"Rory, darling, stop worrying. You'll give yourself wrinkles. Oops—too late." David grinned, the cheeky sod.

Rory laughed. "Am I bovvered? Least no one's gonna mistake my face for a shop dummy."

"Mia*ow*. Speaking of which, you may want to check your shoes. There was a suspicious patch of feathers on the grass outside, and no sign of the bird which should have been wearing them."

"Yeah, cheers for telling me *before* I got 'em on." Rory held up his booted foot. "Right, I'm off. Shouldn't be long unless Mr. Squiddy's gone walkies again. Evie's pretty good about getting the kids ready on time."

"Does Lewis help pack their little bags?" David's expression was so flippin' innocent it had to be guilty of something.

Only trouble was, Rory wasn't sure what. "Nah, think he leaves all that to her," he said, and left.

When he got up to Evie's, the kids weren't just ready, they were sitting outside the front door on their luggage like the Girl Who Waited from *Doctor Who*. Lucy had loved that episode. Evie was hovering, looking a bit fed up. "Finally," she muttered when Rory stepped out of the Škoda. "These two have been running me ragged since they got home from school. Next time, why don't you pick them up from there? I can drop off their things during the day."

Leo flung himself at Rory's legs and clung on like a spider monkey. "Oof." Rory managed not to stagger backwards, and patted his son's tousled head. "Fine by me. You'd like that, wouldn't you, kids?"

"Yeah! Doughnuts!" Lucy shouted, bouncing up from her squished backpack.

Evie made a face. "And don't fill them up with sugar over the weekend. I don't want them hyper when I pick them up."

"Wouldn't dream of it." Rory hoped it came over as sincere.

She huffed, so maybe it hadn't. "Now, you two be good, and we'll see you on Sunday. Usual time?"

Rory nodded. "Yeah, that's fine. Come on then, you two, are you coming or what?" He gently unpicked Leo's grip from around his legs, hoisted him on his hip, and bent down to grab his backpack.

"Is David going to be there?" Lucy demanded as they drove off.

"Course he is, love. He lives there."

She didn't answer, and as he'd just got to a junction, Rory didn't push it.

He'd find out soon enough if she was pleased about that or not.

Neither Rory nor David could work out whose turn it was to cook, and the kids wanted to help anyway, so in the end they all mucked in together. Lucy asked for fish fingers, and her eyes nearly dropped out of her head when David said he'd never eaten them.

"What, never?"

"Never."

"Never *ever*?"

"Never ever ever."

"What *did* you have for tea when you were little?"

David's face went dreamy. "Hen—that's my mother—used to do some yummy black bean and avocado quesadillas. And I used to love her quinoa bites with salsa. But they were only for a treat, obviously."

Rory and the kids exchanged blank looks. "So . . ." Rory said slowly. "Is that the sort of thing you used to cook before you moved in here?"

"Oh, God, no. I lived on Lean Cuisine and smoothies. Hen did *try* to teach me to cook, bless her, but we ended up not speaking for a week. She's really more into acquiring knowledge than passing it on."

"Uh-huh. Right. Moving on . . ."

Then David had to ask why they weren't having custard with the fish fingers, cos he'd seen that episode of *Doctor Who*, and the kids started on at him too, and before Rory knew it, he was opening a can of custard and bunging it in a saucepan.

That Moffat bloke's got a lot to answer for, Rory thought darkly as he struggled not to gag on his dinner. He felt a bit better when he realised how green David's face was, and that even Lucy was scraping off as much of the custard as she could and eating it separately.

Leo flippin' *loved* it, asking for seconds in actual words and everything. Okay, he whispered in Rory's ear, but it still counted. Rory felt a bit better after that.

Then they played games until bedtime. Rory showed the kids a bath—they didn't look that dirty, or whiff or nothing, so he didn't reckon they needed more than a quick dunk—and got them into their jim-jams and back downstairs with a couple of pillows and some fluffy blankets.

"Leo wants David to read to us," Lucy announced.

"Love, you can't ask him to—"

"It's no trouble," David cut him off, letting Mr. Willis catch the long pheasant feather he'd been teasing him with and disappear under the coffee table to mangle it at his leisure. "I'd be delighted to. What literary treats are in store for us tonight?"

"*Francesca the Football Fairy*." Lucy scrabbled around in her backpack and brought out the book, which was a bit worse for wear these days. "It's our favourite."

Rory gave him a commiserating look. "There's a whole series of them. Football, painting, kitten, even musical flippin' instruments. You name it, they got a fairy for it."

"Sounds like a place in Soho I used to frequent." David hoisted a happily squirming Leo onto his lap and opened the book. "Now, children, are you sitting comfortably? Then I'll begin."

Rory listened, bemused, as David's animated voice brought life back to words he could have recited backwards in his sleep.

It was cosy, the four of them lined up on the sofa. Nice. Like being a family again. And all right, David was only the lodger, but . . . but he *wasn't*, was he? Not really. Would he read the kids stories if he was just a lodger? No way.

He was a mate. A good mate.

Rory wasn't sure what Evie did about bedtime at weekends anymore, but his rule was lights out at nine o'clock sharp, so he and David tucked the kids up under their blankets and said good night.

Once they were out in the hall and the door shut behind them, David turned to him and whispered, "So what do we do for the rest of the evening? Go to bed?"

"Nah. Well, sorta. I usually go upstairs and watch telly on the laptop. Join me if you like?"

"Ooh, that'd definitely be more fun than going to bed alone. What are we watching?"

"Whatever you want. You into, like, Marvel and stuff?"

"Does a hobby horse like spotted dick?"

"That was a yes, right? So, uh, *Agents of S.H.I.E.L.D*? *Agent Carter*?"

"*Agent Carter*. That lipstick is to *die* for."

"Nah, it don't kill you. Only knocks you out. Come on, then. Before one of 'em gets up for a wee and finds us hanging around out here like we want to read more stories."

They tiptoed upstairs, and David turned to him. "You get it set up. I'll go and get Gregory."

"He's a big Marvel fan and all, is he?"

"He's more into period drama, but what is *Agent Carter* if not that? He *adores* Hen's DVDs of *Brideshead Revisited*."

"Fine, but I'm not waiting while he gets changed. He can come as he is."

"Spoilsport. It'd serve you right if he turned up naked."

"He's a bear. With fur. I don't think naked's an option. I'll see you in a jiffy." Rory flung himself on his bed, punched the pillows a few times until they made a good back support, and opened up his laptop.

David was there before he'd even got the website to load, holding Gregory in his arms. Rory patted the bed beside him. "Come and pull up a pillow."

"Now there's an offer I don't get from you every day." David sat down, carefully placing the teddy bear between them. He—the bear, that was, not David—was wearing a tiny set of striped pyjamas, so either David had changed him in double-quick time or Gregory had been a lazy sod and never got dressed today.

Rory smiled at himself. He was getting as bad as David. "How long have you and Gregory been together?"

"Oh, years. Decades. Well, nearly. I found him hiding under the Christmas tree when I was four. He wasn't called Gregory then, of course. We had a little confab about it and changed his name a few years ago. Apparently he thought *Boobie Bear* wasn't dignified for a bear of his advanced age."

When he was four. That must have been about how old David had been when his dad had died. Rory sneaked another peek at the teddy. He was looking pretty good, for a twenty-year-old soft toy. Still had plenty of fur, although it was thinning in places. Not that Rory was in any position to throw stones. "He always had the piercing?"

"Oh, the button in his ear? Yes, that's original." David smiled down at the toy, and there was something in his face that made Rory feel strange inside. Sort of hot and lumpy. But in a good way. "Do you think I should get one to match?"

Rory laughed. "Yeah, why not? I reckon it'd suit you."

"Well, if I do, you're explaining it to Hen. She has Views on permanent body art."

"Good thing I never got a tattoo, then. Right, we starting from the start?"

"Oh, yes. We have to see poor tragic Colleen's brief arc."

"Here we go, then." Rory got it set up, hit Play and Full Screen, and settled back to watch.

Weird how much better it was, watching a show with someone who was as into it as he was. David wasn't exactly quiet. He threw out comments on everything from what the characters said and did to the way they dressed. Rory got into the spirit of it and added some of his own. It was fun.

After they'd watched the first two episodes back-to-back, he paused it and had a bit of a stretch. They'd both slipped down a bit on the pillows, so they were more lying than sitting, and he was getting a crick in his neck. "You all right, there?" he asked David.

"Mm, perfect." He straightened Gregory, who'd started to lean over, then turned to Rory with a wicked grin. "Tell me honestly, Rory. Am I the only man you've ever had in your bed?"

Rory gave him a look. "You're on my bed, not in it."

David met his gaze with a defiant air, pulled down the duvet a few inches, and shoved his toes underneath.

Rory had to laugh. "Cheeky sod."

"Mm, fair comment. On both counts."

Okay, that made Rory feel a bit . . . weird. He hadn't meant that *literally*. Hadn't even thought about the sort of thing David might like to get up to in bed.

Now he couldn't *stop* thinking about it.

David gave a nervous laugh and pulled his feet back out from under the duvet. "Ignore me. You don't want to listen to anything that comes out of my mouth. So, next episode? Or should we call it a night?"

He was all tense and still, like he was holding his breath, and suddenly Rory felt ashamed. So what if David *did* like to do stuff in bed with blokes? Didn't mean he was gonna jump on Rory and do it to him just cos they happened to be sitting on the same bed and having a laugh together, did it?

"Next episode," he said firmly, pushing down all the weird feelings and trying to forget them. "You wanna grab a drink or something first? Still got some of that whisky left."

David scrambled off the bed, smiling like a kid who'd been told to go find a bag of sweeties. God, sometimes Rory forgot how young he was. "I'll get it. You're having a glass too? I'd offer to make Scotch cocoa but it'd be a crime with whisky this good."

"Neat's fine. Bring the bottle, yeah?"

"*Oui, mon capitaine.*" David snapped off a sharp salute, turned on his heel, and scampered off.

Shaking his head, Rory cued up the next episode.

They ended up watching the next two, but Rory was nearly falling asleep by the end of the second one cos it had to be well late by now. He looked at his clock and groaned. "Call it a night? The kids'll be getting me up about six hours from now."

"Oops. I forgot little ones tend to do that." David yawned and stretched, his T-shirt riding up again. "Can I just not move? I'm not sure moving at this juncture is actually possible. Why am I so tired? I'm never this tired on a Friday night."

Rory laughed. "Kids, eh? They take it out of you."

David lounged back against the pillows. "But they are adorable. Do you think they like me?"

"Course they like you. They don't make just anyone read that flippin' football fairy book."

"Don't you dare say a word against Francesca. She and I are soul mates. Apart from the whole *liking football* thing."

"Uh-huh. Soul mates. Definitely."

David grinned up at him. "Sooo . . . Tell me, Rory, Rory, Rory: who would be your soul mate? Out of our *Agent Carter* heroines, that is. Angie or Peggy? The sassy blonde, or the cool, competent brunette?"

Rory didn't know about soul mates, but then he didn't reckon that was what David was really asking. "Peggy."

"Oh, that was *fast.*"

"Proper old-fashioned stunner, ain't she? What about you, then?"

David raised an eyebrow. "Peggy or Angie?"

"Nah, you tosser. Uh, Stark or Jarvis? The, uh, the moustached millionaire—"

"Oh, very good."

"—or the British butler?"

"Let yourself down a bit on that one. Hm, that *is* a hard one. Which is what *he* said. Either. No, both."

"Yeah?" Rory frowned. "I mean, yeah, Stark's fit enough, even I can see that, and he's got all the charisma, but Jarvis? He's just a bit ... I dunno. Boring?"

"But look at the way he fills out a three-piece suite. Suit."

"Never been much for suits. Too . . . stiff."

"You say *stiff* like it's a bad thing." David sniggered.

Rory found himself laughing too, and it was great, until flippin' *Barry* popped into his head. He could guess what Barry would say about him and David sitting in bed together sharing dirty jokes. And . . . it was stupid, wasn't it? It wasn't like there was anything actually going on between him and David.

Thinking that didn't make him feel better, though. Cos, so what if there *was* something going on? Who was Barry to say that wasn't right?

Not that there *was*, mind.

But—

"I'm off to get my beauty sleep," David said, grabbing his teddy bear from where it'd fallen down between the pillows, and getting up. "Sleep tight."

"Yeah, mate. You and all," Rory said, his voice a bit funny for some reason he didn't want to think about.

He'd sleep on it. Things would be clearer in the morning.

Right?

CHAPTER TWENTY-TWO

David lay in his lonely fairy bed, and wondered why he felt so . . . flat. True, Rory had *looked* as if he was about to have a Gay Panic attack earlier in the evening, but he'd got over it remarkably quickly.

It had just put a bit of a damper on the evening, that was all. David was hugely relieved he hadn't made a mess of things with Rory, of course he was, but he'd had to censor his behaviour after that. Make sure he didn't do anything too threateningly gay.

Asking Rory which of the female characters he fancied had been a good move. He should be glad he'd thought of that. And Rory hadn't seemed to mind David saying he'd be up for a threesome with the men, or the innuendos that had somehow slipped in at the end there. That was good too.

David just didn't *feel* good about it all. He grabbed Gregory and held him tight, in case he'd been affected by the atmosphere as well. Teddy bears could be such sensitive creatures.

The next morning, David continued to feel a little as though he were walking on tiptoe around Rory.

Fortunately, the children were still there (obviously, as they hadn't been abducted by aliens in the night), and they weren't having any of that nonsense. It was amazing how hard it was to stay on tenterhooks while playing Hungry Hippos.

"Did you used to play this when you were little?" Lucy asked, her tone not entirely gruntled. David had just won again.

"Oh, no. Hen dislikes plastic toys. Hen is my mother, remember?" he reminded a momentarily frowning Lucy.

Rory's eyebrows performed a *petit saut*. "Blimey, what did you play with, then?"

"Oh, lots of things. Wooden trains, wooden cars—"

"Lemme guess, they wooden go?" Rory laughed.

David winced, and Lucy gave her father a disgusted look. "*Dad*-dy." Even Leo groaned audibly.

"And I used to love dressing up. There was a wardrobe in the spare room where Hen kept a lot of her old clothes—some very pretty dresses, you know the old Laura Ashley styles? And shoes, too, and handbags . . ." David beamed in fond memory. "I used to create whole new personas, and Hen would play along and pretend she didn't know it was me."

Lucy was frowning. "Why do you call her Hen? Why not Mummy?"

"*Loads* of children have mummies. I was the only one with a Hen."

"What did you call your daddy?"

"Armand. But he died when I was younger than Leo." David hastened to add, lest he plant worries in tiny heads, "He was quite old, and he had a poorly heart."

"Did you miss him?" There was an odd, sad tone to Lucy's voice.

"Oh yes." David couldn't precisely remember losing his father now, but he was certain he must have. "But I was glad to have known him as long as I did."

"Mummies and Daddies aren't supposed to die. Or—" Lucy glanced up at her father and bit her lip.

Rory didn't seem much happier than his daughter. Neither did Leo.

David jumped up. "Drinks and biscuits, everyone?"

After they'd finished their drinks and biscuits, it was pretty much lunchtime, which wasn't the *best* management but what could you do? David and Rory quickly put some sandwiches together.

"You know," David said, cutting the cheese-spread-and-no-butter sandwiches into triangles for Leo, "we don't have to eat these now. We could have a late lunch."

"Nah, ain't gonna work." Rory looked a bit embarrassed. "Meeting Barry and his nippers down the swings in an hour."

"Oh. Well, that'll be nice for you." David suppressed a wince at how flat that had come out. It was ridiculous of him to feel abandoned.

He was only the lodger, after all.

Rory didn't seem to have noticed, though. "Bet you'll be glad of the quiet while we're out, won't you?"

David summoned up a smile. "I shan't know what to do with all the space on the sofa, either. Now, if we've got enough food, we should probably get on with eating it, shouldn't we?"

Lucy found some cartoons to watch while they munched their sandwiches. David's tasted like ashes, which was odd, seeing as he hadn't toasted them. Perhaps realising his distress, Leo gave him a slightly squishy triangle, which tasted a little better.

"Right, you lot," Rory said at length. "Time to get your coats on. We're going down the swings to meet Sam and Kelly and Uncle Barry."

Lucy let out a *Yay*, although whether at the prospect of the swings, the other children, or even Uncle Barry, David wasn't sure. As the children scrambled off the sofa and ran for their coats, he told himself firmly that it was ridiculous to feel hurt over their joy at leaving him behind.

"Guess we'll see you in a couple of hours, yeah?" Rory said, pulling his own jacket on. He hesitated. "Um, you know, if you wanna . . . just, I know you and Barry didn't exactly hit it off . . ."

David opened his mouth to say, *No, no, I wouldn't want to intrude*—and Lucy burst into the room. "Hurry *up*, David. It's time to *go*."

"Uh, sweet pea, David's not coming," Rory said awkwardly. "He's got his own stuff to do, yeah?"

David swallowed. Leo was standing in the doorway, one arm in his coat and a look of absolute betrayal on his face.

Oh God. If he didn't go, the children would be upset. If he did go, Barry might burst a blood vessel or something equally unpleasant . . .

Put like that, it was no contest. David jumped to his feet with a smile. "Of course I'm coming, *mon lapinou*."

"Is that another cabbage?" Lucy asked suspiciously.

"No, this one's a bunny rabbit. And I wasn't talking to you, Miss Cabbage Patch 2016."

Leo beamed. Lucy didn't. "That's not this year."

"And far be it from me to say your bloom has faded. Jacket, jacket, where's my jacket? Ah, thank you, Leo." David ruffled the hair on his happy little head.

"You didn't have to do that," Rory said quietly as Lucy skipped down the road in front of them. "But, you know, cheers."

"I do feel a teensy bit bad about interrupting your bro-bonding time with Barry," David admitted.

"Nah, he can handle it. Barry's a big boy." Rory grinned. "Getting bigger all the time. And it ain't like it was going to be just me and him."

Tell that to Barry, David thought privately when they got to the park, which was an attractively irregular patch of green behind the churchyard with a fenced and gated children's play area. The Neanderthal wasn't so much staring daggers at him as launching intercontinental nuclear missiles with the power of his beady eyes.

"Oi, oi," Barry said by way of friendly greeting. "See the honeymoon ain't over yet."

Rory laughed. Apparently the undercurrents of hostility had gone over his head. Would that make them overcurrents? David forced a smile. "How lovely to see you again. Which are your charming offspring?" He gestured at the children playing on the park equipment.

Barry's eyes narrowed, which they could ill afford. "That's Sam on the swings, and Kelly's on the slide. Planning to join 'em, are you?"

Rory coughed. "Uh, Barry, you all right, mate?"

Leo, bless him, saved the day by tugging on David's hand and leading him to the swings.

Dutifully, David sat on a swing, grateful for his narrow hips. "Well? Aren't you going to push me?"

Leo made an unimpressed face, hands on his hips like a very small fishwife.

David beamed and hopped off the swing. "Oh, you want me to push *you*? Okay, then, on you hop. Let's see if we can get you doing somersaults."

From his position behind Leo's swing, David had ample opportunity to observe proceedings. Lucy had run over to the slide to join Sam or Kelly—David had already forgotten which was which.

Barry and Rory had their heads together, sitting on a bench. That was moderately ominous, and David wondered if his ears should be burning. Although, of course, there *were* other topics of conversation than his excellent self.

Barry seemed to be doing most of the talking, judging from his excessive hand gestures. Clearly it was something he felt strongly about. Bringing back hanging? Electric shock therapy for homosexuals?

"Why don't you like Uncle Barry?" Lucy asked from behind him, making him jump and almost miss-time a push.

"I don't think Uncle Barry likes me."

"Mummy doesn't like Uncle Barry either." Then she ran off, leaving David more curious than ever about the woman Rory had married.

CHAPTER TWENTY-THREE

Rory wasn't much enjoying sitting on the bench, listening to Barry bang on about how David might not be the kind of role model Rory wanted for his kids. He was talking out of his arse, cos David was bloody fantastic with the kids, and as for being a role model, well, they could do a lot worse than a bloke who dressed smart and used all them big words. Expanding their vocabulary, he was. Rory's too, if he was honest. *And* teaching them a bit of French on the side.

Trouble was, Barry didn't seem to want to let Rory get a word in edgewise to explain all that. So when Lucy ran over and asked him to push her on the roundabout, he ignored Barry's complaint that she was old enough to do it herself and jumped straight up. It was fun, anyhow. You could get that roundabout going a fair old whack if you ran fast, and it was big enough for Rory to jump on for a ride as well. Lucy loved it.

After a while—a long while—she decided she wanted to go on the slide. Probably cos Leo was over there on his tod, having given up his swing to Kelly. Barry was standing by the side of the swings yelling stuff like, "Put your legs out—no, not now, when you're going forward. Jesus, don't they teach you anything at school these days?"

Rory caught David's eye, and they went to sit on a free bench, Rory still breathing hard and waiting for the park to stop spinning. "All right? Sorry if it's a bit boring for you."

"No, no. It's a whole new world. I've never had children before. Actually the roundabout looked like fun."

"Yeah? Next time they want a go on it, it's all yours. Any more of that and my lunch'll be making a reappearance."

They both watched Barry for a mo. He'd given up on getting through to Kelly with words alone and was now running backwards and forwards alongside the poor kid's swing, making hand gestures. "You can't say he doesn't put the effort in," Rory said at last.

"Mm. So, you and Barry: bosom chums forever?" David sounded . . . not exactly sarcastic, but a bit on the sharp side, maybe.

"It's not . . ." Rory stopped and tried to get his thoughts in order, cos David didn't *get* it, and he had to make him see he was wrong. "I owe him. Like, a lot. You know when Evie left me?"

"It must have been a rough time."

"Yeah . . ." He screwed his eyes shut, cos he couldn't look at his kids and say this. "It nearly killed me. Her saying she'd found someone else, and she was gonna take the kids and live with him. It was like . . . remember that bit in the Indiana Jones film where the priest bloke rips some poor bastard's beating heart right out of his chest? It was like that. Only she took me lungs too, and me liver, and all them other bits nobody knows what they do."

David nodded. "I've often wondered why we really *need* a gall bladder. Isn't the world full of enough bile? Or is that the pancreas? But I'm rambling on. Just ignore me."

Rory managed a weak smile. "Never, mate. But it was bad. I'm not saying I'd've . . . done nothing stupid, topped meself or what have you, but, well . . . Oof." All the air rushed out of his lungs as David clamped himself around Rory's chest. He patted David's back breathlessly. "Oi, mate, 's okay, yeah? I'm good now. But if it hadn't been for Barry . . ."

David nodded and gave a loud sniff. What was it with him and Jenni, getting all teary when Rory talked about emotions and stuff? Huh. Rory blinked his own eyes—must be dust or something. He cleared his throat. "So what I'm saying is, I owe him, and if he needs a shoulder to cry on cos he's got his knickers in a twist over the wife's latest health fad, or he wants someone to rant at about the world going to the dogs and then some, I'm gonna be there for him."

"That's so sweet." David sniffed again.

Rory offered him a hanky. Then he glanced over to where the kids were and saw Barry standing stock still, staring at them with a weird look in his eye.

As if, say, he'd just seen his best mate getting a cuddle from the gay bloke who was living with him.

Well, crap.

Barry was in a right mood the rest of the time they were at the park. Kept brushing off Rory's attempts to talk to him. At first, Rory felt bad about it, and he wanted to explain stuff, but the longer it went on, the more he stopped feeling guilty and started feeling angry.

It wasn't like David and him had done anything wrong, was it? And even if it *had been* wrong—which it *hadn't*—it'd only happened cos Rory was trying to get David to like Barry, the ungrateful git.

So why should he be all in a hurry to tell Barry there hadn't been anything gay going on? What if there had been? It wasn't against the law. Maybe it had been, yeah, decades ago, but that'd been a stupid law. Cos what was so flippin' wrong with two blokes having a cuddle in public? Or doing other stuff, for that matter. Although maybe best not to do *that* in public.

Rory ran his finger round his collar. He'd thought he'd cooled off from all that roundabout pushing, but he was definitely feeling a bit hot and bothered now.

David was off with Leo again when Barry finally came over to talk to Rory.

"Right, then," he said heartily. "Me and the kids are off. See ya."

Rory frowned. "Oi, hang on, we'll walk back up with you." That was what they always did, wasn't it? Why did Barry have to go changing things now?

"Nah. No need to drag the kids off the slide." Barry stomped off, trailing a kid by each hand. Sam and Kelly didn't look too happy about having to leave while Lucy and Leo were still playing, either.

Rory was staring after them when David left off larking about with Leo on the slide and came over to join him. He wasn't smiling, and it was strange, but it was the first time Rory had noticed how good-looking he was. Like a picture in a magazine, or . . . or a painting, or something. Not like someone real, someone Rory knew.

It made Rory feel funny inside, and he didn't like it. He wanted David to go back to being real, being the bloke he was mates with. Except . . . in a weird sort of way, that wasn't right either.

"Is everything all right?" David asked.

Rory definitely didn't like to see David looking worried, so he forced a smile. "Barry got the hump about something. Daft git. He'll get over it."

David bit his lip. "Will he? I mean, it was my fault, wasn't it? I think he saw me getting handsy with you, although not in the sense he must have thought."

Bloody Barry. "You didn't do nothing wrong, and if he don't get over it, he's just a stupid great . . . twat-muffin."

David gave a startled laugh. "*Twat*-muffin?"

"Yep. You heard me."

"I hope the children didn't."

"Yeah. Lucy'd give me that disapproving face she gets from her mum. Course, Leo would probably think it was what we were having for tea."

"Twat-muffins and honey. Hm. I'm afraid I've never been that fond of—" David caught himself as Lucy ran up to join them, Leo trailing after her "—muffins."

She gave him a withering look. "That's silly. *Everyone* likes muffins."

"One man's muffin is another man's poison."

Lucy stared at him. Then she turned pointedly to Rory. "Are we going home soon, Daddy? Leo needs a wee and I want a drink."

"Right, love. Not left anything behind, have we? Then let's get home."

Getting the kids home and sorted out with drinks and the loo and making sure they washed their hands took up all Rory's attention, which he wasn't sorry about. What with Barry, and David . . . Nah, he could do with a break from thinking about all that, ta very much.

CHAPTER TWENTY-FOUR

David felt like a complete and utter bastard. There Rory had been, telling him how important Barry was to him, and David had had to get overemotional and hug the poor man. Rory, that was, because the thought of hugging Barry made David shudder, and not in a good way.

Barry hadn't *quite* edged his way out of the park with his back against the wall, but that was probably because the park didn't actually have any walls. David was lucky Rory hadn't done the same. When would he learn that straight men didn't often appreciate physical affection from gays?

Except, Rory hadn't *seemed* annoyed with him. In fact, he seemed to have been trying to make David feel better. Which was nice, although it came with its own side order of extra guilt. Like treading on someone's toe, and having *them* apologise to *you* while clearly in agony from some abused in-growing toenail or bunion, only times about a million.

He wanted to ring Hen. She was wonderful for talking things through with. Failing that, a conversation with Fen—funny how the two women in his life rhymed; perhaps he should introduce them one day, or alternatively write a poem—might help him sort through his feelings. He could just imagine how it would go too:

David: I hugged Rory.

Fen: Ew, why?

David: He's really very sweet when you get to know him.

Fen: We have *got* to get you a boyfriend. And did I mention, *Ew*?

But he couldn't seem to find an opportunity. When they got back home from the park, Lucy needed help with her homework, which had to come from David as sums had apparently never been Rory's strong suit, bless him. And then Leo needed someone to read to, and while Rory was technically capable of listening to him on his own, it was so adorable to hear Leo sound out the words in his barely there whisper, that David ended up making the other slice of bread in a Leo sandwich on the sofa.

Lucy gave him a funny look when Leo had finished his book and skipped off to find Mr. Squiddy, who'd apparently been left in the loo—David only hoped Leo didn't mean that literally. "He never does that at Mummy's house."

"What, read?"

"Not with anyone else there. Only me and Mummy. *Lewis* has to leave the room."

David glanced at Rory, but couldn't quite interpret his expression.

And then they needed to make tea, and apparently Rory had told the children about David's scromblet, so they insisted he make that, and they all had a big discussion about how scrambled a scromblet could be before it turned into scrambled eggs, and then they watched *Frozen* with the children, which took them up nicely to bath time.

By this point David had decided to go with the tried and tested approach to problem-solving: ignore it and hope it goes away.

Later, Rory closed the living room door gently behind them, the two little mites tucked up securely on the sofa. "So, you up for some laptop telly?"

David blinked. He hadn't expected to be asked again. Most straight men, in his experience, would have used tonight as an opportunity to re-establish boundaries. "Um, yes?" His voice came out a bit squeaky. Must be all that bedtime story reading.

Rory laughed. "You don't sound too sure. Go on, it's your turn to choose what we're watching."

It certainly *seemed* like the offer was sincere. "You don't want to carry on with *Agent Carter*?"

"It ain't like the 1940s are gonna get any more out-of-date for waiting a few days, is it? Your choice."

At times of uncertainty, it was often best to stick with the familiar. "*Sherlock*?" David suggested.

"Yeah, go on. I ain't seen any of them for a while. Season one?"

"Ooh, I think so, don't you? If only to hear Mycroft say that famous line."

Rory laughed, and they chorused it together: "'Sherlock Holmes, and Dr. Watson.'"

David could hear the jaunty notes of "The Game Is On" playing in his head, and his fingers twitched for a piano. "But you have to wait for Gregory to get properly attired. He'd be heartbroken to find himself watching *Sherlock* without his little costume on."

Rory's eyes crinkled up rather adorably. "I'll put the kettle on while I wait, then. But if he ain't ready in ten minutes, we're starting without him."

"You're a hard man, Rory Deamer." David bit his tongue to prevent any untoward innuendo slipping out of his mouth.

And could have knocked himself over with a feather boa when Rory came straight back with, "Good to find, or so I've heard. Right, see you in ten."

Rory turned and made his unhurried way to the kitchen.

David stared after him for a heartbeat—had Rory realised what he was saying?—then blinked and ran up the stairs, remembering to tread lightly for fear of disturbing the children.

He decided Gregory should go for the classic Arthur Conan Doyle Holmes outfit, mostly because the tweeds were a lot quicker to put on than the BBC *Sherlock* costume, which consisted of an extremely tight purple shirt, tailored trousers, and a mini Belstaff coat, with optional blue scarf and deerstalker (borrowed, obviously from classic Holmes, as nobody needed two deerstalkers. David had had to be very firm with Gregory on this point). As they emerged from his room, Rory appeared at the top of the stairs, holding a couple of mugs of tea in one hand and the still two-thirds-full bottle of Lagavulin in the other.

David wasn't entirely certain how he felt about adding alcohol to this evening's mix. That warm, fuzzy, affectionate state he usually got into after a snifter or two might lead to more than Rory had probably bargained for.

On the other hand, there was a lot to be said for something to make him feel less awkward about the whole sitting-on-Rory's-bed thing, so when Rory offered him a tot in his tea, David accepted. "Although it's sacrilege, really, using single malt in tea. Don't you feel wonderfully decadent?"

"Yeah, no. Kind of knackered, to be honest."

"Oh? I didn't think the day was unduly taxing? The children were little angels. Well, most of the time."

"Nah, no complaints there. I just can't get the hang of having a lie-in, that's all." Rory yawned.

"Well, we don't have to watch more than one episode." Paradoxically, David found he was disappointed by the prospect, and tried to tell himself that less time on Rory's bed with him was a Good Thing. *Boundaries*, he reminded himself, and plonked Gregory firmly in the middle of the bed as chaperone.

"Hey, nice costume." Rory grinned. "You got one like that too?"

"Ugh, no. Tweed itches. And looks ghastly with my complexion. No, I'm keener on the BBC version for personal wear."

"Yeah? You got the coat and all?"

"Mm, and it wasn't easy. You know it had been discontinued by the time the show aired? They brought it back later on, of course—ka-*ching*—and there's any amount of knockoffs around on the internet now."

"I'd like to see you in that getup. You gonna dress up for that Comic Con thing you're going to?" Rory sounded a little wistful.

"You know, you should definitely come too," David said without thinking, and then caught himself up guiltily. "Um. I'll work on Fen."

"Nah, 's okay. I don't wanna spoil her day." Rory took a deep breath, the sort usually accompanied by girding of loins.

David did *not* look at Rory's loins. Or consider what an absolutely perfect Watson he'd make to David's Sherlock, if he could only be persuaded into wearing a wig.

He could probably manage even without the wig. The cuddly sweater would likely be sufficient. Or he could simply go as Rory, which wouldn't detract from his cuddliness one iota—

"Here we go," Rory went on with cheerfulness that seemed a little forced, and hit Play on the laptop. "Episode one, coming up."

Glad to be distracted from that line of thought, David settled back into the pillows and let the theme music lull him into a state of pleasant anticipation, aware of Rory doing likewise on the other side of Gregory.

"So, um, Sherlock," Rory said later, as the music died away at the end of the first episode. "You'd say he was good-looking, right?"

David cocked his head and grimaced at the ceiling. "It's an interesting question, actually. I mean, a million fangirls can't be wrong, but you'd have to say that Benedict's features are more *arresting* than classically handsome. Where was he when they were handing out strong, manly jawlines? The styling, obviously, is calculated to be attractive—seductive dark colours, and so very swishy—but I think it's the whole package that appeals to people." He was proud of himself for not adding any further comment on the actor's *package*.

"Yeah . . ." Rory paused. "So you don't fancy him yourself?"

"Oh, God, no. Not at all my type."

"Seriously?"

"Rory, Rory, Rory, did I name my teddy bear Sherlock? No, I did not."

"Gregory?" Rory frowned, and David could see the moment when the penny dropped and the light lit up. "Wait—Lestrade? Really? Ain't he a bit old for you?"

"He's a very attractive man." David was a little hurt by that *Really*. "A perfect silver fox. Only improved by age."

"Huh." Rory stared straight ahead for a mo. Then he lifted the bottle of Lagavulin. "Top-up?"

David braced himself, tossed down the cold dregs of his tea, and held out his mug. "Please. Just a dash, mind."

"Yeah, don't wanna overdo it." Rory gave them both modest splashes of whisky, then reached towards the mousepad. "What about Watson?"

"He's got a certain cuddly charm. But he's not Lestrade." *He isn't Rory, either*, David found himself thinking.

Rory nodded, and hit Play. "Fair 'nuff."

It was gone midnight by the time the second episode finished, and Rory looked on the verge of nodding off. "Call it a night?" he said with a yawn.

David said good night with the warm glow that came from knowing his behaviour had been entirely without reproach. No straying hands, no excessive innuendo . . . He'd been a perfect gentleman.

The hollow feeling inside was undoubtedly caused by tiredness. Undoubtedly.

When he got into bed, though, David couldn't seem to switch off his mind and go to sleep.

Rory had seemed so . . . sad about not going to Comic Con. David had a strong suspicion he'd never been to one before, and that was a crying shame for someone with as many fannish interests as he had. Presumably the women in his life hadn't been the fandom sort.

"Maybe we should try to find Rory a girlfriend?" he whispered to Gregory. "A *proper* girlfriend." Someone who liked the things he did, and would be happy to go to Comic Con with him?

His insides twisted themselves in knots at the thought. David frowned. This wasn't like him. Just because *David* wasn't doing well in the romantic stakes right now didn't mean he had to begrudge Rory a bit of loving. Rory was *made* to be someone's boyfriend. He was sweet, funny, caring . . .

Oh God.

David slapped his forehead. Hard. It was so blindingly obvious. How on earth had he not seen it before?

He didn't want Rory to have a girlfriend because *he* wanted to be the only woman in Rory's life.

Which, given that he was a man, presented quite a problem, didn't it? David lay in his lonely fairy bed, and pondered. He'd slept with so-called straight men before, of course. Some of them had even still spoken to him afterwards.

But . . . Rory had turned out to be unexpectedly good company. David didn't want to ruin that by pushing him headlong into a crisis of sexuality.

Probably.

He *did* have a lovely smile, though. And David had always liked his eyes. And he was kind, and fit, and altogether adorable . . .

But straight. At least, that was obviously how Rory thought of himself. Which brought David back to the whole crisis-precipitation thing.

It wouldn't be fair. Rory was a nice man who'd generously welcomed David into his home and his family life. Paying that back by shaking the foundations of his self-image wouldn't be very nice on David's part, would it? And yet . . . "What do you think, Gregory?" he whispered. "Surely a little broadening of the horizons wouldn't hurt?"

Gregory's glassy gaze, in the dim light thrown by David's digital clock, didn't seem to indicate agreement. In fact it rather reminded David of his mother that time he'd told her he was fed up with working for Charles and wanted to go and be a market gardener. Or possibly a fossil hunter, an idea he'd got from a sarcastic remark Ryan had thrown his way referring, somewhat harshly, David had felt, to his usual romantic pursuits. She'd told him he should learn to stick things out.

And then he'd been fired anyway. Hah. That had shown her.

"What would Hen say?" he wondered aloud.

The answer was depressingly obvious. *Whatever you do, don't do it frivolously, darling.*

Which was all very well, but most people who knew David seemed to consider him incapable of doing things in any other fashion.

So it would probably be best to do nothing. Carry on being friends with Rory, and forget all thoughts of further intimacy.

Ignore the growing ache in his chest at the thought of spending more and more evenings watching television with an invisible wall between him and Rory.

It was so confusing. Usually when David saw someone he wanted—and all right, yes, he wanted Rory, so sue him—and who wanted him back, it just *happened*. A brief but intense prelude of eye-fucking and then straight down to the real thing.

Like with Xav.

And that had all ended *so* well, hadn't it?

Why were relationships so *hard*? And not in a good way.

Even the innuendo brought him little joy. David pulled the pillow over his head and resolutely started counting sheep.

CHAPTER TWENTY-FIVE

Sunday morning, hitherto a fairly nonexistent time as far as David was concerned, now apparently involved being hauled out of bed by the children to watch *X Factor* reruns. Still, they didn't seem to require him to be more than physically present, so he was free to doze off as much as the frequently awful singing would allow.

At some point, Rory came to sit next to him, a steaming mug of coffee in his hand. "I'd've got you one and all, if I'd thought you could hold it without spilling it all down yourself."

"Mm. Just waft it in my direction now and then. That'll do," David said sleepily.

An indeterminate time later, Rory coughed. "That one there— he's pretty good-looking, ain't he?"

David manfully tried to blink his eyes into focus on the male singer pole dancing around the microphone in skinny jeans and a tight T-shirt. The singer, not the microphone, although David wouldn't personally put anything past the production design team on this programme. "Objectively speaking, I suppose."

"Like, his face, and all. Not just that he's fit."

Lucy butted in with an air of annoyance. "*Shush*, Daddy. We're *listening.*"

"Sorry," Rory stage-whispered, and shot David a grin.

David wasn't so amused. He'd had a horrid thought. All this talk by Rory about attractive men . . . Was he deliberately trying to divert David's attentions from himself, in hopes of avoiding any further unwanted hugs?

No, it couldn't be that. For one thing, pointing out hot men would probably get David *more* in the mood, rather than less, and for another, that would be far too subtle for a man like Rory.

Was he trying to find out David's type, with a view to setting him up with someone?

David was just as unhappy with this idea as he had been with the prospect of *Rory* going out with someone who wasn't him. Even the thought that at least he'd be getting frisky with *somebody* didn't console him.

He didn't want *somebody*. He wanted Rory.

And he wanted Rory to want him back. Was it such a far-fetched idea? Rory definitely *liked* him. Maybe a little nudge or two, a suggestion that other romantic prospects than women were available . . .

But then Leo climbed onto his dad's lap, and Rory beamed, a picture of happiness and contentment. David knew he couldn't do anything that risked shattering that.

They had an early lunch, and then it was time for Lucy's football.

"Is David coming too?" Lucy asked, scrambling off the sofa to go and get ready. "Or is he staying home with Leo?"

"Uh . . ." Rory looked embarrassed. "I think David might want some time to himself."

"Why?"

"Yes, why?" David echoed, stretching expansively. For some reason Rory's gaze skittered away. "I'll have you know I'm a keen aficionado of sport. Football is the one with the H-shaped goals, isn't it?"

"If you're in America, maybe," Rory said. "Over here we call that rugby. Lucy Lou, you let David have a bit of peace and quiet, yeah?"

It was very sweet of him, but David didn't actually *want* to be left on his own. "I'll do what Leo wants to do," he said firmly as Lucy stomped out of the room.

Leo, judging from the way he thrust his school reading book into David's hands, would rather stay at home and do homework than stand on a draughty field watching other people play football.

David beamed at his anxious little face. "A man after my own heart. You two go and enjoy being muddied oafs, and we'll indulge in some vicarious adventure courtesy of Biff and Chip." He glanced up at Rory, and couldn't work out what he saw there.

"We'll see you later." Rory's voice was hoarse, and he cleared his throat.

David stamped down ruthlessly on the temptation to see that huskiness as cause for optimism. Rory was probably just coming down with a cold. David would have to check they hadn't used all the honey, and lay in a crate of lemons.

"Play well," he told Lucy when she reemerged, clad in a violently yellow football strip, from wherever she'd disappeared to. "Break a leg—preferably not your own."

"Mate, don't even go there," Rory muttered with unexpected feeling. "Right, Leo, you be good for David. And we'll be back in a couple of hours."

Leo snuggled up to David's side and opened his book.

David had a good feeling about the result of Lucy's football match even before an excited Lucy told him her team had won three nil. Possibly the fact she and Rory came in singing "We Are the Champions" had something to do with it.

"And she didn't get booked or nothing," Rory added with, if anything, more pleasure than the win itself seemed to have given him.

David narrowed his eyes, but let that one go for now. "Congratulations, *ma petite choupinette*. I'm glad to hear you've upheld the honour of the Deamer name. Now, I think it's time for your proud father and me to do unspeakable things to that chicken. At least, according to the website I found when I did an internet search on *Roast Chicken for Dummies*."

Lucy sniggered.

Rory coughed. Definitely a cold. "Right, then, love, you go and get changed, and I'll wash me hands. Leo been good for you?"

"Couldn't have been better. We had a nice, relaxing time, didn't we, my little Leo-lapinou?"

Leo nodded so hard it was a wonder his head didn't come off. Bless.

The chicken was, in the end, if not an unqualified success, perfectly edible. Granted, the extremities were a smidge on the dry side—but that was what gravy was for, wasn't it? David felt entirely vindicated over buying the Waitrose gravy. It hadn't been *that* expensive, and the children seemed to love it.

Rory beamed at them. "There you go kids. Good as your mum's?"

There was a pregnant pause, and the beam went down a lumen or two. "Good as your granny's, that time she had a funny turn halfway through cooking and Grandad had to finish it off?"

They looked at each other, and nodded.

"That'll do me," Rory said. David felt rather proud of his part in encouraging family bonding via food.

After they'd finished, David selflessly volunteered to wash up to give Rory more time with his kids before they were picked up. They'd eaten early, so it was only just starting to get dark. Rory took the children out into the garden, a pocket-sized patch of (mostly) grass with some scrubby bushes at the end where apparently all kinds of small creatures lurked.

David was halfway through when there was a ring on the doorbell. Drying his hands on a tea towel, he went to answer it.

The woman at the door smiled at him. "You must be David. I'm Evie—Lucy and Leo's mum." She held out a hand.

Evie was surprisingly youthful in appearance. Although come to think of it, David wasn't entirely sure how old Rory was. That shaven-headed look tended to be aging at first, but then the person seemed to exist in a timeless limbo, not getting visibly older for decades and inspiring worried thoughts about portraits in attics. The erstwhile Mrs. Rory looked to be in her midthirties, with long, dark hair; a thin, pretty face; and a belly the size of the London Eye.

So this was the faithless hussy who'd broken poor Rory's heart. Not that David was biased or anything. He slung the tea towel over a shoulder and took her hand gingerly. "*Enchanté.* Do we anticipate a happy event?" he asked politely, standing back—well back—to let her enter.

She laughed. "I hope so. It's either that or I've eaten a whale."

"My congratulations. Or is it felicitation? At any rate, do come in and sit down. Rory and the tots are in the garden doing something with snails. It's probably best not to ask. And best to check their pockets before you put their clothes in the wash. I'll tell them you're here."

Evie eased herself onto the sofa. "Tell them to wash their hands when they come in," she called after him.

Having informed Rory and the children, David decided that cowardice was the better part of valour. He left Rory to face Lucy's loudly voiced complaints and Leo's Victorian urchin impression, and went back in to keep Evie company.

Possibly nosiness was also a better part of valour in this instance. David couldn't deny that he was agog to find out what Rory's ex was like.

"Cup of tea while you wait?" he offered. "We may have to hire a digger to get all the dirt off Leo's hands, so they could be a while."

"No, I'm fine, thanks. Drinks lose some of their appeal when you've got a baby sitting on your bladder. Have they been good, over the weekend?"

"Like little angels." After all, Lucifer had been an angel until he took that fateful tumble, hadn't he? David joined her on the sofa.

Evie laughed. "You sure you've got the right kids?"

"One loud, one quiet, about so high and so high?" David made the appropriate hand gestures as he spoke.

"Yeah, sounds like my two horrors. They must have made quite a difference around here."

Her tone made it clear she didn't expect it to have been for the better. David found himself wanting to defend her own children to her, but that would be just too weird. "Have you had a good weekend without them?" he asked politely, instead.

She smiled. "Yes. Lewis took me into London on Saturday and we had a meal and saw a show. It was so nice to go to something grown-up for a change, you know? Although I suppose you don't, not having kids."

"It must have been quite a big adjustment for Lewis, too, when you got together," David said tactfully, if also leadingly.

"Oh, God, yes. It hasn't been easy for either of us. I never realised what it'd be like being married to someone who worked in the City. Lewis doesn't even get to see the kids during the week—they're always in bed by the time he comes home—and we only have every other weekend with them, so it's been difficult for him to get to know them properly. And for them to get to know him. They don't do what he says if I'm not there, and he gets frustrated about it. It's not his fault. He's just not used to being a dad."

"Mm-hmm," David encouraged. None of his business, of course, but this was all rather interesting, in a schadenfreude-y sort of way.

"And sometimes I have to go out, to see Mum, or . . . or sometimes I just need a break, you know? All through the week I'm on my own with them these days." She gave a sad little laugh. "S'pose it never really hit me how much Rory did with them, back when we were together. He was always there to walk them home from school, and play with them while I got dinner on. It does my head in, trying to cook a meal with the kids on at me all the time. And I get so tired at the moment." She gestured at her swollen midriff.

David would be the first to admit he wasn't the expert on such things, but he couldn't see how adding a newborn baby to the mix was going to make life any easier.

Might be best not to say so, however. "How did you two meet?"

"Me and Lewis? I'd been in London, meeting up with an old friend from school, and when I came back, there was a problem on the line and we had to get off the train three stops down from Bishops Langley. And naturally, all the taxis were snapped straight up, and I didn't know how on earth I was going to get back home. But I thought there had to be a bus service, so I asked the man next to me if he knew which one I needed for Bishops Langley, which was where my car was."

"Let me guess—Lewis?"

She smiled and nodded. "He swears I must have been using it as an excuse to chat him up, but honestly, I hadn't even looked at him before I said anything. If I had looked, I'd have probably picked someone else—I mean, there he was, this tall, handsome bloke in a posh suit and a Burberry mac . . . He was just so different from all the blokes I knew."

"Rather dashing, was he?" David tried to imagine it and failed utterly, but perhaps he was biased about these two after all.

"Yeah. Not really the kind of person you'd expect to know about buses, though, you know?"

"Why do I have the feeling you're *not* about to tell me he had, in fact, an encyclopaedic knowledge of the timetable?"

"Because it's true? No, he said Bishops Langley was on his way so it'd only make sense for him to drive me there."

"And was it?"

"What, on his way home?" She stared down at her feet. To be fair, it wasn't as though she'd be able to see them when she stood up. Perhaps she'd forgotten what they looked like. "No. But I didn't know that at the time. And, well, there was a lot of traffic. The drive took a lot longer than it should have. And we got talking, and when we got to Bishops Langley, we ended up going for a drink . . ." She looked up at David. "I never set out to cheat on Rory. I just . . . Lewis was so different. So . . . driven. Ambitious. Rory . . . he's happy with what he's got, isn't he? And Lewis was such a gentleman."

David wasn't entirely certain the Oxford English Dictionary definition of *gentleman* included the term *seducer of married women*. Then again, with his own recent history, he was hardly in a position to cast the first stone. "Did he know you were married?"

"Oh yes. I never lied to him."

So that was all right, then. *Not.* "These things happen," he said diplomatically.

"I told Rory about it. As soon as Lewis and me started being more than friends. I didn't lie to him either." She gave David an earnest look. "I wouldn't have done that to him. Not carried on behind his back."

Apparently all the initial flirting and clandestine meetings hadn't counted as *carrying on*.

David was saved from having to reply by the arrival in the living room of Rory and two freshly scrubbed natural historians, one appearing rather woebegone and the other militant. Both, however, were equally silent. He wondered if Rory had used bribery or blackmail.

Evie heaved herself to her feet. "Come on, you two, time to get you home. You say good-bye and thanks for having you to your dad, okay?"

"They don't have to thank me for having 'em," Rory protested. "I'm their dad."

Lucy immediately flung her arms around him. "Thank you," she said loudly. When she released him, Leo took her place. David wasn't sure but thought he could discern a whisper of a word or two.

Then, to David's surprise, Leo relinquished his father and came over to hug *him*. Touched beyond measure, David hugged him back, and was further astonished to hear a quiet but unmistakeable "Bye-bye." He glanced up at Rory, and saw from his look of surprised delight he'd heard it too.

Lucy, the little minx, immediately caught on and hugged him too with a, "Bye-bye, and thank you," as if butter wouldn't melt in her scheming little mouth.

"You've clearly been a hit with them," Evie said with a false laugh.

If her nose was any further out of joint, it'd probably fall off. David was willing to bet the man in *her* life didn't rate too many hugs from the children.

Not that David was, strictly speaking, the man in Rory's life. But still. "What can I say? I adore children."

"Uh-huh. Well, come on then, you two. You got their things, Rory?"

David watched from the hall as they trooped out to the waiting BMW. Rory exchanged a couple of words with Evie, made sure the kids were strapped in, and then they were off.

He came back in with a heavy tread.

The house *was* awfully quiet now the children were gone.

"So," David said brightly. "*Doctor Who* marathon?"

"Yeah." Rory dropped onto the sofa. "That'd be great."

CHAPTER TWENTY-SIX

Rory had never thought he'd miss squinting at his laptop instead of watching on a proper big screen, but it wasn't the same watching telly on the sofa. It wasn't so... so cosy, somehow. Like him and David weren't so close. And he missed that. Feeling close to David.

It was well daft, if you compared it with the way he'd felt with Evie or Jenni. He hadn't felt like there was this weird invisible barrier between them while they were snuggled up on the sofa, maybe sharing a blanket if it was a bit nippy.

But then... Rory and David didn't snuggle, did they? Except that one hug in the park, and that had just been out of sympathy, right?

Just cos Rory was starting to think he wouldn't mind snuggling with David, didn't mean David wanted to snuggle with *him*.

It was all so flippin' confusing, anyway. How did blokes even know if they were into other blokes? For all Rory knew, he was simply getting confused cos David lived with him and the only other person he'd lived with since leaving home had been married to him. Like, his brain had got it into its head that if he was living with someone, there ought to be snuggling going on.

Yeah, and the rest, a part of him much lower down butted in with. And *that* wasn't helping either.

Rory was straight. Had been all forty-one—nearly forty-two now—years of his life. It was like one day finding out your dad wasn't who you thought he was. Or that your granny wasn't a Yorkshire lass like you'd always assumed, but had come over on the Kindertransport from Germany during World War Two, oh, and strictly speaking you were Jewish, not Christian, cos it came down the female line. That one had actually happened to Barry, and it'd been all he could talk about for weeks.

Hadn't made him start going to synagogue or give up bacon butties, mind.

But, yeah. Finding out you weren't as straight as you thought: bit of a knock to the old self-image, that. *If* it was true.

Cos he might think he fancied David, but what if, once they got their kit off, he discovered he really, really didn't? It'd be a bit late then to say, *Hah, funny thing, turns out I'm straight after all*, wouldn't it? There'd be hurt feelings and stuff. And if there was one thing he *was* sure about, it was that he didn't want to hurt David.

Who probably didn't fancy him anyhow, cos face it, Rory was no one's idea of a silver fox. He rubbed his head self-consciously and for a moment actually wondered how much hair transplants cost and if everyone would laugh at him if he got one. Except the answer was bleedin' obvious: lots, and they'd piss 'emselves. He was better off carrying on shaving. And wearing a hat in winter, cos it got a bit nippy.

He'd tried watching some gay porn on the internet last night after David went to bed. As research, to see if it got him going. And, well, he'd got a fairly enthusiastic response from the appropriate bits. But then he'd tried watching bog-standard porn, and that worked too. So he'd given lesbian porn a go—still purely as research, mind—and to be honest, after that he'd felt a bit too . . . drained to carry on. Was he into blokes as much as women, or was it just . . . porn?

Granted, he'd found himself noticing men on the street and that for a while now—there'd been this really fit lad out jogging the other day, and even one in Asda, at least until he'd turned round and showed his face, poor sod—but was it just cos ever since David moved in Rory had blokes fancying blokes on the brain?

He kept on going round in circles, and it was seriously doing his head in. He needed to talk to someone, but who the hell could he talk to about *this*? Patrick would be the obvious choice, if he didn't hate Rory's guts at the mo. He'd had girlfriends and was with a bloke these days, so he must know how it all worked.

Or there was Mark, who'd even married a woman and had a kid with her, but he was David's boss, and that made it awkward.

His mum and dad? God, no. He'd never spoken to them about his love life, and he didn't reckon now was the time to start. They wouldn't understand at all, and anyway, he didn't want to have this conversation on the phone. It'd be bad enough face-to-face.

Barry? Yeah, right. After the way he'd been at the park . . . Rory hadn't seen him since then, and wasn't sure what he was going to say to him when he did, but it wasn't going to be a heart-to-heart about possibly fancying blokes.

Evie?

No. Not in a million years. Not after . . . He didn't *hate* her for what she'd done, cheating on him and then leaving him like she did. She couldn't help falling in love.

He just couldn't trust her anymore.

When he thought about it, there was only one person he could turn to.

Jenni.

Seven o'clock Monday night, Rory stood on Jenni's doorstep while she stared at him with her arms folded, her foot not quite tapping but with a bit of a quiver in the toe of her fluffy slipper, like tapping was definitely something it had in mind.

It was almost like they'd never stopped going out together, which given what he'd come to ask her about was well confusing. "Can I come in? Only I gotta talk to someone. I'm going mental."

"Come on, then." She opened the door wide and jerked her head in a *Get in here* motion. "How come you're not crying on Barry's shoulder, though? He busy or something?"

"Nah, see, Barry's part of the problem, ain't he?" Rory wiped his feet on the doormat and then took off his boots and stood them by the wall.

She snorted. "Finally, he buys a clue. Cup of tea?"

"Smashing. You got any of them—"

"Chocolate chip cookies you like? Yeah. Had a couple of packets left over, didn't I? You go sit down while I put the kettle on."

Rory padded into the living room and sat on the sofa. That felt weird, though, cos that was what he'd have done when they were together, wasn't it? He'd have sat on the sofa and she'd have come and sat next to him and snuggled up. So he got up again and sat on one of the armchairs. Yeah. That was better. Plus, he wasn't tempted to put his feet up on the table from here, cos the angle was all wrong, and putting your feet on the table wasn't right. Not at your ex's place.

Jenni brought in the mugs and a packet of biscuits. "Here you go, love," she said, handing him a mug. She perched down on the sofa, in the corner nearest to him.

"Cheers, love," he said, and then they looked at each other and laughed, cos, well.

"This ain't awkward at all, is it?" Jenni said, still smiling. "So come on, out with it." She took a sip of her tea.

Oh God. Probably best to get the lot out at once. Like cleaning a dog bite. "I think . . . I think David's gone and turned me gay."

And, okay, he'd *thought* he was prepared for any reaction, but Jenni spitting her tea out over him hurt a bit, and not just cos the tea was hot. He gave her a wounded stare as he mopped himself down with a hanky.

"I'm sorry, but . . . Jesus Christ on a crutch." She shook her head. "First, that's *really* not how it works, nobody *turns* you gay, and second . . . You? Gay? *You?*"

"I know, right? But since he's been living with me . . . I dunno, I wondered if maybe I was just, you know, frustrated, but . . . He's nice looking, isn't he?"

"If you like 'em young enough to be your *son.*"

And, yeah, that'd been worrying Rory and all, but he couldn't help thinking that wasn't the biggest issue here. "And he's fun. Like, we get on really well."

"Yeah, but—"

"And now I keep seeing blokes I fancy *everywhere*!" Rory's mouth had gone dry and his voice cracked on that last bit, so he took a gulp of tea, swallowed it wrong, and just about managed not to snort it out of his nose again.

"Which blokes?"

"What? Oh, you know. People I see around. Mates, some of 'em. That one on *Strictly Come Prancing* with the—"

"Oh my God." She'd gone pale. "Mates. Not . . . *Barry*?"

"What? No, that'd be . . . No. Really. No." Rory shivered. That would be just wrong. Him and Barry were mates. It'd be like fancying your mum.

"Thank Christ for small mercies." Her eyes narrowed. "What about Si?"

"Si? Yeah, he's pretty fit. Needs to shave that face-fungus, mind."

"You can keep your hands off that one, Rory Deamer. *And* off his lovely beard."

Rory grinned. "Seriously? You got a thing for Si? Does he know?"

"If he doesn't, he wasn't paying attention last night. Or the three nights previous." Her eyes went a bit dreamy. "Or last Sunday teatime, or—"

"Yeah, yeah, I get the picture. Uh. Congratulations?"

"Ta, love. But no saying anything, you got that? It's been bad enough Patrick giving you the cold shoulder just cos you and me didn't work out. I don't want that happening to Si. We're keeping it quiet until we're certain it's going to last. So, you and blokes. You honestly telling me you've never fancied one before?"

"S'pose I never thought about it. I mean, fancying girls was just what everyone did. Uh, the blokes, I mean. But now, it's like . . . Like when you hear a new word on the radio, and next thing you're reading it in all the papers, everyone and his dog's saying it on the telly, and it even turns up as that week's flipping Countdown Conundrum."

"Yeah, but be fair. Catfishers were a big news story that week. Course everyone was talking about them. Although the Countdown thing was a bit weird, I'll grant you. What was the anagram again?"

"Uh, race shift, I think?"

"Yeah, that was the one. I dunno how they come up with them all. So anyway, you're saying you reckon there's gay people everywhere now? That's just cos they're less afraid to come out—"

"Nah, that's not what I meant. It's like I'm noticing blokes more? And getting, um, interested. It's like . . . You know the first time you have a curry, and then after that you realise there's this whole world of spices and stuff out there you never knew about? So you never wanted a curry before, but now you do cos you know they're there."

"*Ohhh*. So David's your extra-hot chicken vindaloo, and you want to nibble on his naan?"

"Uh, maybe. I dunno. See, I've never had . . . vindaloo before. What if I tried it and I didn't like it?"

"You're never going to know unless you have a taste, though, are you?"

"Yeah, but . . . See, if you're going to try a vindaloo, you ain't gonna do it on, like, a big occasion, are you? You don't book some fancy restaurant where you need a second mortgage to afford a starter, in case you can't make it through the first course."

Jenni had this weird look in her eye. Sort of watery. Had Rory put on too much aftershave again? "Maybe that's where you're going wrong, love. Maybe you ought to take out that second mortgage and just go for it. If you don't like vindaloo at the fanciest Indian restaurant around, you're probably not going to like it anywhere."

"Yeah, but . . . Say the manager's a mate. And he knows you don't like, like, spicy food and stuff, but he's been going on at you for years to try some. And then you try it, and you don't like it, and you gotta tell him that, and it's worse than if you never tried it, you know?"

"*Has* the manager . . . Sod it, this is doing my head in. Has David been acting like he wouldn't kick you out of bed given half a chance?"

"Yeah. Bit. I mean, he flirts with everyone." Rory smiled. It was cute, the way David acted. "But he's different when it's just me and him."

"Different how?"

"I dunno, really. Less . . . less put together. Like, you know he always wears posh clothes? Even his jeans look like they came from some fashion shoot. But round the house, he's way more of a slob."

Jenni nodded gravely. "I can see how that'd appeal to you."

"And his hair goes sort of fluffy when he's not got that stuff in it holding it in place, and he's into *Doctor Who* and Star Trek and all that geek stuff you never had a right lot of time for. Yeah, he likes these reality shows too, but he cracks me up, the way he talks about them."

"Okay, that's why you like him, but what makes you think he likes *you*?"

Rory slumped. "I dunno. Maybe he doesn't? Look at me. He could have anyone he wanted. Why'd he want some sad old geezer like me?"

"*Excuse* me. Are you trying to tell me you think *I* go out with sad old geezers?"

"Uh . . . no?" Oops. Rory hadn't thought about it like that.

"If you're good enough for me, you're good enough for Mr. Fancy-pants David Greenlake, aren't you? So no doing yourself down."

"But you dumped me," Rory felt he had to point out.

"Not cos I didn't fancy you. Tell you what, why don't you try and talk to David about it all?"

"What, just tell him I fancy him?"

"*No.* Rory, love, subtlety's a lost art as far as you're concerned, isn't it? Work round to the subject. Try talking to him about what he finds attractive in a bloke."

"I've done that a bit." Rory was proud of himself for being able to say that. "We've talked about blokes on the telly. You know *Sherlock*?"

"Yeah, but everyone fancies him."

"David doesn't. He likes Lestrade better."

"He never. Isn't he the one with the grey hair?" She cocked her head. "Well, I wouldn't kick him out of bed. All right, that's good. So we know a bloke being older than him isn't a deal breaker."

"Think I should ask him what his turn-offs are?"

"Maybe."

"What if he says, I dunno, short blokes? Or blokes with no hair? For the turn-offs, I mean."

"Then at least you'll know. Would he say something like that? Most of what I know about him I know from my Patrick, and bless him, he's not exactly an unbiased observer."

Rory laughed. "Nah. He still reckons David's after his bloke. Uh. You don't think he *is* after Mark, do you?"

"You know him better than I do."

There was a pause while Rory thought about it. "Nah," he said at last. "He only flirts with him to wind Patrick up. And cos he can't help it. It's just how he is."

"Right, then. So you ask him, and then take it from there." She sat back and folded her arms, like it was case closed.

Rory wasn't so sure. "I dunno, though. If me and David . . . you know . . . what's everyone gonna say?"

Jenni's face fell. "Oh my God. I didn't think about that."

"Yeah, see, I know it's a lot more accepted these days, blokes together, but—"

"I don't mean that! No one who cares about you is going to give a monkey's about you being with David. Maybe Barry, but he can shove it where the sun most definitely doesn't shine. But have you thought about what it's going to mean for me?"

"Uh . . . you'll stop worrying about me fancying Si?" Rory rubbed a hand over his head.

"No, you muppet. I'm the last woman you went out with, aren't I? I'm going to be the one everyone thinks turned you gay." Her eyes were wide and horrified.

"Hang on, you just said that wasn't how it worked."

"Doesn't stop people thinking it, though, does it? They're going to look at me and go, 'That cow, whatever she did to Rory was so bad he doesn't like women anymore.'"

"Oh. Sorry?"

She took a deep breath. "Nah, don't you worry about it. Can't do nothing about stupid people. Speaking of which, don't you let that Barry talk you out of it."

"You never liked him, did you?" Rory frowned. "Don't think David likes him, neither. I know he's a bit . . . He makes these jokes and stuff, but he doesn't mean 'em. Not really. He's a good bloke at heart."

"Oh, love. It wasn't the jokes so much. Well, maybe a bit, cos you can say what you like, but nobody makes that kind of joke without it coming from somewhere. It was more the way he treats you. And you just let him."

"How do you mean?"

"He takes advantage. You're too easygoing for your own good, and blokes like Barry walk all over that. People like your ex-wife and that Lewis, too."

"Barry doesn't do it on purpose." Rory didn't want to think about the rest of what she'd said right now. "And he's been a good mate to me. 'Specially when me and Evie split up. You didn't know me back then. It was rough."

"Join the club. It wasn't a picnic leaving Patrick's dad, may he rot in jail or whatever gutter he's washed up in lately." She made a face. "Mind you, staying with him would've been even less of a picnic."

"Yeah, but . . . Never mind." Rory didn't know how to explain how rough it'd been, and wasn't sure he wanted to anyway. It was one thing coming to her for advice, but stripping himself raw like that? Nah. Maybe if they'd still been together. But they weren't. He stood up. "Cheers, Jenni. You've been great."

"Yeah? It helped, did it? Good. You go get your man." She laughed. "And I still can't believe I'm saying that to you of all people. Just goes to show, doesn't it? You never can tell. Oh, and take the rest of those cookies with you. They go straight to my hips."

"There's nothing wrong with your hips," Rory said, cos there wasn't.

"Oi, none of that, or I'll start thinking you're after me again. Oh, and remember, you keep stumm about me and Si? And I won't go blabbing about you and David."

"If there ever is a me and David, you can tell anyone you like. But yeah, not before. That'd be well awkward if he turns me down now I've gone all gay for him."

"Bisexual, you mean. You still fancy women, don't you?"

Rory thought about it. If there hadn't been a David, and Jenni had been free and single too and had asked him if he fancied a bit of slap and tickle for old times' sake, would he have gone for it? Probably, although it was hard to tell cos every time he imagined shagging he couldn't help thinking about David. "Yeah, I guess."

"Then you're bi, like my Patrick. Look it up. It's a different flag and everything."

"Right. Bi. Huh. It's weird, you know? I never really got it before. Now, though . . . it's like, why isn't everyone?"

"Yeah, well, don't get carried away and start evangelising. That sort of thing gets up people's noses. Gets 'em all in a paddy about the so-called gay agenda and all that guff."

"Nah, I checked that on the internet. It's all about buying milk."

Jenni laughed. "Rory, love? Do me a favour, will you? Never change."

CHAPTER TWENTY-SEVEN

Wednesday morning, David was already feeling a little off-balance. Rory had been acting strangely around him since the weekend. David kept getting the oddest feeling that Rory was about to say something to him, something important—but then it always ended up being about what they were having for tea, or if they were out of loo roll, or on one occasion, if he'd realised that Mr. Willis had been sick in the bathroom.

David was beginning to wonder if he was imagining things. And then just as he'd halfway managed to convince himself he was being paranoid and was starting to relax, Patrick turned up at Mark's literally *seconds* after Mark, being egalitarian, had left to nip to the bakery for coffees.

"Can I have a word?" Patrick asked, standing a little closer than was polite, his arms folded and his feet planted firmly on the floor.

"But of course," David said, feeling generosity in the face of the enemy couldn't hurt. "Take a whole sentence."

"There's something going on, and I want to know about it."

David froze. That did *not* sound good. "There's nothing going on!" It came out rather more of a squeak than he'd have liked. Was this about his lunch out with Mark last week? He cleared his throat. "My relationship with your better half is entirely platonic. Trust me."

Patrick huffed. "You? About as far as I could throw this house. Mark though, I trust completely, so untwist your knickers. It's about Rory."

David froze. "Rory? My Rory? I mean, not *my* Rory, but the one in whose house I—"

"Yeah," Patrick cut him off rudely. "That Rory. What do you know about his love life?"

"Can I ask why you're asking? It seems a little, dare I say—"

"Look, is he back with my mum or not?"

David blinked. "Not," he said after a moment. "You can trust me on that. Or you could, and this is only a suggestion, mind, *ask her.*"

"Yeah, well, sometimes she says what she thinks I want to hear. And how come you're so sure? Just because he hasn't brought her home doesn't mean he's not spending time with her. Which, by the way, I know he is, cos my mate Con saw Rory coming out of her house the other night. He asked *me* if they were back together."

David's stomach lurched. *Was* Rory getting back together with Jenni? He'd said he was going round to see a mate when he went out Monday night. And all right, exes *could* be mates, but why make such a thing of not telling David it was Jenni? Oh God, this was a reaction to David's little faux pas in the park, wasn't it? Rory was trying to prove he was straight—to himself, to David, it didn't matter.

He *knew* he and Fen should have tried harder to fix her up with Si.

"David?" Patrick's voice sounded concerned.

David forced a smile, but found himself blinking rapidly and had to clear his throat again before he could speak. "It's, ah, probably just . . . I expect he left some clothes at her house, and wanted to pick them up. Or something."

Patrick was still staring at him. "David," he began again, then stopped.

"I'm fine," David said quickly, only realising a moment later that Patrick hadn't asked.

"Mate . . ."

And, oh God, this couldn't be good. One thing Patrick never called him was *mate.*

"Honestly. I'm fine. Now, got to get on with work, so much to do, don't want to disappoint Mark . . ." David turned resolutely back to his file, the contents of which had become unaccountably blurry since he'd last looked. He jumped as a hand landed gently on his shoulder.

"Rory's straight," Patrick said. "I mean, I used to wonder sometimes if he and Barry were more than just mates, on Rory's end at least, but . . . I've been watching them, and trust me, they're the straightest couple of blokes around. I'm sorry, but it ain't gonna happen."

"You can't say that for sure." David spun to face him. "You don't know him like I do. He's different, when . . . when Barry's not there."

Patrick was shaking his head. "Mate, you're setting yourself up for heartache there. I'm telling you. Don't do it. Even if you get him feeling experimental, it ain't gonna end well. He's in his forties. You think he'll thank you for screwing with his world view now?"

He squeezed David's shoulder, and somehow that was the worst part of it all.

If Patrick was being nice to him, it *had* to be hopeless, didn't it?

David took a deep breath. "You won't say anything to anyone, will you?" It was bad enough that Patrick knew. He couldn't face Mark's sympathy on top.

Or Fen's total incomprehension, come to that.

"Silent as the grave, mate," Patrick said, squeezing his shoulder again.

The front door slammed, and Mark strode in. Patrick's hand dropped from David's shoulder so fast he must have got friction burns.

"Getting a bit nippy out there now— Oh, Patrick. I wasn't expecting you home." Mark gave an awkward laugh. "I hope you two have been getting on all right while I've been gone."

"Great," Patrick said, at the same moment as David said, "Fine."

Mark looked from one to the other of them slowly.

"Yeah, just came back for my phone. Left it here this morning." Patrick pulled said phone out of a pocket with a flourish. "Better get back to work now."

He shoved his phone back in his pocket, kissed Mark, and left. If he sent a final glance of sympathy David's way en route, David missed it, having buried his nose in his work.

"Did I miss something?" Mark asked, sitting down.

"The destruction of all my fondest hopes and dreams," David said sadly.

"Oh. I see." Mark coughed. "Want to talk about—"

"No."

"Okay. Fine. Um. Almond croissant?"

David took the proffered paper bag and held it gratefully.

It wasn't his teddy bear. But it would do.

David didn't get a chance to quiz Rory on the subject of his possible reconciliation with Fen's Granny O that night, because when he got home from work the house contained three hundred percent more occupants than he was expecting. Close on four hundred percent, in fact, as Evie's pregnancy bump was looking alarmingly close to term.

Evie and Rory turned harried faces in his direction when he walked in the front door. They seemed to have been having a tense conversation in the kitchen while—David ducked his head into the living room—Leo and Lucy watched *SpongeBob*.

"Anything amiss?" David asked, approaching the kitchen with caution.

Evie huffed. "Just those two running me ragged as usual. You won't *believe* what they did when they got home from school tonight. Lewis is going to go spare when he gets home."

"Well, if there's anything we can do to help . . ."

"You know what? Sometimes I worry they're past helping. I mean, look at me. I've got a daughter who's getting herself a reputation for violence, and a son who's hardly said three words to me all year. Or anyone else. I've had the school calling me in and chucking around words like *selective mutism*, for God's sake—"

"You never told me that! And he ain't that bad. You just have to get him on his own."

She groaned. "You think I haven't tried that? He still hardly talks to me—and he won't say word one to Lewis. If he wants something and I'm not there, Lucy asks for it. If he wants to have a flippin' *row* with Lewis, Lucy talks for him. It's driving him mental."

"Oi, Leo talks to me. He's even said a few words to David, ain't he, mate?"

David nodded, but didn't get a chance to speak before Evie was off again.

"And that's what I'm talking about." She screwed up her face. "He's like that with us because he doesn't want to be with us. Neither of them does. Have you got *any idea* how it feels to be their mum, saying that?"

Rory folded his arms. He was doing his pit-bull-cross-standing-firm-against-a-German-shepherd impersonation again, only this time the German shepherd was more of a . . . David wasn't sure what. What Evie most resembled at the moment was a stressed hippopotamus, although it seemed a little unkind to think of her that way.

"Right, then," Rory said briskly. "How about this? You and me, we swap. The kids can spend the week here with me, I'll take 'em to school and back and all that, and you get 'em every other weekend. We still got joint custody—we just switch it around a bit."

"What about him?" Evie jerked her head in David's direction.

David felt very strongly that he shouldn't be part of this discussion, but if she was going to drag him into it, he was going to support Rory.

"I think it's a marvellous idea?" he hazarded.

"See? Not a problem." Rory pushed home his advantage. "With you having this baby, you're gonna have less time for Lucy and Leo, and face it, you're gonna be knackered, and Lewis is too. The kids ain't happy now. They ain't gonna get any better when the new baby's there and nobody's getting any sleep."

"But where are you going to put them? You've got this bloke living in your spare bedroom now—remember?"

David opened his mouth to say if all else failed, he was sure Mark and the newly friendly Patrick wouldn't *actually* let him sleep on the street, but Rory beat him to it. "I'll get a bigger place. Me and David, I bet we could manage the rent on a three-bed semi or something between us."

She gave Rory a look David couldn't work out, and didn't speak for a long moment. Then, "How you going to get them to school? You'll be half way through your round."

"Oh, that's easy," David put in, glad to be able to contribute. "I'll have plenty of time to drop them off before work. It'll be a pleasure."

Now *David* got the searching look. "It's more than just walking them up there," Evie said after a pause. "You'd have to get them out of bed, get their breakfast down them, *and* make sure they've got all their stuff for school."

It sounded, at least to David, that she was actually considering it. He glanced at Rory and saw hope dawning on his face. "Oh, I'm a born organiser. Ask Mark. His files hardly know what's hit them since I started working for him."

"Just think about it, love," Rory urged. "You go home now and put your feet up—"

"Chance'd be a bloody fine thing, what with all that mess to clear up. The dry cleaning bill's going to be through the roof."

"—and me and David'll take care of the kids. Did you bring their school stuff?"

She sighed. "Yes. Thanks, Rory. I'll talk to you tomorrow."

"So what did they do?" David asked curiously as Rory shut the door behind Evie. "What's Lewis going to go spare about? And what's all this about dry cleaning?"

Rory laughed. "You know we had this charity bin bag come through the letterbox? Evie had one too, so she asked the kids to get out any stuff they didn't want and bung it in the bag for the charity shop to take away."

"And?"

"They got out three more bin bags, and emptied Lewis's stuff out the wardrobe while Evie was cooking their tea. All his poncey suits— no offence, mate, your poncey suits are all right—and his designer shirts and his silk ties, crumpled up together with his shoes and his squash gear and his muddy hiking boots. Evie only found out when Leo dropped one of the bags down the stairs and it all spilled out."

David laughed. "Hm, I'd say Lewis going spare is possibly the understatement of the century."

Rory's face turned serious. "That's why she brung 'em round here. Give him a chance to cool down before he sees them. Tell you straight, I don't like it."

David glanced at the living room door, and knew exactly what he meant. "Well, you know that anything I can do, will be done."

"Yeah. Yeah, cheers, mate. Means a lot. And cheers for saying you'll take 'em to school. You okay to do that tomorrow?"

David nodded eagerly, and Rory's face cleared. "I was gonna call in to work, say I couldn't come in, but that helps. Helps a lot."

"No problem." How hard could it be to get a couple of tots off to school? "So, I suppose we'd better start checking out rental listings online."

Rory rubbed his face with both hands. "Yeah. About that. Look, mate, that was out of order, me saying that without even asking you how you felt about it. You don't need to worry about me putting the rent up, neither. I'll manage it somehow."

"Rory, Rory, Rory. Don't be ridiculous. As it stands you're charging me nothing like market rate, and my travel costs to work are precisely zero. You could double my rent and I'd still feel I was getting a good deal." This was literally true. "Although I will miss the kitchen, and the air of intimacy it adds to preparing a meal together. And Mr. Willis, obviously."

"You're a star." Rory gave a relieved smile. "Anyway, I s'pect we ain't gonna end up moving out for a while. *If* she says yes, which she might not." His look turned dark. "Wouldn't put it past Lewis to tell her to say no just to spite me."

"*Au contraire.* I'm fairly certain his sense of self-interest is too highly developed for that."

Rory laughed. "You're not wrong there. Well, cheers, mate. I owe you." He paused. "And you never know. It might not have to happen— the moving, I mean." He glanced down, but David could still clearly see the flush that spread across his cheek.

A horrid thought struck him. Was Rory anticipating moving in with Jenni?

No, he couldn't be planning that far ahead, could he? Not when the reconciliation was still tentative—at least, David *hoped* it was still only tentative? Surely Rory would have at least mentioned it to him if their relationship had been on a firm footing? He opened his mouth to ask, but before he could speak, Lucy burst in on them with "Daddy, Daddy! You've got to come and watch with us," and dragged them both into the living room for *You've Been Framed!*

Next morning David was awoken not by his alarm clock, which he'd set an hour early to be on the safe side, but by a strange prickling sensation on the back of his neck.

He rolled over, blinked his eyes open, and gradually made out a small, pale face in the gloom. Leo was standing by his bed.

The clock said five fifteen. David manfully repressed a groan. "What's wrong, *mon petit lapinou*?"

Leo stared at him for a moment. "Daddy's gone."

"And you can't get back to sleep?" David guessed. "Tell you what. You take Gregory"—he handed over the bear—"and I'll bring my duvet, and we'll both go downstairs and join Lucy, how about that?"

Lucy was snuffling softly on one leg of the L-shaped sofa. David settled himself, Leo, Gregory, and Mr. Squiddy on the other, by now rather crowded, leg. Leo snuggled down with a smile on his little face and was asleep within seconds.

David lay awake for some time, wondering how this had become his life—and trying to come to terms with the realisation that he actually *liked* it this way.

His second awakening that morning was decidedly less pleasant, and consisted of Lucy shaking him violently by the shoulder and shouting, "Wake *up*, David, we'll be *late*." In the distance he could hear the faint strains of his alarm clock upstairs. It sounded as exhausted as he felt—God knew how long it had been ringing to itself.

He pushed himself up groggily to a sitting position, and blinked at the excessively milky bowl of cereal Lucy thrust under his nose. "I made breakfast, but you've got to be *quick*."

"*Absolument*. Thank you. I'll, um . . . I'll eat it in the kitchen. Wouldn't want to make a mess." He picked up the bowl, managed not to spill any milk as he staggered into the kitchen, cast a guilty glance over his shoulder to check the coast was clear, and hid it in a cupboard.

Then he nipped upstairs to turn off the alarm. It was, in fact, only fifteen minutes after the time he'd set it for, and by his reckoning, they weren't running late at all. Rory had made sure the school bags were packed the night before and the uniforms laid out, right down to little cotton socks. David strongly suspected Lucy was channelling her mother.

He even had time for a cup of blessed, life-giving coffee while the children brushed their teeth and made last-minute trips to the loo, and then they were off, out into the cold, fresh light of morning. It was surprisingly pleasant. St. Saviour's (David did his best to ignore the not wholly unpleasant frisson that tingled down his neck at the reminder of his encounter with a certain older gentleman) School was only a hop, skip, and a jump away, opposite the eponymous church. Hordes of warmly clad children were converging on the playground, shepherded by mummies and a few daddies in varying degrees of readiness for the day.

David even spotted a couple who had thrown their coats on over their pyjamas—he'd always thought that was an urban myth.

Leo tugged on his arm, and David crouched so he could hear what the little mite had to say. "That's Mr. Enemy," he whispered, wide-eyed, pointing to a tall teacher who was wearing a bow tie and holding a whistle in a manner that suggested he wasn't afraid to use it.

"Mr. *Emeny*," Lucy corrected. "I was in his class last year."

She tugged David over to the teacher. "Mr. Emeny, this is David. He lives with Daddy now."

The teacher smiled, as well he might. David was suddenly very conscious of his thrown-on clothes and unshaven chin. "Oh? Pleased to meet you," he said.

"Shake hands," Leo said audibly, giving David a gentle shove.

Mr. Emeny's smile grew broader. "Thank you for the reminder, Leo. Where *are* my manners today?"

They shared a firm, if brisk, handshake, and then Mr. Emeny lifted his whistle. "Now, I'm afraid it's time for the children to line up. You may want to stand back if you value your eardrums."

David made a hasty retreat, just as his new acquaintance blew a piercing blast on the whistle. Children immediately started gravitating to the front of the playground and forming wobbly lines.

"You can go now," Lucy said, and ran off to a line roughly in the middle.

"Oh. Bye," David said a little forlornly.

"Bye," Leo said, and gave him a quick hug before running off likewise.

It's a brave new world, David thought to himself as he strolled back home for another coffee and a shave before work.

Just because he felt a small—or not so small—pang at yet *another* person assuming he and Rory were now blissfully coupled-up . . . That would get better in time.

It *would*.

Definitely.

CHAPTER TWENTY-EIGHT

When Rory got home after he'd finished his round, he got a weird, bittersweet feeling on seeing the clear signs of the kids having been there overnight—blankets and pillows still on the sofa, and books and games on the coffee table. David's duvet and teddy bear were on the sofa too, for some reason. Rory set about tidying up with a bit of a pang, cos wouldn't it be great if he could have them over after school to mess it all up again?

God, he hoped Evie said yes to them staying with him. Maybe he should talk to his solicitor, in case she wanted to fight him on it—but he'd wait and see what she said first. No sense making it official before he needed to.

But if he had to, he would.

It wasn't right, them having to live with Lewis when he didn't get on with them. It wasn't good for anyone.

"Kids get off to school okay?" Rory asked when David came in from work.

David smiled and flopped onto the sofa. "*Absolument.*"

"Ate their breakfast?"

"*Mais oui.*"

"Cos I found this bowl of terminally soggy cereal in one of the kitchen cupboards . . ."

"Ah. That would be mine. Sorry."

Rory laughed. "I won't ask. So it went okay, did it?"

"Perfectly. I even got an introduction to Mr. Enemy. I mean Emeny." David yawned.

"Yeah? Leo worships that bloke. He can't wait till next year when he'll be in his class." Rory gave David a fond look. Probably wasn't all that surprising Leo got on with him too, was it? "Thanks for taking them."

"Anytime." David yawned again. "I think I may have to join you in the land of early nights tonight, though."

He was silent after that, which wasn't like him.

Still, Rory knew what'd cheer him up. "Are you doing anything tomorrow night?" he asked. That ought to get him a fun reaction, like David wanting to know if Rory was asking him out, and fluttering his eyelashes and stuff.

But all he got was a sigh and a no.

What was up with David lately? He'd been moody for *days*. It wasn't helping Rory pluck up the courage to tell the bloke he *did* want to ask him out.

Rory had even had one or two dark moments of his own where he'd wondered if it was because David had guessed what he was planning to say, and wasn't looking forward to having to let him down gently.

He took a deep breath. "See, it's my birthday tomorrow, and—"

At least that got him a reaction. "Oh em *gee*, and you didn't *tell* me? I'd have bought you a present. Baked a cake. Blown up balloons. Put up one of those hideously embarrassing signs you see on roundabouts, with an unflattering picture of you and your exact age in really big numbers—come to that, what *is* your exact age?"

"And that's *why* I didn't tell you." Okay, it wasn't exactly true. It hadn't occurred to him to tell David. Partly because he hadn't thought he'd be interested but also, if he was honest, cos he hadn't wanted to rub in how much older he was. "Forty-two."

"Ooh, the ultimate answer. So where are we going tomorrow? Romantic *dîner à deux*?"

And, okay, yeah, that'd been the sort of reaction he'd been going for, but it was all wrong, somehow. Like David was trying too hard to be himself. "Um. No. The pub. Three Lions." He cleared his throat. "There's a Spartans meeting first, so we'd end up there anyway, but seeing as it's my birthday, I'm taking the Saturday off work so I can stay a bit later. I thought maybe you could join us? But if you're busy—"

"I'd be delighted. Will I be the only one there not of Greek extraction?"

"Uh?"

"Non-Spartan."

"Oh—nah. Jenni said she might pop over for a quick one."

David's smile dimmed at that, which was weird cos it wasn't like he'd even met her. "Oh. Well, I'm sure we'll have lots to talk about."

"Oi, no swapping stories about my terrible cooking."

David frowned. "Your cooking's fine. Has either of us died yet?" His tone was weirdly defensive.

"Uh, cheers, mate," Rory said, touched by the way David was getting the hump on his behalf. "Yours ain't bad, neither."

And then they got into a discussion about what they were going to have for tea, and David seemed almost all right for a while.

But he didn't want to watch telly afterwards, just said he had a headache and disappeared to his room, and when Rory went up to go to bed, David's light was already off.

Well, he had said he wanted to get an early night. But Rory still went to bed feeling flatter than a bloke had any right to on the eve of his birthday, and it wasn't the age thing that was getting him down.

He didn't lie awake for hours, because having walked the best part of ten miles in a day, and knowing you've got to get up at four thirty and walk another ten miles meant you got down to the z's pretty quickly.

But his dreams, what he could remember of them the next morning, were strange and sad.

Rory got a few birthday wishes at the delivery office that morning, but mostly it was all low-key. His round went okay, no problems with the cats, dogs, and ferrets on his route, and he got home around half past one. Because he was going out in the evening, Rory put his head down for a couple of hours kip, and woke up just in time to have a coffee before Evie brought the kids over on their way home from school.

"Daddy!" Lucy's voice was shrill with excitement when he opened the door to them. "We've got your presents, and Mummy let us get doughnuts as *well*!"

Leo held up a sticky-looking paper bag with pride.

"Doughnuts too, eh? In that case you can definitely come in." Rory waved them all in, but Evie hung back. "Coming in for a cuppa?"

"No, I'd better get on home. Things to do. When do you want me to pick them up? You're having them for tea, aren't you?"

Rory hadn't been sure if he was or not, but he wasn't going to grumble. "Half seven? Spartans is at eight," he added, so she'd know he needed her to be on time. He almost asked her if she'd thought about him having the kids every week—but she'd most likely spent all yesterday doing damage limitation with Lewis. Best not to pester her too soon.

"Fine. Bye, you two. Be good. Oh, and happy birthday, Rory." She gave him a brief smile that didn't unkink the line in her forehead, and didn't immediately turn to go.

"Cheers, love. Um. Everything okay with the, uh...?" He gestured at her belly.

"Fine, yes. Fine." She took a breath, as if about to say more.

"*Daddy*!" Lucy tugged on his arm. "You've got to open your *presents*."

Evie made a face. "I'd better leave you to it. See you later." This time she did go, and Rory let the kids pull him back into the house.

"Where's David?" Lucy asked when they got into the living room.

"He's at work, sweet pea. He doesn't finish till five."

She frowned. "But he won't see you open your presents."

Bless her heart. "We can wait, if you like."

She glanced at Leo and bit her lip. "Will he be long?"

"About long enough to have a doughnut and play a few games."

"All right."

David turned up bang on time at ten past five, which was just as well as they'd all been eyeing up the fourth doughnut, left on its lonesome in the paper bag. Rory was pretty touched Evie had thought to include David.

He was also pretty hungry.

"We're in the living room," Rory shouted out so he'd know they had company.

David's head appeared around the side of the door. "Ooh, small people. Where did they spring from? Rory, did you leave the back door open again? I told you we'd have all sorts of wildlife wandering in."

Leo scrambled off Rory's knee and went to give David a hug. David ruffled his hair, smiling. "Here to help the birthday boy celebrate?"

Lucy frowned. "Daddy's not a boy. He's old."

"Cheers, love," Rory said with a laugh.

"But it's true. You're . . ." her little forehead crinkled as the cogs went round ". . . seven years older than Mummy and eight years older than Lewis. David, how old are you?"

David struck a girly pose. "Oh, a lady doesn't like to say."

"You're not a lady."

"So I'm often told." David gave her a wicked smile. "Still, I'm fairly sure most people mean it as a compliment. So, is there cake?"

Leo held up the doughnut bag. David took it, had a quick peek inside, then closed it up again. "Later. I wouldn't want to ruin my tea. But thank you."

"Can we do presents now?" Lucy demanded.

"Course you can."

"Mine first, Daddy!" Lucy was practically jumping up and down, Leo hovering shyly at her elbow, as David took a seat on the sofa.

Rory gave her a look. "All right, hold your little horses. How about we do youngest first? That's fair, innit?"

"I sup*pose*."

Leo handed over a crumpled parcel half as big as he was with a quiet but clear, "Happy birthday, Daddy."

Rory took the present and pulled him into a hug. "Thank you. Shall I open it?"

His tousled head nodded against Rory's side.

"Let's see what we got here . . ." Rory had a job getting in to the parcel, cos it looked like Leo had used a whole roll of Sellotape, but he finally found a tearable bit and managed to get inside.

"Ooh, what is it?" David was literally on the edge of his seat.

Rory grinned, and held up a funny-shaped brown cushion. "I *think* I know what this is, but . . ."

David laughed. "Oh em gee, poop emoji! Excellent choice, *mon lapinou*."

Leo was smiling like Christmas had come early.

"He chose it himself," Lucy said. "Mummy didn't want to buy it, but I made her. Now mine."

Her parcel was a lot better wrapped than Leo's, and way easier to get into. She'd given him a Man of the Match mug with a pair of football-themed socks inside. Perched on top was a little net bag of chocolate footballs. "That's smashing, love. Thank you."

"Now David." Lucy fixed the poor bloke with a look that promised really bad things if he didn't come up with the goods.

"Oi, come on. David doesn't have to get me anything. It ain't like he's family or nothing." Rory's guilt-muscles flexed. He wished he'd come up with a better way to put that. One that didn't . . .What was the word people used? *Exclude*, that was it. One that didn't exclude David, make him feel like he didn't belong.

David frowned. "Of course I had to get you something. I'm sure there's a law about it. Now, as *somebody* didn't tell me it was his birthday until last night, I didn't have a lot of time to shop. However, I think you'll agree I rose to the challenge." He handed over an envelope with a flourish.

Inside was a card, and inside that was a folded-up computer printout. Rory opened it out, and was genuinely touched. "A ticket to Comic Con? Cheers, mate, that's brilliant."

"And you're coming with me and Fen, and she's agreed to be on her very best behaviour. Oh, and make sure you read the small print."

Rory looked again at the ticket. Scribbled in faint pencil was, *Under 10s go free.* He caught David's eye and grinned.

"And on the other side," David said, making turning-over gestures.

Rory turned it over. Another handwritten message, this one in cramped, grumpy biro, read, *I promise to be nice to you at Comic Con. David made me write this. Fen. :-(* He had to laugh.

"What's a Comic Con?" Lucy asked.

"It's where grown-ups go to wear fancy dress and talk about superheroes," David said seriously.

Lucy sat there for a moment, wide-eyed and silent. Rory wasn't sure if it was the *grown-ups dressing up* bit she was having trouble with, or the idea of having to go somewhere special to do it. "Can we go too?"

Rory counted on his fingers. "It ain't my weekend, sweet pea, but I'll have a word with your mum, all right?"

"Today?"

"If she ain't in a hurry. Or a bad mood. Now, we need to get tea on. You want cheese on toast or beans on toast?"

Leo tugged on his sleeve.

Rory smiled fondly. "Yeah, you can have both if you want. Seeing as it's my birthday. But we need to get it sorted now, cos Daddy's got a meeting later."

Evie was a few minutes late picking up the kids—she didn't say why, and her face didn't encourage asking, neither. Rory had to practically run down the hill to get to the Spartans meeting on time.

David had told him to just go, and let him wait for Evie with the kids, but Rory didn't reckon that'd help persuade Evie to let him have them full-time. The Spartans could wait for once. The kids were more important.

Maybe I should have explained that to David, Rory thought as he jogged up the stairs in the Three Lions. He'd looked a bit hurt at the refusal.

The upstairs room at the Three Lions, where the Spartans always met, was a big old-fashioned room that was draughty in the winter but had proper old beams, posh chairs, and a good, solid table that made a cracking *thunk* when Barry rapped it with his gavel. The meeting was mainly about organisation for the next big charity fundraising event, which was going to be at the end of November when the village Christmas lights got turned on. Shamwell wasn't big enough to attract a celebrity, even a local one, to flick the switch, but the village organisations still made a night of it, with fairground attractions, carol singing, and all that. Rory volunteered to man the kiddies' teacup ride, while as usual Barry appointed himself head of mince pies and mulled wine, which meant he'd get to stay in the nice warm local café they'd be taking over for the evening. And knowing Barry, do his bit to make sure none of the food and drink went to waste.

Across the table, Patrick kept giving Rory funny looks, but he didn't say anything to him. Maybe Jenni had been talking. Or perhaps she'd mentioned she was coming to the pub tonight, and Patrick had realised Rory hadn't broken her heart, after all.

Rory hoped it was that. He was getting fed up with people thinking he was a git.

Si was there too, sitting next to his mate Alasdair like an advert for Beards Reunited. When Rory caught his eye, Si made an embarrassed face. Rory shrugged in a *That's life, mate, innit?* sort of way so Si would know he wasn't upset or nothing. Wasn't Jenni he was pining over, was it? Christ, Rory hoped he could pluck up the nerve to finally say something tonight.

At the end of the meeting, Barry stood up. "Right, lads, as usual it's downstairs to the pub, and tonight we've got even more reason to go, as it's our man Rory here's birthday."

There was the familiar round of backslapping and gentle ribbing: "Big five-oh, is it? Swear you don't look a day over forty-nine" and "Blimey, how many candles is that gonna be?"

Rory ducked his head, chuffed to bits Barry had clearly got over his huff from the weekend. Maybe he wouldn't be as bothered about David and Rory getting together—*if* it happened—as Rory had thought? He went downstairs with a big grin on his face to get the drinks in for them all.

David wasn't there yet, but that wasn't surprising. Rory had told him ten o'clock, and they'd finished the meeting—Rory checked his watch—whoa, half an hour early. Barry really had been keen to get the beers in.

Rory could get behind that plan. He sloshed down his pint of Brock Bitter a fair bit quicker than he usually would.

As he put his empty glass back on the bar, Barry slapped his shoulder. "Rory, my man. 'Nother pint?"

"Cheers, mate." Thank God things were back to normal between him and his best mate. "Good week?"

"Not bad, not bad at all. See you went ahead and had the surgery, then."

"You what?"

"Got that lodger of yours removed from your hip." Barry barked a laugh, but his eyes were sharp and fixed on Rory.

Uneasily, Rory joined in the laughter. "David? He's coming along later. Uh, how's the missus?"

"Mine, you mean? She's good. Doing the no-carbs diet now, but it ain't too bad as long as I remember to get a bag of chips on me way home from work."

"Right." Rory took a big gulp from his pint and braced himself. "I gotta tell you something. Come outside a mo."

"You what? It ain't bleedin' summer, you know."

Rory huffed. "It's September. You ain't gonna freeze your nads off. Come on."

Barry gave him a suspicious look, but he followed Rory out to the pub car park. Even though it was pitch-dark outside, they were sheltered from the wind, so it wasn't too cold to be out without a jacket—for a while, anyhow.

"So what's this you gotta tell me?" Barry laughed again. It still didn't sound right. "Better not be that that p—David's turned you gay."

Rory swallowed. "Uh. Funny you should say that . . ." He tried to smile.

"No. You're cranking my handle, right? Tell me you're cranking my handle." Barry backed off a couple of paces, staring at Rory.

"Mate, it ain't like it's such a big deal these days."

"'Not a big deal,' he says? Not a big deal?" Barry threw his arms wide and didn't seem to notice the beer sloshing out of his pint glass. "Don't do this to me. Christ, it's bad enough Patrick and Mark are going at it, but at least, well, Patrick's always been a bit suss, and Mark, I s'pose I shoulda known what he was like when he turned up for his Spartans induction looking way too bloody good in that outfit. I mean, honestly, what normal bloke his age hasn't got a bit of a beer gut? But don't you go turning into a bloody ponce on me too. I can't handle it."

Rory winced. The name-calling, that was out of order. "You don't have to handle it. *I'm* the one what's handling it. That's the point."

"No handling, all right?" Barry's voice came out high and squeaky. "No fucking handling. Not while I'm around. Not ever. I'm serious. You and me, we was like . . . Shit. I thought you was my bro. And none of that poncey *mance* stuff."

"'Mance'? Sorry, mate, I'm a bit new to all this gay stuff, you're gonna have to—"

"Jesus. It's not a bloody sex act. 'S what they call it, innit? *Bromance.* But you and me, we was above all that. Shit, I *cried* on you."

"I know. Took me two washes to get the snot out of my shirt." Course, he'd returned the favour when Evie left him, hadn't he? "But that's what mates do. Look after each other."

"Yeah. Yeah. That's what I'm talking about, see? You do this, and . . . and it'll all be over."

"What?" Rory took a step forward.

"I mean it. Bros before homos, yeah?"

Rory couldn't believe what he was hearing. "That's bollocks, that is. And if you think you and me being mates means you get to spout all that shite about gay blokes and lay down the law about who I'm allowed to ask out . . . well, we ain't mates, then, mate." He walked away from Barry and headed for the pub without looking back.

He almost walked straight into David in the main bar.

Rory blinked. David was in full Sherlock getup—not the deerstalker, but he had on the purple shirt and the swishy coat. With his pale skin and dark hair, and yeah, that tall, lean figure, he looked flippin' amazing. Not exactly like Sherlock, but more . . . more like he ought to be on the cover of a magazine or something.

"David?" Rory's voice came out all croaky. He cleared his throat, his face hot. "You made it."

"Of course I made it. Gregory didn't want to come out so late—that's teddy bears for you, always preferring to stay in bed—so I thought as it's your birthday I'd dress up instead. Do you like?" He flicked the collar of his coat up in a gesture that was pure Sherlock.

"It's great. You look really good." Rory took a deep breath. David turning up like this, straight after that conversation with Barry . . . It was all seriously doing his head in. "Lemme buy you a drink."

"No, let me—it's your birthday, after all."

"You can buy the next one." Rory was grimly determined. He'd bought all the Spartans drinks. He'd bought *Barry* a drink. He was bloody well buying one for the bloke he—for David.

"Well, if you insist. Thank you. Glass of pinot grigio, please. I'm not a fan of beer, and that Lagavulin has ruined me for pub whisky. Well, anything that's actually affordable by the glass, anyway."

Rory got him a large one, and another pint for himself, which meant tossing back the last third of his current pint a bit quicker than he usually would. What the hell. He still didn't reckon he was getting drunk fast enough.

David hopped up on a barstool and raised his glass. "Cheers, and many happy returns. How was the meeting of minds? Or was it more like a banging of heads?"

For a horrible moment Rory thought David was talking about him and Barry. Then he realised. "Oh—the Spartans? Uh, yeah. Good."

David frowned. "I hope you don't mind me saying so, but you seem a little distracted. Is anything wrong?"

Rory opened his mouth, wondering what the hell he was going to tell him. Then, of all people, Patrick interrupted them.

"David, glad you could make it." He clapped a hand on David's shoulder.

David froze, then slid off the barstool and onto his feet. "Patrick. Um. Yes. Oh look, there's Mark. I must go and say hi."

Rory stared at him as he swished away with his wineglass to the other end of the bar, where Mark was joking with the barmaid.

Then he stared at Patrick, who'd parked his bum on David's barstool.

"All right, mate?" Patrick's voice was the kind of fake cheery tone most people used when talking to the terminally ill. "Listen, I wanted a word with you." His eyes narrowed.

Okay, Rory had got that wrong. It was the tone of someone talking to a bloke who wasn't terminal *enough* for their liking. He seriously couldn't handle this right now. "Uh . . ."

"Mark reckons I should mind my own business, and you're probably going to agree with him, but . . . Shit. I hope you know what you're doing, that's all."

"Uh . . ." Rory's brain was actually starting to ache.

"I mean . . . for God's sake, people get hurt, you know? And not just the people you think are gonna get hurt." Patrick's face twisted up. "There's always more than two people in a relationship."

Oh God. Patrick knew. He knew—how the *hell* did he know?— about Rory being totally gone on David. Shit, he must have been talking to Barry.

Christ, was Barry going round telling *everyone*?

Already?

At least Rory wouldn't be short of a shoulder to cry on if David let him down gently and said they'd always be friends. Or did he mean *when* that happened? No, *if*, for crying out loud, seeing as how the bloke had dressed up for him tonight. That had to count for something, didn't it?— "So, what, this is you telling me you don't *approve*?" Anger rose in his chest, spilling into his throat. "Bloody hell, that's rich, coming from you."

Patrick stood up. "You may think it's none of my business. You may even be right. But there's stuff you don't know—"

"Ah, Rory," Mark said heartily over Patrick's shoulder. "Thought I'd come over and wish the birthday boy a happy birthday. Having a good time?"

"Uh . . ."

Patrick gave Mark a long look, then took himself and his pint over to where David was sitting all on his lonesome. Patrick clapped him on the shoulder again, and sat down with him, and it was really messing with Rory's head cos since when did Patrick like David any more than he liked Rory?

Mark gave a nervous laugh. "Um. Sorry. Bit of a difference of opinion there. I thought I'd better come and rescue you. He thinks . . . Oh, you know what he thinks. I hope you realise it's nothing personal. He's just worried."

"Yeah, well, he ain't the only one." Rory glanced over to David.

Mark seemed to follow his gaze. "He's settled in okay, hasn't he? David, I mean. I'm amazed he's stuck it out so long. I honestly expected him to go running back to London after a couple of days. Apparently the novelty of village life hasn't quite worn off yet."

That . . . didn't sound right. "What, you gave him a job even though you weren't expecting him to stick it?"

Mark made a weird face, half a smile and half not. "Between you and me, I'm sure I'd have found it a lot harder to talk Patrick round to the idea if we hadn't both been convinced it wouldn't last. David's a terrible flirt. But he's always been flighty. Something, or more likely some *man*, turns his head and he's off, but it never lasts."

Rory's gut felt hollow. A hefty swig of beer didn't help, either—just made him feel even further adrift without an anchor. "So you reckon he's just gonna up and go anytime?"

"Well, yes. And, well . . . for God's sake don't say anything to him, but I have to confess, I'm not sure I'm going to have enough work for him after the end of January—you know, when all the tax returns go in." Mark put down his pint glass and leaned forward, frowning. "God, I should have made all this clear at the start, shouldn't I? This is going to impact on your financial situation. I'm sorry. I really should have said—"

"'S okay," Rory muttered. Except it wasn't. It wasn't anything *like* okay. He stood up. "I gotta . . . I gotta go."

He stumbled out of the pub, his head buzzing so loud he could hear it. This wasn't right. It wasn't *fair*. How could Mark give David a job, knowing it wasn't going to last?

How could he have sent him to live with Rory knowing that wasn't going to last neither?

"Rory? Rory!" He turned to see David running along the street after him, coat tails flying like a superhero's cape. "Rory? Are you okay? Only Jenni just turned up and sat on Si's lap and, well . . ."

Rory stopped. "Oh? Good on her." It came out flat, but Rory didn't give a monkey's because that was how he felt. Squashed flat, like a bug under someone's shoe.

"Patrick was looking *very* confused. He, ah, he seemed to think Jenni and you were back together . . .?"

Right. So that was what all that was about, Rory thought dully. Not about him and David after all, which was good, because there was never going to be a *him and David*.

He'd been stupid to ever think there could be. David was way too young for him, and young people, they didn't stick to things, did they?

It was like Mark said. Even if by some miracle David wanted to be more than friends *now*, it wasn't going to last. David would move back to London and get a job there, and that'd be the last Rory would ever see of him.

It hurt. Fuck, it hurt. All that talk about him and David caring for the kids together, too—that was all it was, wasn't it? Just talk. Yeah, maybe he meant it right now, but sooner or later, he'd get bored, and that'd be it. Rory would be left on his own.

Again. Except worse this time, because he wouldn't even have Barry.

Shit. He'd told his best mate to sod off, and for what? For a bloke who was going to up and leave as soon as it suited him.

"Rory?"

"Uh. Yeah. Sorry. Just tired. Gonna call it a night."

"Um. Patrick didn't say anything, did he? That upset you?"

Christ, who *hadn't*? David himself, maybe, but that was only cos Rory hadn't got around to asking him out and now never would. "'M just tired." It was true enough. Rory felt the sort of bone-deep weariness you got from pulling overtime at Christmas, lugging a bag twice as far with ten times as much stuff to deliver. And no festive spirit to lighten the load.

"I'll walk you home," David said, sounding worried. "Um, it wasn't the outfit, was it? Was it too much for the pub?"

Rory had to laugh, even though it hurt his chest. "Nah. The outfit's great. It ain't you, mate."

And maybe that wasn't exactly gospel, but it wasn't David's fault, was it?

It was Rory's for ever kidding himself that him and David had a chance in hell.

CHAPTER TWENTY-NINE

David lay awake in bed for a long time. Rory had seemed so *sad* coming home from the pub. Not at all how a birthday boy should feel. Was it the Jenni thing?

Conscience stabbed him in the heart. Oh God, he'd been an idiot. A stupid, selfish idiot, running after Rory to tell him the woman he was pining for was carrying on with another man. Of *course* Rory was down in the dumps. How could he not be?

And how could David have been such a terrible friend as to help Fen set Jenni up with the other man? He should have *known* Rory wasn't over her. And he shouldn't have let his own jealous feelings about Rory dictate his actions. David was a horrible, horrible person.

Except... was it really about Jenni? Rory had clammed up tighter than a nervous virgin when David had tried to gently probe him, but looking back, when David had dropped the supposed bombshell, Rory had seemed sad *already*.

There came another stab, this one in the region of David's stomach. "*Et tu*, fear?" he muttered shakily.

Was it, in actual fact, the *David* thing?

Why had he left Patrick alone with Rory? He'd panicked and run, where he should have stood and . . . well, not fought, precisely, but at least staved off Patrick telling Rory about David's stupid, selfish feelings. And Rory was so *nice*—naturally he'd feel down about hurting a—David swallowed—friend.

Or maybe it was even worse. Maybe he was upset about David *having* those feelings. Some men were like that. It was the whole man-equals-hunter, woman-equals-prey thing. They didn't like the thought of crossing the predator/prey divide.

No, surely not. Rory was—

Wonderful, lovely, cuddly, nice, genuine, honest, warmhearted . . .

—not homophobic. And secure in his masculinity.

No, it was the letting-David-down thing. He was almost sure of it.

He woke up on Saturday still troubled. Rory was already up and about, of course—the man really didn't know how to do lie-ins. David stumbled downstairs to find him standing in the kitchen by the kettle, staring at the wall.

"Morning. Has that boiled?"

Rory blinked, looked at the kettle, then at David. "Uh. Probably?"

He flicked the switch on again anyway. The kettle chugged and sputtered, clearly feeling it was a little soon to be doing all this boiling lark again.

"Tea or coffee?" David asked politely, getting out a couple of mugs.

"Uh. Yeah. Cheers." Rory turned to the fridge, stood there for a moment, then wandered out of the kitchen.

David decided to give it his best guess as regards the coffee/tea question. Chances seemed high that Rory wouldn't even remember to drink it, or if he did, notice what it was in any case.

Actually, come to think of it, coffee was definitely indicated here. David made it nice and strong, and carried the mugs through to the living room.

"Bad night?" he asked, handing one to Rory.

"Yeah. Kinda. Cheers, mate." He sounded distracted—and worse, weighed down by the troubles of the world, or at least this small corner of it.

It was as if the mood fairies had flitted in and replaced happy, cuddly, fun Rory with mopey, distant, sad Rory.

David sat down gingerly. "So, er, Jenni and Si? Who'd have thought it?"

"Yeah," Rory said, still not meeting David's eye.

"Must be hard for you, seeing them together," David added, before remembering that as far as he knew, Rory *hadn't* seen them together, having left the pub just before any togetherness was perpetrated.

Rory turned to him. "What?"

"Jenni. And Si. A poignant reminder of happier times? I mean, it must be hard not to feel the teensiest stab of jealousy—"

"What?" Rory's brow had furrowed. "No, it ain't like that. I'm happy for her." He sighed, not precisely the picture of happiness, then seemed to rouse himself. "So, your mum still coming today?"

"Barring last-minute emergencies and train derailments, yes."

"Right. Good." Rory nodded and resumed staring into space.

David took a despairing sip of coffee.

Maybe Hen would be able to cheer Rory up? David drove Mrs. Merdle to Bishops Langley to pick his mother up from the station just in time for lunch, regretting now that he'd arranged to take her to a local restaurant instead of straight home. He was worried about leaving Rory alone too long.

Then he reminded himself sternly that Rory was a grown man and didn't need—not to mention, would probably not appreciate—David fawning over him.

Having arrived at the station, David waited impatiently by the barriers for his mother to appear. As usual, she eschewed the turnstiles in favour of wafting through the wider gate intended for those encumbered by heavy luggage, small children, or mobility aids.

Not having expected her to bring either of the latter two, David frowned, as she walked up to him, to see she didn't seem to have the first, either. "Hen, where is your luggage?"

She kissed him on the cheek, a gentle ambiance of Coco Chanel settling around them both. "I'm sorry, darling. I'm afraid I'm not going to be able to stay the night. You know my friend Ursula? It's her husband's birthday tomorrow, and she's asked me to go over for lunch."

David felt he was entitled to be a little miffed. "Isn't he a bit old to insist on a birthday party?"

"He didn't. Couldn't, actually, on account of having died three weeks ago. Dreadfully sudden, it was. Just like your father." Hen's eyes took on that mistiness that always made David stop whatever he was doing and hug her, so it was a good thing he'd brought up the subject before they'd got in the car and started driving.

She stroked his hair. "Silly boy. That was a long time ago. Now, don't you think we should get out of this crowd?"

David looked around. They were, as it happened, causing something of an obstruction in the busy station. "Good idea. Come and meet Mrs. Merdle. I've left Gregory in charge of her."

Hen greeted David's pride and joy with a raised eyebrow and a "Really?" which was about par for the course. Her spiritual home being a sumptuous Agatha Christie adaptation, or possibly Downton Abbey, she only tended to appreciate cars if they came with a uniformed driver. Gregory did his best, bless his little sawdust heart—he was wearing a cap and everything—but with all the will in the world, his feet were never going to reach the pedals.

"Now, tell me everything that's been happening in your life," she said as David pulled away from the twenty-minutes-only parking spot.

"Oh, it's all been very boring, really," David said. "How about you?"

"David." There was a warning note in her voice.

"Fine. I met a nice man who doesn't love me, is that better?"

"I'm encouraged by you describing him as *nice*. That makes a pleasant change. So why doesn't he love you?"

"Too straight. I don't want to talk about it. Hen, why did you never settle down with a man again?"

"After your father died?" She shrugged—elegantly, as she did everything. "I never meant to settle down at all. Armand was rather a surprise."

"Did he sweep you off your feet?"

"Such an overused, common phrase for something that didn't feel the least bit common at the time. But yes, I suppose he did. Is this where we're having lunch?"

David had pulled in at the Bishops Langley Arms Hotel, which he privately tended to think of as the Bishop's Gangly Arms, and where he'd booked a table for them.

Conversation over lunch was mostly about family matters, which led on smoothly to Rory's family, and his and David's plans concerning the children.

Hen's brow showed the teensiest furrow. "Honestly, darling, are you sure you're ready to be a daddy? Looking after children is not like dressing up your teddy bear."

David was hurt. "I thought you'd be pleased about me showing some responsibility. You're always saying life isn't one constant social whirl. And, in any case, it's all up in the air until Evie makes a decision."

"Is it all up to her? Don't they have joint custody?"

David shrugged. "Oh, Rory has this ridiculous attitude of not wanting to drag the mother of his children into court to try and force the issue."

"Very admirable of him. Still, it's quite a big commitment on your part, isn't it?"

"You haven't met them. They're adorable. Well, Lucy does have her less-than-adorable moments, but Leo's a perfect cherub. And we have to get them away from the wicked stepfather."

"You always did love your fairy tales, didn't you?"

"I did until you started explaining all the symbolism in them. But, anyway, are you ready to go? Rory will be dying to meet you. Although be warned: it was his birthday last night and I think he may have a bit of a head."

David crossed his fingers under the table. Hopefully that was all it was, and Rory would be back to his lovely self by the time they got home.

CHAPTER THIRTY

Rory knew he had to snap out of it. David's mum was going to be there soon, and he didn't want to give her the impression her son was living with a miserable old git, did he?

And . . . he'd had a chance to think about it all now. At the end of the day, he only had Mark's word for it David would up and run. What did he know? He'd never lived with the bloke. Just cos he'd known David for as many years as Rory had weeks . . .

Shit.

Why the bleeding hell couldn't Mark have said something sooner? Like before Rory had had that conversation with Barry? It was the Jenni thing all over again. Here he was doing the time, and he hadn't even got to do the crime. Maybe she was right about him letting people take advantage of him. Her included.

On the other hand . . . the stuff Barry had been saying about gay blokes was well out of order. Maybe he *wasn't* the sort of mate Rory ought to have.

But he'd been the only thing keeping Rory going some days, back when Evie ran off and took his kids with her.

Rory was still going round in circles by the time David got back from lunch with his mum.

"Hen, this is Rory. Rory Deamer. If you only use his first initial his name is an anagram of *dreamer*, which is rather sweet, isn't it? Rory, this is my mother. Henrietta Greenlake."

David's mum was even more impressive in the flesh, all tall and elegant like her son. *Aloof*, that was the word. Rory got the feeling if they went back a few hundred years, his ancestors would probably have done an awful lot of bowing and curtseying to hers.

And her eyes . . . They were the scariest part of her. They crinkled up at the corners, all friendly, but he could tell they saw right through him.

"Hello, Rory. Lovely to meet you." She held out a hand, like it was a business meeting or something. Rory took it gingerly. It was cool and dry, soft skin barely covering tiny bones. "Then again, you're also an anagram of *rearmed*, which is rather less sweet, aren't you?"

"Uh, yeah." What he was supposed to say to that? *Sorry?*

"Wanna come and sit down?" Rory asked instead, cos she seemed to be waiting for an invitation.

"Oh, yes, do, Hen," David added. "Pull up a chair and call Mr. Willis a bastard."

"Thank you." She floated into the living room—Rory could have sworn her feet didn't touch the ground—and sat down on the end of the sofa, smiling up at David. "Isn't this cosy. Although I'd always imagined Liberty Hall as being a trifle more commodious. Darling, would you make me a cup of green tea?"

While Rory wondered what the hell they'd been on about—family joke, maybe?—David frowned at his mum. "Since when do you drink green tea?"

"Since I realised I really should take more care of my health. You do have some, don't you?"

"No."

"Oh, well, I'm sure the shop in the village can provide. No need to take the car—I can wait while you walk down." She gave a sunny smile that reminded Rory painfully of David when he was happy. "The exercise will do you good."

"*Dear* Hen. Always so very concerned for my well-being." David shot his mum a knowing look, and grabbed his coat. "Rory, fancy a stroll into the village?"

"Uh . . ." Rory glanced guiltily at Ms.—Miss? Nah, she was definitely a *Ms.*—Greenlake.

"David, where are your manners? You wouldn't leave a guest on her own, now would you?" She turned to Rory. "I'm so sorry for my son. I did my best to bring him up properly, but . . ."

"But you were sadly hampered by your own limitations in that regard. Yes, yes, I'm going." David stomped out. Then he stomped back in. "You know, you could just *say* you want a chance to speak to Rory on his own."

"But where would the fun be in that?"

"Rory, if she starts shining a light in your face just repeat your name, rank, and serial number. And if she gets out the fingernail pliers, run."

Rory gave an uneasy laugh as David left the room, this time apparently for good.

"So, now it's just the two of us," Ms. Greenlake said, after the door had closed behind her son.

Rory suddenly wished he'd moved a few towns over, where they'd had a lot of trouble with sinkholes lately. At least there, if you were wishing the ground would open up and swallow you, there was some chance it might come true. "Uh. Yeah."

"Tell me a bit about yourself, Rory. David mentioned you have children?"

"Yeah. Yeah, Lucy and Leo. That's them over there on the bookshelf."

"Lovely children. Such sweet expressions. They make me think of David at that age. He was such a darling, odd little boy. Always dancing. I hated having to send him to school." She sighed. "Society can be so crushing, can't it?"

"Uh. Yeah."

Her eyes went all sharp again. "Although perhaps you've never had to go against its expectations?"

Rory thought about telling Barry that he might not be all that straight, and couldn't help a hollow laugh slipping out. "Yeah, right."

She raised an eyebrow, but didn't ask him what he meant, thank God. "I imagine living with someone like my David must be quite a change for you."

Rory nodded. "But it's a good change," he added hastily, worried she'd think he was dissing her son. "The kids love him to bits."

"How wonderful. Children can be very quick to give their affection, can't they?"

"Huh. Not my two. Least, not always. They can't stand their stepdad."

"But I understand you're hoping to have them living here with you soon."

"David told you? Yeah." Rory hesitated. "You've known him awhile. I mean, all his life, I s'pose."

"Indeed."

Rory gave a nervous laugh. "So, uh, would you say he's . . ." He groped for a way of putting it that wouldn't sound like he was doing David down. "Easily bored? Always on the lookout for something new?"

She smoothed her skirt before answering. "He is very young still. Only twenty-four. And young people do crave excitement and change."

That was a yes, wasn't it?

Sod it. One last go to make sure. "But—"

He broke off as the front door opened and David poked his head around the door. He looked a bit red in the face, like maybe he'd run all the way to the shops and back. "Green tea?"

CHAPTER THIRTY-ONE

"You shouldn't have done that, you know," David told Hen as he drove her back to Bishops Langley.

"I'm sure there's any number of things you feel I shouldn't have done in my life, but how about telling me which specific thing you're talking about right now?"

"Made me leave Rory on his own with you like that. It's not fair—it's not like he needed vetting as a potential boyfriend, is it?" David stared sadly out of the windscreen. Leaves were falling from the trees and being tossed by the wind, dancing wildly for all-too-brief moments before they came to rest on the road and were unceremoniously crushed beneath the wheels of passing traffic.

Much like his hopes and dreams.

"And he's not having an easy time of it at the moment. Ever since his birthday yesterday, he's been all down in the dumps."

"Oh dear. Midlife crisis? Birthdays can be so tricky."

Oh God, that was it. David relaxed as relief flooded through him—Rory's sudden mopiness wasn't his fault after all.

"Just you wait," Hen continued. "He'll be buying a fast car and looking for a much younger partner."

"Hah. I wish."

"Oh dear. I thought that was it. I must say I'm rather surprised. He *is* nice, isn't he? Not at all the sort you usually go for."

"You say that like it's a bug, not a feature."

"*Nice* isn't the stuff of which *grandes passions* are made."

"The chance would be a fine thing in any case."

They were silent for a short while as David negotiated the Saturday traffic. It wasn't until they were almost at their destination that he blurted out, "Tell me honestly, Hen—do you think I have a chance with him?"

She hesitated. "I'm sorry, darling."

Oh. And that was it, wasn't it?

Because if there *had* been a glimmer of attraction to him in Rory's eyes, Hen, with her psychology and her . . . her *Hen*-ness would have seen it, wouldn't she?

David drove into the station feeling as though his splintered heart were being crushed beneath Mrs. Merdle's very tyres. With his luck, he'd end up getting a puncture.

He went to bed early again that night.

After all, what was there to stay up for?

On Monday morning, David dragged himself over to Mark's with a weary air, and was so unchatty even Mark, who was usually the one to tell him to stop talking and get on with his work, complained.

There was a noticeably brittle briskness to Mark's manner when David got back from his lunch break, which he'd spent in the park watching tots in wellies as they played in the river. It had all been impossibly old-fashioned and idyllic, and had lulled him into a false sense that the lark was on the snail and all was right with the world. Now, it seemed, he was about to pay for it.

"Ah, David. I've just been on the phone with a potential new client. Could mean quite a lot of business for us. We're meeting him this afternoon." He paused, then said with an air of great significance. "Mr. Renard."

"Who?" David wondered if this was some local celebrity he had yet to encounter.

"Mr. Renard." Mark's expression certainly seemed to think David should have heard of the man. Then he sighed. "Apparently you met him at Charles's summer party?"

"I doubt I'd remember him, then. I was one or two sheets, or more like entire duvets, to the wind, and in any case, the whole affair was rather overshadowed by . . ." David's stomach lurched in a curious fashion. "Um. His first name wouldn't happen to be Xavier, would it?"

"Yes. It would. Is, I mean." Mark's face was red, and he met David's eye via the scenic route. "I hope that isn't going to present a problem."

"Not at all," David said firmly, not completely certain he was telling the truth. He had mixed feelings about Xav. On the one hand, his failure to mention the significant detail of his wife being David's boss's wife's sister—perhaps the necessarily convoluted phrasing had put him off?—had cost David his job. On the other hand, David hadn't much liked his job at Whyborne & Co. after Mark had left the firm in any case, and Charles would quite likely have seized the opportunity to sack him no matter who he'd been found in flagrante with.

And, well. Xav was . . . Xav. David couldn't help a little frisson at the thought of seeing him. Would he, seen in the sober light of day, live up to the hazy memory David cherished of their one drunken encounter?

He hoped so. He badly needed something to take his mind off his hopeless love for Rory.

Mark was speaking again—clearly David had been mulling it over too long. "Frankly, this has come as a bit of a godsend. I haven't quite known how to tell you, but if we don't get Mr. Renard's business, I'm afraid I'm going to have to let you go. There simply isn't the work for two of us."

David, who'd been enjoying a few warm, fuzzy, and rather naughty feelings, felt as though plunged into an icy bath by a puritan nanny who'd caught him doing something unspeakable. "What?" he said intelligently, then rallied. "Why did you give me a job, then?"

"I'm sorry." Mark gave an awkward laugh. "You see, it's all your own fault for failing to live down to my expectations. I honestly thought you'd be fed up of village life by now, and would have gone back to London."

"Oh." David swallowed, then forced a smile. "Well, that's me, isn't it? Flitting around the darling buds like a mayfly. Or do I mean gadding about like a gadfly?"

"I was thinking of a butterfly." Mark coughed. "Ah, not in any censorious sense, obviously."

"Obviously," David agreed mechanically.

"Butterflies perform a very useful function," Mark went on. "Ah, pollinating, and so on."

"Like pretty little sex toys for flowers."

"That wasn't *quite* what I . . ."

David stopped listening. It was silly to feel so hurt. He knew that. Why *should* Mark have taken him any more seriously than anyone else in his life?

It was just that David had thought he *had*.

The meeting was held at a hotel just outside Bishops Langley proper. Once a stately home enjoyed only by the idle rich, it had now been surrendered to the needs of the corporate, mingled with the odd gaggle of yummy mummies sharing a guilty cream tea before picking up the tots from school. Mark and he were shown into a spacious lounge with ceilings so high David half expected to see eagles nesting in the chandeliers, with views over gardens that were a riot of autumnal colour. The furniture was all in keeping; no forced modernisation here.

David wondered what Rory would make of the place. Would he be overawed and made uncomfortable by the opulence, or simply delighted with the loveliness of the house and gardens? David couldn't decide.

And then he saw Xav and could think of nothing else.

Xav looked utterly delectable in a traditionally cut suit that showcased his broad shoulders and narrow hips, his perfectly coiffed hair just begging to be mussed in the throes of passion. There was something so . . . *thrusting* about an attractive older man in business wear. David had always been a sucker for the type.

In more ways than one.

"Ah, Mr. Renard," Mark greeted him.

"Nugent. Delighted you could make it. And that you brought young David here."

David swallowed. "Xav, how lovely to see you again."

"Likewise," Xav purred. "How are you, David? You're looking well. *Very* well. No lasting effects from a certain overindulgence when we last met?"

"No." David cleared his throat, his voice having betrayed him on being reminded so directly of that infamous event.

"I was so sorry to hear of the aftermath," Xav went on.

Not so sorry as to offer a good word for David in his brother-in-law's ear. "Very kind of you, I'm sure."

Mark coughed. "I'll, ah, go and see about ordering us some tea."

"Thank you," Xav said, and turned straight back to David as Mark strode off. "I've been dying to make it up to you."

"Oh, you don't need to—"

"Nonsense. And I'm not just being altruistic. You see, Charles told me something interesting about you. He said that, for all your faults—and he went into great detail about those; it was rather amusing—you were the most efficient administrator he'd ever had working for him. And I know he's always thought highly of your current employer. I'm sure I shall be amply rewarded for placing myself in your hands." Xav's smile was somehow strongly reminiscent of Mr. Willis's after he'd jumped on the kitchen counter and divested David's tuna sandwich of its filling one lunchtime.

No doubt another kind of divesting was on Xav's mind. Possibly also filling.

"Your business, you mean," David said a trifle uncertainly.

"I beg your pardon?"

"Placing your *business* in my hands." He fixed Xav with a steely gaze. "Or were you thinking of something else entirely?"

"Right," Mark's voice came breezily—perhaps a little too breezily—from over David's shoulder. "I've ordered us all the full cream tea. Shall we sit down?"

The talk, as they ate, was almost exclusively about Xav's business interests. David made notes, occasionally sipping at his Earl Grey. Xav seemed to be rather in the nature of a peripatetic insect himself, flitting from one money-making endeavour to the next—and apparently never short of capital. Presumably that was Marthe's department.

"But the books are in a shocking state," he said earnestly, leaning forward, his knee nudging David's. "I'm afraid they need a thorough overhaul."

"I'm sure we can do that for you," Mark said bracingly.

"Thank you. I feel we've covered some good ground here today. But, David, you've barely touched a thing. You must at least have one of these scones. They're delicious. Have plenty of cream," Xav added, as David reluctantly reached for the smallest scone on the plate.

He'd been hoping Xav had been about to take his leave, but in fact he turned the conversation to nonbusiness matters so David not only had to eat that scone, he had another, larger one pressed on him as well. And *then* Xav moved on to the cakes . . .

David couldn't decide how he felt about it all as they drove back to Shamwell in Mark's stolidly reliable BMV. Stuffed to the point of imminent explosion, clearly, but also . . . troubled. Which was silly. Xav's attention had been flattering and not at all creepy. Obviously. David didn't even know why he'd thought of the word *creepy* in the first place.

Xav wasn't Rory, of course. But he scored over the object of David's hopeless affection in two significant aspects: one, he was definitely not straight, and two, he was equally definitely interested in David.

Just . . . he wasn't Rory.

The stairs seemed extra steep when David got home from work, so instead of going upstairs to change, he headed straight for the living room and flumped on the sofa, covering his eyes with one arm with a dramatic flourish.

Rory, who was sitting at the other end of it, gave him a curious look. "Bad day at the office?"

David groaned. "Don't ask. And for the love of all that's holy, don't offer me any food."

"Business lunch?"

"Business *afternoon tea*. About an hour after I'd eaten lunch. I'm amazed I haven't burst out of my trousers."

"Yeah? Where'd you go?"

"Langley Place."

"Oh, Jenni went there once with the girls. She said it's dead posh. Good scones?"

"Never mention scones to me again. Or clotted cream. Or strawberry jam. Don't even *hint* about cucumber sandwiches or *tartelettes aux fruits*."

"You're safe with that last one, mate. I don't reckon I can say it."

David lifted his arm to shoot Rory a one-eyed glare. "Stop laughing at me."

Rory spread his hands out wide. "Me? Would I? Hey, don't s'pose you brought home a doggie bag?"

"If only I could have. Then I wouldn't have had to eat so much."

"Guess I'm on me own for tea, then." He grinned. "Want me to eat in the kitchen so you don't have to look at it?"

"Oh God, I'll still be able to smell it. I'll be in my room. Possibly forever more." David hauled himself to his feet and waddled up the stairs to collapse on his bed.

A couple of hours later he felt vaguely human, and once changed into yoga pants and T-shirt, he even dared to venture downstairs.

Rory, who'd been flicking through TV channels, gave him a welcoming smile. "Okay to mention the f-word now?"

David blinked as hope flared, briefly and ridiculously. "Are you propositioning me?"

"What? No. *F* for food, right? I was gonna ask who the client was who rated the posh scones, that was all."

Hope crashed and burned, then salted the earth where it had fallen for good measure. "Ohhh ... Well. Funny story, actually." Not, however, one that he felt inclined to tell for some reason. David sat down on the sofa next to Rory. "Mark said something today that was a little ... Oh, I don't know. Worrying, maybe? Or just depressing? I'm not sure."

"Yeah, mate? What was that?"

"He said when he took me on, he never expected me to stick it out. He thought I'd have run back to London by now."

"Oh. He told you."

Rory's flat tone made David look at him sharply. "You knew?"

"Yeah . . . Remember when we went out for drinks on my birthday? He told me about it then. But he said I wasn't to tell you. S'pose he reckoned if you were gonna leave anyway, what was the point in getting your back up about it? Guess he changed his mind, though."

"It's the new client," David said mechanically. "They're going to provide enough work to keep me on."

"Yeah? That's good, right?"

"Is it?"

"Well, yeah. Cos now you can stay in the village. You know, with me." Rory's face went red. "I mean, as long as you want to. Till you want to move on. The kids'll be glad. That you're staying a bit longer, I mean."

David could have sworn he heard a discordant sound, like unto the dropping of a piano from a great height. So Rory thought he was fickle, flighty, and faithless too? It stung. More than Mark saying it had. He'd thought . . . He'd thought Rory believed in him. Hadn't he meant *anything* he'd said, and all those plans they'd made? For him to take the kids to school, for them to get a bigger place together. Almost like they were a proper couple . . .

Except they weren't, were they? And they never would be. It was past time David started getting used to that. All he was to Rory was the person who'd be taking his kids to school for a while. And helping him pay the rent. And then leaving, because God forbid *David* be allowed to find something he wanted permanently in his life.

Rory coughed. "So, uh, who's the rich client, and what's the funny story?"

"It's Xav." David felt no enthusiasm to explain, but what did it matter, now? "Did I tell you about Xav? No? Well, ah, he was the reason I was sacked from Whyborne & Co."

"Why, what did he do?"

"It's more what we were doing together. At the firm's annual party. We were discovered in flagrante."

Rory seemed to be practising for a new career as a living statue. "Right." He coughed. "Right," he said again, very much in the manner of one wishing he could forget what he'd heard.

"You did ask." Was Rory was now regretting having said he wanted David to stay?

It hurt, and coming on top of the earlier blow . . . Once again, he'd thought better of Rory—and had a rude awakening. But then, weren't so many straight men like this? Fine with gay men in theory; far less so in the face of any evidence they were putting said theory into practice.

"I'm afraid I just couldn't help myself," David went on, in a knife-twisting mood. "Xav's rather an old-fashioned charmer. Devilishly handsome and ridiculously fit, of course. My clothes practically flew off of their own accord. So many sparks were flying it's a wonder we didn't burn down the house. And he has an extensive portfolio of business interests. So I'll be seeing quite a lot of him in future, I expect."

Rory stood up. "Right. Better get me tea on."

He walked out of the room.

CHAPTER THIRTY-TWO

Rory got the eggs out of the fridge and seriously considered chucking them, one by one, at the wall.

He didn't, cos egg was a bugger to clean off, but he really, really wanted to.

Only cos he couldn't chuck them at this Xav, mind.

What kind of a name was *Xav*, anyhow? A stupid name, that was what.

Well, now he knew what kind of bloke David fancied. Handsome. Charming. *Rich*. And, face it, even if Rory won the lottery tomorrow, he'd only have one out of three.

What the bloody hell had they been doing at that party, anyway? *In flagrante* didn't exactly go into details. Not that Rory wanted details. Much.

At all, he told himself firmly and wished he could believe it.

And that was the worst bit, cos getting turned on thinking of David doing . . . whatever . . . with some other man was just *wrong*, and he hated it. Especially when it had been with this poncey new client David was apparently going to be seeing so flippin' much of in future.

Why was David being such a git about it?

Was he being a git? Or was Rory imagining it?

No. He'd been saying that stuff deliberately. To hurt.

And it'd worked.

It wasn't fair. After Rory had . . .

Well, what *had* he done? From David's point of view? He didn't know Rory had told Barry where to go, did he? And that wasn't even so much something he'd done for David. It was something he'd done cos the way Barry had been talking hadn't been the sort of thing any decent person would put up with.

So what had Rory done, specifically, for David?

He'd charged him rent and used him as free childcare, that was what. And then gone and developed a crush on the poor sod, just one more sad old loser lusting after someone way too young for him.

No wonder David had said all that stuff about this Xav geezer. He hadn't been trying to hurt Rory—he'd got that all wrong. David had been warning him off.

God, Rory had been an idiot, ever expecting David to want to be with a bloke like him.

CHAPTER THIRTY-THREE

There was something *off* about Mark the next day at work, which suited David fine, as he wasn't feeling very chatty either. He found out what it was after coffee, when Mark cleared his throat and said, "Mr. Renard has asked if you could drive over to his place this afternoon. He wants to give you a tour and show you the books. I, ah, normally I'd take care of that, but he specifically asked for you."

"My, he is moving fast, isn't he?" David narrowed his eyes. No wonder Mark had needed fortifying before he brought the subject up. "And that's *all* he wants to show me?"

"Would you mind if it wasn't?" Mark reddened. "Obviously, if you're in any way uncomfortable about the situation—"

It was sweet of him to offer an escape route, but David could hardly take advantage of it with Mark looking so very uncomfortable himself. "No, no. Never let it be said that David Greenlake has failed to rise to a challenge."

"If you're sure . . ."

"*Absolument.*" Nevertheless, David pondered that question all the way up past Bishops Langley and along the dual carriageway. He mused about it as he took the turnoff that led past fields filled with placid cows and bored ponies. He cogitated, while negotiating the unexpectedly narrow and bumpy country lane that led to Xav's converted farmhouse, situated high on a hill, all the better to look down upon the neighbours. Not that there were many of those, apart from the aforementioned cows and ponies.

Then he wondered why he was making such a big song and dance about the whole thing. It was only sex, wasn't it? David *liked* sex. He'd been missing it. And sex with Xav, at least as far as he could remember, had been rather fun. So why not just go for it?

Rory wouldn't like it, a small inner voice reminded him.

Rory could bloody well get over himself. Why should David censor his behaviour, just because his fr—his *landlord* had turned out to be unexpectedly judgemental?

In fact, it'd serve Rory right if he had sex with a *hundred* Xavs. All at the same time.

It wasn't as if *Rory* was going to be the provider of orgasms, was it?

David shut Mrs. Merdle's door behind him decisively.

He was going in. And he was going to get laid.

Xav answered the door in a pale-grey suit that was clearly bespoke. David felt a brief pang of envy for the tailor who'd been lucky enough to measure that inseam.

Xav's smile of welcome was appropriately vulpine. "David. So good to see you again. Do come in."

David looked around curiously as he stepped into the house. There was a definite rustic, European flavour to the décor, with an emphasis on pale colours and pastel checks, and not a table or sideboard to be seen unless decently clad in an embroidered runner.

Ah. That would be the wife's touch, wouldn't it? David had a little too conveniently forgotten about her.

"Is Mrs. Renard at home?" he asked as Xav led him to a comfortable sitting room with views out over the fields.

An arm slipped around his waist, and a cultured voice murmured in his ear, "Impatient to get down to business, are we? No, Marthe has a committee meeting this afternoon. Something frightfully dull and longwinded. She won't be home for hours."

Unaccountably skittish, David twisted away from Xav's grasp. "I thought I was here to look at your books?"

"Ah."

"Ah?"

"I'm afraid I've rather lured you here under false pretences."

"Meaning?"

Xav didn't answer straightaway. "You know, you've been a very naughty boy."

"I have?" David was reasonably sure he'd have known about it, if that had been the case. Opportunities for naughtiness had been sadly lacking of late.

"Oh yes. Ever since Charles's party I haven't been able to get you out of my head. Such a pretty young thing, and so delightfully eager. And how I've missed that sweet little mouth. You realise it's taken me all this time to track you down?"

"It has?"

"Moving house, now, that really wasn't fair. And I couldn't risk asking young Brian for a forwarding address. If it hadn't been for a chance remark of Charles's, mentioning that Mark Nugent had taken you on . . ." Xav stepped forward and stroked David's cheek.

David gulped. "What about the work?"

"Sadly, there isn't any. I already have a perfectly competent team managing my affairs, and I'm hardly about to fire them all in favour of a tiny village operation. Although I'd be very willing to set you up in a flat I keep in the City. For . . . personal convenience. You would have to move back to London, of course. It simply wouldn't work having you too close to home."

He beamed, clearly expecting David to say yes.

And for an awful, horrible moment, David was tempted. It would be so easy. And it was so nice to be wanted. Of course, it wouldn't last forever, but what in David's life ever did?

Then his outrage grew. How could Xav have lied to Mark like that? True, all was said to be fair in love and business . . .

"But what about the little woman?" David hedged. "Mrs. Xav, I mean, not any diminutive female employees you may currently have."

"Oh, Marthe has never concerned herself with what I do in the City. So long as I'm discreet. And if she finds out . . .well, that's what Cartier is for."

And no doubt, that'd be what it was for if *David* ever had cause to complain of Xav being less than faithful.

He'd known open relationships that had worked, but this . . . It was the underhandedness of it all. It wasn't his idea of love. Set against this . . . what he had with Rory didn't seem so bad, even if it wasn't what he really wanted. They lived together, they were friends . . . What was mere sex against that?

Looking back, David was sure he must have misread Rory's manner last night. Something else must have been troubling him. Or maybe he just didn't like talking about sex. Some people didn't.

Rory wasn't a bigot. David should have known that.

And so what if everyone thought he was flighty? He'd show them all. David Greenlake was no flower's sex toy. He'd be there for Rory—in whatever way Rory wanted him—and he'd prove himself.

David backed away from Xav. The scales had fallen from his eyes. Which sounded every bit as unpleasant as David was feeling right now. Xav's kind of relationship . . . it was all wrong. Or was it, if it worked for him and his wife and his lovers? David didn't know. All he did know was that it would never, not in one million years, work for him. How could they live like that? Without a word, he gathered up his things and stalked out of the room.

"David? Is something wrong?" Xav called after him, and there was the sound of expensive leather-soled shoes running lightly over a tiled floor.

David didn't turn. "I'm going. I'm sorry. This was a mistake."

He walked down the driveway without looking back and climbed into Mrs. Merdle. Pausing only to text Mark with, *Client meeting off. Will start job hunt tomorrow*, and then turn off his phone, he started her engine and let the gentle purr soothe him as he pulled onto the road.

Rory was pottering about in the kitchen when David got home, so there was no avoiding him. "David? You're home early."

"Funny thing . . ." David looked around the hall, feeling oddly as if he were seeing it for the first time. "I— Yes, well . . . I decided I didn't want to work so closely with Xav after all."

"You what?" Rory frowned. "So you're not . . .?"

"No." David hunched in on himself, very much needing a hug. The warm glow of virtue triumphant had gradually waned during his drive home, and now he just wanted his teddy bear. For preference, he'd rather the hug came from Rory, but in the spirit of maintaining realistic expectations, he'd take what he could get.

Reality had slunk in with a vengeance on his way back, in the form of a mocking voice that derided him as an idiot for ever thinking he could stay with Rory now he was out of work. At the end of the day, how many straight men were in the market for a platonic house-husband? None, that was how many. Probably less than none. Oh, Rory might be grateful for someone to take the children to school for a month or so—*if* Evie let him have them, and that was by no means certain—but sooner or later he'd work out another arrangement. Then he'd start dropping hints about it being time David moved on and, specifically, *out*, in favour of someone who could contribute to the household.

And . . . David wasn't sure he could bear it anyway. To live with Rory, but not *be* with Rory. Being friends was good, yes. But it was also a constant reminder of how much more he wanted and couldn't have.

David had been building castles in the air. And now he was getting thoroughly drenched by a short, sharp shower of celestial bricks.

Rory strode out of the kitchen and into the hall, but regrettably stopped two feet short of actually hugging David. "Oi, he didn't do nothing you didn't want, did he?"

David took a moment to work out all the negatives in that sentence. "No. God, no." Blinking rapidly, he managed a wobbly smile. That was so like Rory. Rushing in to save people. "If nothing else, Xav *is* a gentleman. In that respect, at any rate. No, I just realised he wasn't what I wanted."

"He ain't?"

David shook his head. "So it looks like I'll be job hunting. I'll pay the rent up to the end of the month, obviously. Next month, that is, as we're nearly at the end of this one. I'm bound to have found a job somewhere by then," he added in possibly the least convincing tone ever heard.

Which was silly, when he thought about it—surely there were always jobs available for people who didn't care any longer? Pig herding was supposed to be a classic, wasn't it? Somewhere like Outer Mongolia would do. If they had pigs there. Or the Outer Hebrides. Or anywhere else with a name that started with *Outer*. Because all of a sudden, having Rory so near but untouchable was like a giant fist clenching around his heart and squeezing it dry.

"So . . . wait a minute." Rory looked angry. "He tried it on, you said no, and he said, 'Right, you can kiss good-bye to your business'? That ain't on."

"Worse, actually. There never was any business. He lied. It was all a ploy to get into my elegantly fitted trousers."

"What? The bastard."

David gave a sad little one-shouldered shrug. "I suppose I should feel flattered he went to so much trouble."

"Uh . . ."

"But I don't," David burst out bitterly. "Why does *everyone* have such a low opinion of me? 'Oh, it's only David, you can't take him seriously, always flitting around like a sex-crazed damselfly shagging flowers left, right, and centre. He'll drop everything the minute anyone drops his trousers.'" He swallowed, unable to look at Rory. "Anyway, must dash. I think I hear Gregory calling me."

David escaped upstairs and finally got his hug, although it was woefully short on reciprocity.

Sometimes a boy needed more. He reached for his phone. There were umpteen missed calls on it, mostly from Mark, but David couldn't face dealing with work stuff now. He had someone else he needed to talk to.

"Hen?"

"Hello, darling. Is everything all right?"

"Fine. Why shouldn't a boy just want to speak to his mother?"

"Why not, indeed?" Her tone said quite clearly that she saw straight through him.

"How are you?" he asked hurriedly, before she could pick him up on it. "Did you have a good time on Sunday? Well, as good as could be expected."

"Yes, thank you, darling. Ursula was very sad, of course, but there were some happy memories there too."

"It must be nice, having a relationship that really does last until death us do part. What was he like? Her husband, I mean."

There was a pause.

"Hen?"

"Oh, it's just that it's funny—I never could understand what she saw in Vaughn. He wasn't at all my sort of man. And yet she adored him, and they were happy together."

"What was wrong with him?"

"It feels awful to speak ill of him, but he was rather on the dull side, I always thought. Not a jot of passion. I'm afraid, darling, that if I'm honest, your Rory reminded me of him."

"Rory isn't dull!" David said indignantly. Then he sighed. "And he isn't my Rory."

"You know I didn't mean it in that way. But, in any case, I'm sure you're over that little infatuation by now."

"Is this the tough love I keep hearing about?" David asked shakily, feeling as though he'd held up his arms for a gentle motherly cuddle and been unexpectedly embraced by an iron maiden. It was a bitter blow to find that even his own mother apparently subscribed to the view that David was nothing more than a human hummingbird, flitting around deep-throating every flower in sight.

"Darling?"

Clearly David had developed an allergy to something in his room. He sniffed and shot Gregory an accusing, if moist, glare. "Is it because Rory's older than me? I thought you'd accepted I prefer the more mature gentleman now."

"Oh, I have, darling. I have. But if you're only going to have a short time together, then the man you choose should be someone you can make the most of that time with. Someone ... oh, like your father, I suppose."

"That's not fair. You know I don't remember Armand."

"No, but I do. He was the opposite of dull. More like a force of nature. You know I had lovers before him, don't you?"

"I should hope so." David made a brave attempt at humour. "Otherwise the first forty years of your life would have been depressingly tedious."

"But they were nothing like him. Dull, little men who I only bothered with because I thought there must be more to them than what the world saw—only to find the world had been right all along. That was why I never planned to marry. But when I met Armand ... oh, he was an adventure all by himself, and he took me adventuring with him. We travelled the world before you were conceived, laughing at all the plodders who never moved out of their own narrow circles. He was so very different from all the men I'd known.

Even our rows—and goodness knows, there were plenty of them—were exhilarating."

"I always wondered . . ." David took a deep breath. "The men you've always encouraged me to go out with, it was because they were like Armand, wasn't it?"

"You're quite right. I've always hoped you'd find someone like him. A mother wants what's best for her son. And Rory . . . well, he just isn't the sort of man I've ever imagined you with."

"But what about what *I* imagine? Or your friend Ursula?"

"Darling, I don't think she has any strong opinions on who you end up with."

"Not me. Her. She met her Armand, didn't she? And he wasn't anything like *your* Armand. So why should mine have to be?" Why was he expending so much effort trying to convince her Rory was right for him? It was Rory who needed convincing, wasn't it?

And . . . wasn't it worth one last try? If David was going to have to leave anyway, what did he have to lose? His resolve strengthened. "I've got to go."

"So soon?"

"Yes. Hen, darling, I love you. But despite what certain Disney villains may tell us, Mother doesn't always know best." David put the phone down with trembling fingers, his insides all aflutter and his heart pounding so loud it was a mercy Mrs. Willis was hard of hearing, or she'd have been banging on the wall to get him to turn the volume down.

Time to spread his dreams under Rory's feet.

CHAPTER THIRTY-FOUR

Rory hovered at the foot of the stairs, hopping from one foot to another while he waited for David to finish his phone call and come down. His stomach was all in knots.

David hadn't gone off with this Xav bloke. Which meant . . . well, to be honest, Rory wasn't sure what it meant, but it had to be good, didn't it?

Cos Rory's chest hurt at the thought of David with another bloke. But it hurt just as bad when he thought of David leaving. He wanted to deck this Xav bastard for making him and David think they could stay together, could be a family together, when it'd all been a lie just to get his leg over.

It would've been so good, him and David and the kids. Maybe not perfect, no, cos they'd still have been only mates. Rory wasn't daft enough to mess something like that up by telling David he wanted more, and risk having David laugh in his face. But it would've been enough.

Then it hit him like a sack of second-class post in the head. At least now, if Rory messed things up between them, it couldn't be worse than if he never said anything, would it? Cos David was leaving anyway.

What did Rory have to lose?

His heart pounded. It was time to go for it. He *couldn't* let David leave without telling him he, well . . . Light-headed and a bit queasy, Rory paused and took a couple of deep breaths. He had to tell David he fancied him.

There. He'd said it to himself. That had to be the hard part, didn't it?

Yeah, right.

Soon as he got downstairs. Maybe give David time to settle down, relax on the sofa, have a cup of tea . . .

There was a footstep on the top stair.

"Can I ask you a question?" Rory blurted out, his mouth having apparently decided his brain couldn't be trusted to get round to it.

David appeared, his expression wary and his eyes a bit on the red side, which made Rory want to punch something. Preferably that Xav git. The impulse didn't fade when David gave him a twisted smile that wouldn't have convinced his teddy bear. "Ask away. But if it's about what happened to the last Babybel cheese, I reserve the right not to answer."

"We out of them already? Blimey." Rory struggled to work out how to say all the stuff that was filling his heart to bursting point. Maybe he ought to edge up to it sideways. "Nah, I been wondering . . . When you started fancying blokes, like, not girls, how did you know?"

"Know what?" David paused on the bottom step, leaning on the stair rail.

"That it was blokes for you. Not girls. Or as well as. Either. Both. Whatever."

"I . . . What?" David frowned. "Are we talking about trans issues, here?"

"What? No. Just, how did you know it was blokes you were into?"

"Because I *was*. Am. Will be. And any other tense you care to mention, up to and including the future perfect continuous, although I've never really felt au fait with that one. Um. I think I need to sit down for this conversation."

"So . . ." Rory frowned with the effort of getting this right as they trooped into the living room. "You mean, like, if there's *a* bloke that makes you, you know, horny, it means you're into blokes?"

"Rory, dearest, is there a *reason* you're asking?"

"Well, I sort of think I might be a bit into blokes."

David went still for a long moment, like someone had pressed the Pause button. Then he put his hands on his hips and puffed up his chest like an aggravated pigeon. "Then why did you get all huffy about *me* being into blokes?"

"You what?"

"Last night. When I mentioned Xav. You went all *Eww, no homo* on me."

"Nah, you got it wrong, mate. That wasn't . . ." Rory realised he was getting dangerously close to spitting it all out, and his voice seized up in panic. He sat down on the sofa quickly.

"What wasn't it?" David sat next to him. Really *close*. Or did it just feel like that to Rory? There was an odd expression on David's face. Sort of excited, or hopeful . . . or was that just Rory? "More to the point," David purred, "what *was* it?"

Rory couldn't look at him any longer. "Um. Well. Um."

"I'm going to need a *little* fuller detail than that."

"It's . . ." Rory slumped and closed his eyes. "Oh, bugger it. I was jealous, all right? Didn't wanna think about you going off with some other bloke, cos I . . . like you, you know? Like, in a fancying-blokes way. Sorry, mate. I know you ain't gonna—"

He broke off with an *oof* as David flung himself onto Rory's lap and kissed him.

CHAPTER THIRTY-FIVE

Rory's eyes opened wide in astonishment, and he'd have gasped out loud if David's lips weren't locked firmly on his.

David was kissing him.

David was kissing *him*.

And it was . . . It was great, it was magic, it was *right*. Him and his mate David. Kissing. Rory had his hands in David's hair, and it was all silky and smelled great, a waft of his shampoo coming every time Rory ran his fingers through it. And his mouth . . . His lips were great too, soft but firm. They knew what to do, these lips did. And they'd had a word with David's tongue, maybe, cos that knew just what it was up to, thrusting into Rory's mouth and roving round like it was searching for something.

They weren't close enough, and then they were, almost, as David climbed astride Rory's lap and straddled him on the sofa. It felt dirty, but in a *good* way, and somehow Rory's hands let go of David's hair, releasing one last waft of that posh shampoo as they went, and grabbed hold of David's arse. And that . . . that was a bit strange, cos David's bum was lean and firm like the rest of him, not lush and round like a woman's would be, but Rory couldn't keep thinking about it cos David was kissing his neck now. Stubble rasped on Rory's collarbone, sending a shiver all through him which, yeah, Rory totally got now why Jenni used to rave about blokes on the telly rocking the unshaven look.

There were too bloody many clothes between them. Rory pulled at David's shirt, yanking it out of his trousers, and could have wept when he finally touched hot, bare skin. Jesus, that felt good.

There was no way on earth Rory's big hand was going to fit down the back of David's fitted trousers, so it slid around to the front and moved up on autopilot. Rory froze when it met flat pecs instead of soft squidgy bits. Then he chuckled under his breath. "Sorry, mate. Wasn't thinking."

David pulled back to grin at him. "I bet you feel a right tit, now."

"Yeah, I . . ." Rory blinked and laughed out loud. "Wanker."

"I hope not. At least, not at this precise moment. No, leave your hand there. I like it." David covered Rory's hand with his own. Encouraged, Rory gave his nip a squeeze. "Oh, God, yes. I like it *lots*."

Yeah, Rory liked it lots too. It was a bit different, the chest being so flat and David being so tall, but some girls were tall and not all that well-endowed, weren't they? Didn't make them any less feminine.

Rory wasn't quite sure how that applied to David, or if the bloke would even want it to, so he stopped thinking about it. Kissing, kissing was good. And squeezing David's bum, and letting David push up his T-shirt and yank it off.

And David going, "*Oh, yes, Daddy*," and leaning in to bite his neck, that was good too. In a weird sort of way.

Letting his hand wander downwards and undo David's trousers so it could dive straight in, that was a bit all right too. It was even better when David got the message and stripped his trousers and pants off, although Rory probably shouldn't have been so surprised to find out David was *really* into all this manscaping lark. Rory had seen plucked chickens with more hair on them. But that was okay, that was good. Smooth, groomed skin was pretty familiar.

It was just the rest of it that wasn't. One specific bit of it, to be honest.

It was, well, it was a dick. Long and thick—way thicker than he'd expected from such a skinny bloke—and dark. Hard as a rock, with ropy veins coursing along it. Heavy balls hung underneath, in case he hadn't quite got the message this wasn't the sort of body he was used to groping. Rory swallowed.

"Okay?"

David was looking a bit worried, so Rory forced a smile. "Smashing."

"You don't have to touch it," David said, and his voice sounded wrong. "Just let me do everything."

Rory frowned, cos that wasn't right either, but . . . it was a dick.

Another bloke's dick, and it wasn't like Rory had been to public school with all them posh bastards who ran the country and had poncey dining clubs where they wore tail coats and did dodgy things to dead animals. He'd never touched another bloke's dick. Not unless you counted Barry when he was too drunk to pee straight, but that was different.

Well different. Rory shuddered at the memory.

David drew back even farther, his mouth turned down. "Or, you know, we could just—"

Rory wasn't having this, David going all sad on him. Not when he'd been happy and laughing a minute ago. "Come here," he growled, and pulled David closer to kiss him again.

And yeah, the dick touched him, but it was just a dick, right? Nothing to get your knickers in a twist about.

Heh. Nothing to be a dick about. Rory half laughed into David's mouth, and leaned back so David was on top of him. Yeah, that was good. This way, he could grab handfuls of bum and grind up into him. Stop thinking about *David's* dick, and concentrate on his own, cos at this precise moment in time it felt bloody good.

David slithered down, kissing bits of Rory as he went. And then he got to *that* bit, and fuck, that was good. That was awesome. That was *amazing*. Jesus wept, was David deep-throating him?

Fuuuck. Rory wasn't sure if he said it, shouted it, or only thought it. And he didn't fucking care. What David was doing with his, Jesus Christ, his *throat* . . . It was great, it was awesome, he was gonna . . . All David had to do was *not stop* . . .

"Stop," Rory croaked. "You gotta stop."

David froze, staring up at Rory with those pretty eyes, mouth still stretched around Rory's cock. It twitched as he looked at it, as if it was saying, *Oi, what the bloody hell do you think you're playing at telling him to stop?*

But this was important. "Come back up here," Rory said. "Wanna kiss you again."

David blinked, then slowly pulled his mouth off Rory's cock with a little swirl of his tongue at the end that nearly finished Rory off there and then. "I live to obey," he purred, his lips all red and shining with moisture.

Christ, Rory could stare at those lips for*ever* . . .

Focus. He slung an arm around David's neck, drawing him down for that kiss, then he braced himself, shoved his other hand down between them, and grabbed hold of David's dick.

David tensed. "It's all right," he murmured, kissing Rory's neck, which made it bloody hard to concentrate on his words. "I told you, you don't have to do anything you don't want to."

And that was wrong, cos . . . cos if David could get his laughing gear around Rory's wedding tackle, the least Rory could do was give him a flipping handjob. Wasn't fair, otherwise, was it? And yeah, David was gay, so he'd probably sucked a lot of dicks—Rory didn't know why that thought made him feel funny, sort of turned on and mad at the same time—and Rory . . . hadn't, but it'd be like . . . it'd be like he was only using the bloke to get off, and Rory didn't want to do that to anyone, and especially not to David.

"'S okay," he muttered, getting a better grip and moving his hand up and down gently. It felt weird, but not weird at the same time. Like when Jenni had got out her vibrator and laughed her head off at his face cos he'd never seen one up close before. Evie hadn't been into toys and stuff, and before Evie . . .

There hadn't really been a *before Evie.*

"That good?" he asked, cos he knew what he was doing when it was *his* dick, but that was cos he could *feel* if he was doing it right.

"You can be a little rougher. I promise I won't break. Mm, that's it." David leaned in close, his breath hot on Rory's neck. "Go on, admit it. This isn't the first time you've had your hand on another man's cock."

Rory had to laugh. "Mate, I've slept with two people in my life before you, and you've met both of 'em. So yeah, it's my first time. You're gonna have to excuse the inexperience."

He might have just imagined David tensing, cos the next minute he was kissing Rory again—big, sloppy kisses with loads of tongue that had Rory's dick sitting up and begging for attention. And yeah, apparently David could speak dick: maybe it was some gay thing, cos his hand landed on Rory's hard-on like a millisecond later. That was well weird, cos Rory was jerking a dick, and his dick was being jerked, but they weren't the *same* dick, and it was like . . . like something he'd seen on the telly where you fooled your hand into thinking it hurt, but he couldn't think, cos Christ on a bike, this was so fucking good, he was gonna— "Stop," he said again, except it came out like a yelp.

David backed off, except he couldn't get far cos Rory wasn't letting go of that dick. He had that worried look again.

"Want you to come first," Rory managed to gasp out. "Not me."

David smiled. "Rory, Rory, you are a man of unexpected chivalric depths. Where would you like me to come?"

Rory frowned down at him, and glanced around the room. "Here?" Then he twigged. "Oh. Yeah. Better do it on me, cos it'll be a bugger to get it out the sofa if it soaks through the throw."

"Mm, practical too. Kiss me, then," David murmured, and leaned back in close.

God, Rory had missed this. Having someone give his dick a good seeing to was great, it was fucking brilliant, but this . . . Just kissing someone while he made them feel good. He could do this all day. And David felt fantastic on top of him, hot and heavy, gasping into his mouth as Rory jerked him off faster and faster until David's breath seemed to catch and his whole body tensed.

Rory jumped as David's dick pulsed in his hand and the first hot splatters hit his belly, but he didn't stop working David through it, wringing out every drop. Fuck, that felt amazing, like he'd scored the winning goal in the World Cup. Him, Rory Deamer, he'd done that.

David collapsed on top of him like a puppet who'd had his strings cut, only carefully so he wouldn't land in the mess on Rory's belly and chest. Rory had to laugh.

"What's so funny?" David asked, gazing up at him from under tousled hair, his smile broader than Rory had ever seen it.

Rory couldn't help grinning back. "You. Me. Life."

His dick twitched again, as if it was trying to say, *Oi, not all of us are finding this funny.*

David snuffled a laugh. "Mr. Impatient. Give me a moment to catch my breath, and I'll—"

"Nah, just, you know. Use your hand." Cos David might have fucking awesome lips, but this way Rory got to cuddle him while he did it, which was . . . Yeah. Yeah, that was great. And it was weird, cos he'd never felt so desperate to come but so relaxed at the same time, so in the moment when it wasn't yet *the* moment. While David worked Rory's dick, he slithered down a bit and teased Rory's nipple with his tongue and bloody hell, his teeth too, and that was . . . Yeah, Rory had done it *to* the women he'd slept with, course he had, but he'd never had it done to *him*, and this was a serious fucking oversight because it felt *fantastic*. "God, yeah, keep doing that," he gasped out.

And David writhed against him, like he was enjoying it all too, even though he'd already come, and that was it, that was all it took, and Rory tipped over the edge from fucking amazing to *fucking amazing* as his orgasm zipped through him like two thousand volts and sparked out of his dick in hot spurts.

Rory wasn't sure, but he thought he might have shouted. He came down slowly, breathing hard, like that time he'd done his round at a run so he could get back in time for Lucy's nativity play, and his whole body fizzed with aftershocks. "Fuck me, that was good. Um. I didn't yell out anyone else's name, did I? Cos, you know, sorry if I did. Brain wasn't exactly firing on all cylinders, there."

"No, but something was." David smirked and gave Rory's chest a significant look.

Rory glanced down. "Uh. Right. Yeah. Need a bit of a clean-up on aisle five. So I didn't . . .?" He'd be well gutted if he'd yelled out *Evie* or *Jenni* when the poor bloke had just given him the best orgasm of his life.

Course, if he'd yelled out *Barry*, he might have to kill himself.

"Not unless you were previously clandestinely involved with someone called *YIIIIIIIISSSSSSSS!*"

"If I was, mate, it was so bloody secret I never knew about it." Rory stared happily at the ceiling. He wasn't sure, but reckoned the spider in the corner might've given him a thumbs-up. "So, yeah, why ain't we done that before?"

"My terminal case of British reserve?"

"You wouldn't know reserve if it jumped up and bit you on the bum."

"Well, I do always try to get the first bite in. If there's any biting to be done in that area." David ran a finger through the mess on Rory's stomach, swirling it around. Mixing them up. "So, no regrets, then?"

"What for?"

"Some people can get a little maudlin about the popping of the cherry. Or . . . react in other ways that are equally unfavourable."

"Yeah? Can't think why. That was great. We gotta do that again sometime. Uh, soon, yeah?" he added, cos people often said they wanted to do things *sometime* and actually meant *never*. Jenni had explained that to him, and a few things had made more sense after that.

"*Mais bien sur.*"

David snuggled back down against him, and Rory would've liked to let him stay there forever, but—"Uh, sorry, mate, gotta move. Getting a bit cold. What with all this . . ." He gestured at his belly.

"Mm, sorry." David pushed himself up on one arm and blinked around blearily before grabbing something from the end of the sofa. "Here we go."

Rory took the proffered T-shirt. It was his, but that was fair enough—David's posh work shirt might have stained, and he had a fair idea that, unlike Rory, David hadn't bought it at Primark for a couple of quid. "Cheers, mate." Rory wiped up the drying mess, then chucked the T-shirt on the floor. "Come here, then."

That big, gorgeous smile still on his face, David cuddled back up to him and, in a nifty move, pulled the throw down from the back of the sofa to wrap it round them both.

Magic. Rory kissed the top of his head and held him tight.

CHAPTER THIRTY-SIX

David's bed was snoring. In a gentle, lull-you-to-sleep way, rather than a decimation-of-entire-Brazilian-rainforests way. Still, it was uncommon enough of late that David blinked open his eyes.

Ah, yes. David's bed was, at time of noticing, a postman. That explained the snoring, not to mention an unusually hirsute and slightly sweaty feel to the lower sheet. It also explained why his feet were cold, as they were sticking out from the end of the bed or, as might be, postman. David was tempted to pull his feet in and warm them up, but the chilly light of experience told him that would inevitably end with his bed (or postman) waking up with a yelp.

Rory, asleep, made a truly enchanting picture in the faint light that filtered in through the living room curtains. The worried or, as might be, puzzled frown he often wore had smoothed from his brow, and his lips were curved up as if he were having a particularly good dream. Hopefully with David in a starring role. And, well . . . experience also told David that while a man might be all right with finding another man on top of him while certain activities were going on, and even immediately following, this did not always hold true after sleeping on it.

Particularly if awoken in a sudden and less-than-pleasant manner, say by a pair of frozen extremities to the knee pit. No, David decided to stay with the lesser of two evils. Who needed feet, anyway? All right, most people, obviously, if they ever planned on walking anywhere, but apparently prosthetic legs were coming along in leaps and bounds these days. Literally.

And David found himself loath to precipitate any pearl-clutching on Rory's part. It wasn't the first time he'd found himself in bed with a man who'd previously claimed to be one hundred percent heterosexual. It didn't bother him to play the role of Hamlet to their Horatio, demonstrating how much more there was in heaven and earth. Apart from the one or two unpleasant incidents...

But this was Rory. Who called him *mate*, and had let him into his house and his life...

David swallowed. He shouldn't have done this, should he? Led Rory astray, as if he was just another so-called straight man whose horizons could benefit from a little expansion. Patrick had been right about people not, as a rule, liking it when you messed with their sense of self. Hen, too, had been quite clear on that, the last time he'd taken his bruised ego to sob on her shoulder.

She'd also told him he should press charges, mind, but the other bruises had faded soon enough. Nothing had been broken.

And now the first flush of delight from discovering Rory had feelings for him was over, it struck David that all Rory had actually said on the matter of those feelings was that he'd been jealous, and that he fancied him. It was perfectly possible to feel jealousy over someone, and *eminently* possible to want to have sex with them, without being in love or anything close to it with that person.

David was suddenly very, very worried that his friendship with Rory might be broken.

Oh God. There was nothing for it, though. He had to get up. For one thing, he was rather desperate for a pee. And although he had no idea what time it was, Rory was almost certainly going to need to get up for work soon. That was pretty much a given, anytime after supper.

David swallowed and tried to gently untangle his limbs from Rory's.

He'd managed to put a few inches of space between them, and was just wondering how to proceed without sending a blast of cold air rushing over Rory in his wake—*wake* being the operative word—when Rory decided to put him out of this misery and straight into a worse one by waking up anyway.

"Um," David said eloquently. "Morning?"

Rory's eyes were wide—but then, unbelievably, so was his mouth, as it stretched in a grin. "Blimey, and here was me thinking I'd just had the best dream ever. Oi, where you off to?"

"Pee," David said, and scrambled upstairs to the bathroom in the hopes his thoughts would be clearer by the time he came down again.

Rory wasn't mad at him? Wasn't even regretting it?

Maybe it simply hadn't sunk in yet? Perhaps he should give him a few minutes. David made a point of washing his hands really *thoroughly*, and making sure he dried right in between the fingers. At length, though, he made a tentative return to the living room.

Rory was still smiling. "Get lost in there, did you? Come on over here before you get cold. Wouldn't want anything to drop off, now would we?"

David slid carefully between Rory and the throw. "You're taking all this remarkably calmly."

"This?"

"You. Me. Bed. Or sofa, rather, but in a beddish sort of way. Both of us men. Not that I'm complaining, mind, but most straight men tend to find it a little harder to deal with, once they're no longer blinded by lust."

Rory stared at him. "You're asking why I'm not having a bleedin' mental breakdown over sleeping with a bloke? Mate, where have you been the last few days?"

David stared back. "I thought you were worried about me fancying you. And Hen suggested a midlife crisis. Which was a very sensible idea, so then of course I thought it was both. You're telling me all the moping was about *you* fancying *me*?"

"Oi, I wasn't moping. And yeah. That and Barry."

Damn it. "You fancy Barry? I should have known."

"What? No! No, I meant . . . I told him, didn't I? On my birthday. He didn't take it so well." Rory slumped.

If that wasn't a cue for a cuddle, nothing was. David duly cuddled. Rory was delightfully warm and pliable. "Have you spoken to him since?"

"Nah. Dunno if I'm gonna."

David was in two minds about this. The first mind was busy jumping up and down waving pom-poms at the thought of a little less Barry in their lives. The *second* mind, however . . . "But he's your best friend."

"Not any more he ain't." Rory's chin was up, but he definitely had sad-face too.

Rory had done that for *him*? David blinked eyes that had suddenly become blurry, and was about to say something—he wasn't entirely sure what, but he'd know it when he heard it—when there was a loud and insistent knock on the door. They both jumped.

"Who the hell is that?" David was outraged and just a teensy bit worried. That kind of knocking rarely boded well. "In the middle of the night?"

Rory glanced at his watch. "Nah, it's only ten past seven."

"P.M.?" David blinked as Rory nodded. His internal clock was *way* off. "Thank God we closed the curtains, or I'd be worried it's the neighbours round to complain. When *did* we close the curtains?" He didn't think *he'd* done it. He'd had his mind firmly on other things. Bless Rory's practical nature.

The knock sounded again, louder and even more peremptory this time.

"Uh, think we'd better answer that." Rory was hurriedly pulling on his clothes.

David joined him. "Oh God, we used your shirt for . . . you know. Better let me answer it." He pulled on his shirt, realised it was inside out and was about to take it off to right it when the knocking recommenced, impossibly loud now. Were they using a battering ram?

He got to the front door just in time to save it from a fourth, and possibly fatal, assault and flung it open. "Yes? Oh, hello, Mark. Um. You got my text?"

Mark looked grim. "I got your text. And I've been trying to call you ever since. What the hell *happened*?" His nostrils flared, and his eyes narrowed.

Oh God, the place probably reeked of sex. *David* probably reeked of sex. "Nothing," he squeaked.

"David, did he—"

"No, that was Rory," David blurted out.

"*Rory?*"

As if answering to his name, Rory emerged from the living room, his arms folded self-consciously across his bare chest. "Uh, hi, Mark. Everything all right?"

Mark stared. "Apparently, yes. David, what the hell...?"

"Um. I'll give you the gory details tomorrow, but here's the short version: Xav is a lying liar who lies and, well, the extra business isn't going to be forthcoming and never was. Although he did offer to set me up in his City love nest. Spoiler: I declined."

Mark's face darkened. "That's despicable."

David was impressed, having never met anyone who could use that word and not subconsciously slip into a cartoon lisp. He gave a helpless shrug. "That's Xav. Anyway, um, sorry to worry you, but as you can see, I'm fine, so maybe we should let Rory stop flashing the neighbours?"

"Oh. Yes. Of course." Mark backed off from the doormat, then paused, looking between David and Rory. "So you two are...?"

"Yes," David said quickly. "See you tomorrow."

He shut the door.

Then he turned back to Rory, who was watching him warily. "So..."

"Uh. Yeah. So...?" Rory's tummy gave a loud rumble, and they both laughed a little hysterically.

"Dinner?" David suggested.

"Yeah. Dinner. Um. Think I'll go get a clean shirt."

CHAPTER THIRTY-SEVEN

It wasn't until they were halfway through cooking dinner that Rory plucked up the courage to ask the question that was on his mind.

Cos he *thought* David had been saying he didn't just want a shag, but, well, plenty of people had told Rory over the years that he wasn't the brightest spark in the shed, and he'd feel a lot better getting David to confirm that wasn't all it was for him.

Rory took a deep breath. "So, right, when you told Mark we were . . . what you told him, did you, um, mean it?"

David paused in his stirring. "Yes?"

"Sure?" Rory had to ask, cos he didn't exactly sound it.

"Not really. I mean, what precisely did I tell him?" It all came out in a nervous rush as David dropped the spoon in the pan and spun to face him.

"That you and me are boyfriends now?" Rory asked hopefully.

"Oh! Yes. That. Definitely." David beamed. "Yes. I'd like that."

"Good," Rory said, and put his arms around his bloke. "Me too."

Course, then he had to nuzzle into David's neck, cos it was right there and asking for it, and that led to them having a bit of a snog, and they ended up burning dinner, but that was okay. It was still mostly edible. And Rory had never liked that pan much anyhow.

The rest of the evening was pretty amazing. They spent it on the sofa, cuddled up in front of the telly, David making outrageous comments on everything. Rory was in fits.

A bit later, Rory was cleaning his teeth and idly staring at himself in the bathroom mirror while David waited for him in bed, it hit Rory all at once—he was a bloke with a boyfriend. He was a—well, not a gay bloke, cos he still fancied women, but not a straight bloke neither.

A bisexual bloke. No *curious* about it. And everyone was going to know, cos there was no way he was hiding it, cos he wasn't ashamed or nothing. Just . . . was everyone going to feel differently about him now?

Barry obviously did—had done even before there was anything to feel different about. And that was . . . Rory hated that, cos Barry was his best mate, and the thought of them not being mates anymore was like a flippin' big weight pressing down on his chest, but the bloke was *wrong*. He had to see that.

Didn't he?

Rory was pretty sure *he* felt different, mind. It was like . . . like the time he'd let the lads talk him into going on that ginormous bloody roller coaster, when they'd had a Spartans trip down to Thorpe Park. Sitting in that carriage after they'd chugged up to the top thinking, *Oh my God, what have I got myself into?*

His reflection grinned at him. That'd been bloody *brilliant*, that ride. And this would be too. Him and David. Wasn't like they'd be the only gay couple in the village, now was it?

Yeah. It was gonna be magic.

He rinsed his mouth out, turned out the light, and climbed into bed with his bloke.

David snuggled in to his side. "I could hear you in the bathroom, you know. Thinking."

Rory laughed. "Don't worry, mate. It ain't likely to happen again."

Next morning was . . . in one way, it was good, cos he woke up next to David. And in another it was bad, cos it was four thirty and he had to get straight out of bed for work while David rolled over with a pillow over his ears muttering, "*Oh, God, make it* stop."

Maybe he ought to get a quieter alarm clock. Or buy David some ear plugs. Yeah, that might be the answer.

He got ready for work as quietly as he could—he'd been getting used to doing that anyhow, since David had moved in—and set off for the delivery office.

It felt weird, walking in, knowing how much his life had changed and knowing they didn't have any idea. Like, this was just a normal day for all them, but for him, it was . . . it was the first full day of him and David being, well, him and David, which was flippin' *amazing*.

And nobody knew. Except him and David, obviously, and Mark, and probably Patrick now, and like as not Fen, but nobody *here*.

They didn't have a *clue*.

Then he realised Collette was giving him a funny look and waving her hand in front of his face. "Earth to Rory, anyone home?"

He blinked. "Uh, sorry. All right, love?"

"I'm fine, but I'm not sure about you. Magic mushrooms for breakfast, was it? It's either that or you're in love . . . Oh my God, are you in love? You are, aren't you."

"Um. Maybe?" Rory made a face, cos it just didn't sit right, lying about how he felt about David. "Yeah. Yeah, I am." He could tell he was grinning like an idiot, cos his cheeks were starting to ache.

"Oi, everyone, Rory's got a new woman in his life!"

Uh-oh. Heads, everywhere, turned, and there was a chorus of wolf-whistles and *Good on you, mate*. Some of the lads were clapping. "Uh . . ." Oh, sod it. "It ain't a woman," he said, and it felt like ripping off a scab.

There was silence for a long, long moment. Then Tel at the back yelled out, "Lock up your sheep"; somebody, Rory wasn't sure who, made a loud "Baaa"; and Raj chipped in with, "All the more for us, then," which got him bombarded with calls of *You wish* and *In your dreams, mate* mostly, but not exclusively, from the women.

Collette screamed out, "I knew it! It's that lodger of yours, innit? Rory Deamer, you old goat," and hugged him, which was nice, but also whispered in his ear, "You're gonna tell me *all* the details," which he wasn't so keen on.

Nobody said anything bad, like, at all. There had been one or two of the lads, not particular mates of his, he'd been worried about, but if they didn't approve, they kept it to themselves, which was good enough for Rory.

Still, it was a bit of a relief to get out on his round.

When Rory got home from work, he probably should've had a bit of a kip, cos he'd had a later night last night than he should have, what with . . . one thing and another.

Especially the other.

Course, when he put his head down on the sofa, he couldn't sleep, could he? Thinking about David getting back . . .

The clocks were on a bloody go-slow today, the bastards, and by the time five o'clock ticked round, Rory was practically camped out on his own doorstep, waiting for David.

Twelve hours was a long time, all right?

Maybe David thought so too, cos he was in the door by two minutes past and in Rory's arms two seconds later.

"Had a good day?" Rory asked, when David had stopped kissing him long enough for him to get a word out.

"Fantastic. Wonderful. Absolutely fabulous. Mark took me out to lunch, and Patrick came too, and he's being a *lot* nicer to me now. And guess what? It looks like I may not be job hunting after all. You know that charity Patrick works for, doing the fundraising? His assistant, Lex—that's Fen's friend—has decided to go and train as a locksmith, of all things, which leaves Patrick in a bit of a bind as apparently he's had *lots* of offers of better jobs from much bigger charities, but he doesn't want to leave SHARE totally in the lurch. So in the New Year, I'll start working with him on a trial basis—just to see if he *can* actually work with me without committing murder most foul—and if it works out, he'll train me up as his successor. Isn't that wonderful?"

"That's great, love." Rory didn't realise what he'd said until David's smile turned all tender and he got pulled into a clinch.

"Mm. Patrick said the trustees are going to *love* me." David frowned. "He said it with such an odd tone of voice, though. Oh well. I'm sure I'll find out. How was your day?"

"Uh, you know. Same old routine. Uh. Told the lads and lasses at work about us."

"Really?" David gave him a kiss that might have turned into something else if he hadn't broken it off. "Ooh, what did they say? Anything actionable?"

Rory laughed. "They were all dead good about it. Course, I dunno what they're saying behind me back, but what I don't know can't hurt me, right?"

"The Darwin awards would beg to differ, but I take your meaning. Thank you."

"What for?"

"For . . ." David looked away for a moment. "For having faith in me."

"Oi, why wouldn't I have faith in you? You're my bloke, aincha?"

It was a lot later, and Rory's bed was a lot more rumpled—just like they were—when Rory brought up the other thing that'd been on his mind. "I was thinking about giving Barry a bell. If you're okay with that. I know you and him never got on." Rory held his breath.

David's face softened. "Darling, he's your *friend*. Yes, he's a . . ."

He seemed to be struggling for words, which wasn't like him, so Rory helped him out. "Narrow-minded git? Yeah, but nobody ever changed anyone's opinions by telling them to piss off, did they? I wanna give him another chance."

"And you should." David kissed him. "I'd be a total hypocrite if I told you not to. And no, I'm not telling you who I'm talking about, because she was only doing what she thought was best for me, as always."

Huh. Rory had *known* David's mum hadn't exactly thought he was the greatest thing since sliced bread. "So you're okay with it? Even if it means us spending more time with him and stuff?"

"*Absolument.*"

Rory waited to make the call until after dinner, when he was pretty sure Barry wouldn't pick up his phone, cos this was one of his missus's nights out and it'd be bath time for the kiddies.

Maybe it wasn't the bravest thing to do, leaving a voice mail, but on the other hand, Rory wanted to give Barry time to think things over, instead of knee-jerk reacting. Cos Barry . . . He wasn't a bad sort. Mostly. But he tended to say stuff before he'd properly thought it through.

Rory took a deep breath and spoke after the beep. "It's me. Uh, Rory, but you probably know that, right? Anyhow, I wanted to let you know that, well, me and David, we're a . . . a thing now. Going out together and stuff. So. I just . . . Well, we both said a few things, that night at the pub, and I just wanted to say . . . I miss you, mate, all right? So if you wanna, you know, go for a beer or something . . . but if you don't, yeah, that's okay. So. You take care."

He hung up, breathing hard.

Then he went to find his boyfriend for a cuddle.

CHAPTER THIRTY-EIGHT

The following day at work, it was as if nothing had changed at all. Rory laughed at himself a bit for thinking it would. So, a bloke comes out as bi and the world keeps turning? Imagine that.

He'd just got home from his round when he got a call from Evie. "Oh, hello, love—"

"Rory? You've got to pick the kids up from school and have them overnight."

"Okay, but is everything all right?" She sounded a bit stressed.

"I'm in labour. Six days early. And flippin' Lewis is in flippin' Birmingham."

"What? Are you on your own, then?"

"I've got a friend coming over. She's going to take me to the hospital. But you—" she did some heavy breathing "—you've got to come and get their stuff."

"I'll be there in five."

He was there in not much more than that, and found her in the middle of packing the kids' bags, hauling clothes out of cupboards and pyjamas out of beds.

"Oi, let me do that. You sit down."

"Don't want to sit down. I've got to have something to take my mind off it. Jesus Christ, why did I ever agree to go through all this again?"

Rory kept silent.

They finished up together, and Rory loaded the bags in his car. Then he came back.

"You off, then?" Evie asked.

"Don't be daft. I'll wait here until your friend comes over."

"You don't have to—bloody hell—do that."

"Course I do. Not leaving you like this, am I? You want anything? Cup of tea? Back rub?"

She seemed tempted, but shook her head. "No. Ta. I'm okay."

"So is Lewis on his way home?"

"He'd better be. In a meeting, wasn't he? I had to leave a message." She huffed, then gave him a significant look. "Heard something interesting down the village."

"Yeah? Is it about them new houses they were talking about building?"

"No, you muppet. It was about you. And David."

"Oh. Right."

She gave him a funny sort of smile. "Congratulations. Hope he makes you happy."

"You're not . . . I dunno. You don't mind?"

"Why should I mind? It's the twenty-first century, isn't it? Plenty of blokes come out as gay now."

"Bi," Rory corrected her.

"Yeah? Whatever. It's not like the writing wasn't on the wall, anyhow, about you and him." Evie paused. "Aren't you going to ask me what I've decided about the kids?"

"Thought you had enough on your plate at the mo."

She laughed grimly. "Not wrong there. Rory, why didn't you fight me when I said they ought to live with me after we split up?"

Rory blinked. "You really want to go there now?"

"Yeah. Yeah, I do."

He took a deep breath. "I wasn't in a good way back then. It hurt, love, you going off with him and muggins here not having clue one until the day you left. Don't reckon I had much fight in me for a while. And, well, Leo was only tiny, and you're their mum . . ."

Her face screwed up in pain for a long moment before she spoke again. "Bollocks."

"What?"

"It's all a load of bollocks, that is. No, let me finish, will you? It's like . . . everyone assumes kids are better off with their mum, don't they? And that's just . . ." Evie shook her head. "I said I wanted them with me cos if I hadn't, everyone would've said what a crap mum

I was. What a cow, putting herself before her kids. But they were always more your kids than mine." Her hands on the kitchen counter went white-knuckled.

Rory waited for the contraction to pass.

"I used to watch you and them sometimes," she went on. "Playing in the garden or some stupid game round the house, and I'd feel so left out. You didn't *need* me, Rory. You *never* needed me. And I hated it. Hated you, sometimes."

"Evie . . . you know we all loved you."

"That's not the same. You . . . you and the kids, you're like this unit. This *family*. I was just there, doing the laundry and the cooking while you and them had fun."

"Hang on a minute, that ain't fair. I pulled my weight round the house. And you never *let* me do the cooking. I'd say, 'Why don't you let me get dinner?' and you'd be all, 'No, don't be daft, all I want is for you to get the kids out from under my feet.'"

Evie's lip wobbled. "I know, all right? It's just . . . when you're a mum, you're supposed to be great at everything—love being with the kids, love cooking. Bugger it."

Rory was fairly sure that was another contraction. "I never said you had to be, like, Supermum or nothing."

"No, but everyone else does. Even my mum—remember how snippy she got when she came round and caught you doing the hoovering?" Panting, she gave a soggy smile. "She used to say you'd go off and find yourself another woman, someone who didn't expect all that.

Rory laughed, although it came out bitter. "Got that one the wrong way round, didn't she?"

"I never meant to hurt you, you know that, don't you? It just happened, me and Lewis. And he was so . . . I felt like he needed me, you know?"

"Right." Rory really didn't want to hear it. "How about we concentrate on this little one, yeah? They're gonna need you pretty soon."

Too bloody soon, Rory reckoned. Those contractions were coming a bit thick and fast for his liking. And weren't babies quicker coming the more of them you had?

Evie smiled and glanced down at her bump. "This one . . . It's going to be different. I'm going to do things right this time. Lewis can pay for a cleaner and for meals out. I'm going to play with my kid. Be a mum who *likes* being a mum. And that's why I'm going to go along with what you said. Jesus *bloody* Christ."

Rory's breath caught. Had he heard that right? "You're—"

"Yeah. Me and Lewis talked it over, and we both think it makes sense. At least for the next six months. Well, Lewis reckoned a year, but we'll see how it goes. You have Lucy and Leo during the week. We'll have them every other weekend. Maybe not for the first few weeks after this one's born, mind. *Bugger* it."

Bloody hell, he was getting his kids back. It was like winning the lottery, flying to the moon, and getting drunk on champagne all rolled into one. He couldn't wait to call David and tell him the good news. Grinning wildly for pure happiness, Rory looked at his watch. "This mate of yours, how long's she gonna be?"

"She's got to drop off her baby at her mum's first. Maybe an hour?"

He came back down to earth with a bump. "An hour? Not sure this nipper's gonna wait that long. You got a bag packed? I'm taking you in."

"You sure you want to . . . Oh, fuck it. Yeah. Bag's in the kitchen. *Shit*."

It was well weird taking Evie to the hospital, just like he had with Lucy and Leo. Not that he was in any danger of forgetting this wasn't his kid on the way, but apart from that . . .

"Do you want me to come in with you?" he asked her, as they checked her in to the maternity ward.

"What? Christ, no. You've done your bit. All I want is a shitload of drugs, and then I won't care who's with me. You go and make sure you're on time for Lucy and Leo."

Rory felt a bit bad about the wash of relief. He'd always hated seeing her in pain, wanted to do whatever he could to make it better, and he wouldn't have abandoned her if she'd wanted him . . . But yeah, watching her have Lewis's kid? He hadn't fancied that. It wasn't jealousy—he had David now, didn't he? But it would've brought back a lot of memories, the bad ones tainting the good.

"Cheers, love. Good luck and all," he said.

"Thanks." She screwed her eyes shut and panted for a minute. "You've been really great. Makes me feel . . . I'm sorry about how it all turned out. You know that, don't you?"

"Course, love," Rory lied. She probably meant it at the moment. Or meant something like it, anyhow. "Now you concentrate on having that kid, all right?"

CHAPTER THIRTY-NINE

David had been fondly anticipating a warm welcome when he got home from work.

He hadn't anticipated it coming from two excited children, however. Leo ran to hug him as he stepped in the door, and while he was still reeling from the unexpected onslaught, Lucy yelled out, "We're coming to live with you!" and proceeded to bounce up and down.

Rory emerged from the living room with a somewhat shifty expression. "Uh, guess what? Evie said yes."

"That's wonderful! Leo-*lapinou*, could I possibly have my legs back for a moment? I'd like to kiss your daddy." Released, David went to embrace his boyfriend, swiftly banishing a pang of regret for one or two highly pleasurable activities which would now have to be deferred until after 9 p.m. Then he drew back. "Is this okay? In front of *les enfants*?"

Rory grinned. "Don't worry. I warned 'em."

True enough, Leo was totally ignoring their semipublic display of affection in favour of gleefully clomping about in David's second-favourite pair of loafers, while Lucy eyed her father and David with satisfaction written all over her face. "Daddy says I can have my room back now."

"But of course." David pulled Rory back into his arms. "The handover appears to have been accomplished remarkably quickly," he murmured in Rory's ear.

"Nah, well, it wasn't quite like that. Evie's gone into labour early."

"Mummy's in hospital having *that baby*." Lucy, bless her, didn't sound like she'd been looking forward to the event.

"That's good news, isn't it? I mean, it's not *too* early, is it?" David glanced at Rory for confirmation.

He shook his head. "Nah, only six days. Should be fine."

"Babies smell," Lucy said with disgust. "And they cry *all* the *time*." She cast a guilty glance at her brother. "Except Leo. He was okay."

David raised an eyebrow. "I'm guessing that when we move your toys over, dollies aren't really going to feature, are they?"

"Dolls are boring. They don't *do* anything. Can we have fish and chips for tea? Daddy said we could if you said yes." Her folded arms and beady little eyes made it clear that *no* was an option best avoided.

"Of course we can, *ma choupinette*." David quite liked fish. And there would undoubtedly be no shortage of volunteers to eat up his chips for him. "Just let me get changed first."

"*And* you finish your homework, love," Rory put in. "I'll, um, pop up and help David get changed."

"That's what Lewis says when he wants to have cuddles with Mummy," Lucy said, pulling out her school books.

She said it offhandedly, and for once it was Leo who sent them the suspicious look.

David stifled a laugh at Rory's impressively guilty expression.

"Uh, yeah, love? Fancy that."

Leo tugged on Rory's arm. "Can I play on your phone, Daddy?"

It was the longest sentence David had heard him utter voluntarily. He beamed and blinked his eyes rapidly against a speck of sentiment that appeared to have got lodged there.

Rory was smiling too as he handed over his phone. "As long as you don't disturb your sister."

They managed to snatch a quick snog in David's bedroom, which they had to stop a *lot* sooner than David would have liked. He reminded himself there would be plenty of opportunity later for all that and more, and cast a fond glance at the fairies flitting across the walls. They had been pleasant companions, but David couldn't regret leaving them behind.

Gregory, for his part, had a conspiratorial glint in his eye. Bless. Then again, he undoubtedly knew full well he'd be moving into Rory's bedroom too. He was probably looking forward to the show.

"You sure you're gonna be okay with all this?" Rory asked. "It's a lot to take on."

David stroked his stubble-roughened cheek fondly. "I suppose you are, but the children make up for it."

Rory laughed. "Git."

"*Moi*?" David forced himself to be serious. "I know it seems a lot all at once, but . . . it feels right. And I *have* always loved a challenge."

Rory took a breath, as if he was about to say something, but then there was a loud shout of "I've finished!" from downstairs, and he went down to check over Lucy's homework instead.

They strolled down the hill to the chip shop in the gathering dusk, the children running on a few yards ahead with strict instructions to stop when they got to the road.

Rory coughed. "So, uh, Evie called while you were upstairs. She's had the baby. Turned up two minutes after Lewis did, she reckoned. Both of 'em are doing well. They've called him Logan."

"That's nice. Their own little Wolverine," David said vaguely, distracted. He'd just noticed something. He turned to give Rory a quizzical look. "You're holding my hand. In public."

"Oh. Sorry, mate. You don't do that?" Rory let go.

That wasn't exactly what David had been aiming for. "*I* do. But since when do *you*?"

Rory's forehead creased. "I always held Evie's hand when we was out. And Jenni's. 'Cept when she was mad at me."

"Yes, but they're *women*."

"Oh. Right. So it's not, like, a thing gay blokes do?" The frown deepened. "Huh. I never really thought about it, but you never see Mark and Patrick holding hands. Or Mr. Emeny and his bloke. Sorry, mate. You gotta tell me if I start treating you like a girl again. Old dogs, new tricks, all that."

David stared. "Rory. Dearest, darling Rory. Sweet, innocent Rory. It's not that gay couples don't *want* to hold hands. It's just that one develops a certain caution against doing it in public. If, God forbid, we should split up and you find yourself enamoured of another man, *please* tell me you won't go striding through the centre of, say, Brixton engaging in public displays of affection."

Rory scratched his head. "Uh. You're saying we'd get a kicking? That wouldn't happen round here, though, would it?"

"It can happen *anywhere*." David felt, for once, cast in the role of blinkered Horatio. What must it be like to be so certain of public approval for one's love life? "It's happened in Brighton, which is generally agreed to be the last place in Britain to visit if you don't want to witness any non-straight goings-on. People, even those who pride themselves upon being *tolerant*, don't like to have two men together thrust upon their notice."

"That ain't fair."

"Congratulations. You are now a fully fledged graduate of the University of Life."

"That's . . . that's shit."

"Ooh, a double first."

"I mean, that's *really* shit."

"Sorry, no extra credit available. Would you like instead to hold a minute's silence for your lost straight privilege?"

Rory's jaw firmed. "No. I'd like to hold my bloke's hand, though. And I don't give a monkey's who gets their knickers in a twist about it." He suited his actions to his words.

David felt a *frisson* at his hand being captured so masterfully, and twined his fingers into Rory's as firmly as possible, in case they started getting skittish once more. He hoped this was the right thing to do.

Just as he was starting to relax, he noticed the children had come to a halt a few yards ahead of them.

A dark, vaguely man-shaped figure lumbered into view.

It was Barry.

He looked at Rory and David, his gaze dropping to their joined hands. David swallowed and felt Rory give him a reassuring little extra squeeze.

Barry squared his shoulders and marched over to them. "All right, Rory? Dave? Listen, mate, I, uh, I been talking to the missus—gave me a proper ear-bashing, she did—and, uh, I think I might have been a bit out of order on your birthday. Wanted to, you know, um, apologise." Barry swallowed, his Adam's apple bobbing, and David was surprised to find himself feeling a soupçon of sympathy for the man, quite beside being far too happy for Rory to correct Barry on his name.

"It ain't been the same without you to have a pint and a laugh with," Barry went on with a plaintive note. "So what if you're a bit bent? Who gives a monkey's? You're still me best mate, same as you always been." He sounded as if he might be quoting Mrs. Barry there. Clearly she was a woman of great good sense—apart from her somewhat questionable choice of husband. "So. No hard feelings, yeah?" The Adam's apple got another workout.

Rory took an audible breath. "Course, mate. Uh, we're just off down the chippie, wanna join us?"

Barry nodded jerkily. "Yeah. That'd be great."

David's heart swelled. He could almost hear sweeping music playing. It was a beautiful moment.

"Daddy!" Lucy snapped. "Come *on*. We're *hungry*."

Rory laughed, and David found himself sharing a sympathetic glance with Barry, of all people. "All right, all right." Rory ruffled his daughter's hair, ignoring her scowl. "No need to get your kecks in a kerfuffle."

Later, while Rory was bathing the children, David rang Hen to tell her the news—not without a certain amount of foreboding. He was fairly sure she wouldn't disown him for his choice of romantic partner, but he'd never been able to bear disappointing her.

"Rory and I are together," he blurted out instead of his usual greeting, and braced himself.

"Then I'm very happy for you."

"You are?" It possibly came out as something of a squawk.

"Oh, darling. What must you think of me? I've had some time to think since we last spoke—I won't ask what *you've* been doing since then," Hen added in a tone so arch it would have a neo-Gothic architect in raptures. "But you were right. Ursula would have been miserable if she'd married my Armand. And so would you."

"You mean, aside from the incest factor?"

"Yes, darling. I should never have let you think your Rory didn't care for you. I'm sorry. I won't do it again."

"You won't? Can I have that in writing?"

She laughed, and all was well with the world. "I think that would be setting a dangerous precedent, don't you? But I will try. If he's what makes you happy."

"He is. He does." That pesky allergy was playing up again. David fumbled for a tissue.

"Then give him my love, and I'll come and see the two of you soon."

"Four," David corrected. "The children are coming to live with us. Evie said yes."

"And here I was worried your life with Rory might lack excitement. Then may I hope you'll be looking for a larger house?"

"Ideally, yes, but we'll have to wait and see how my new job works out. Ooh, did I tell you I got a new job? Anyway, we'll probably put twin beds in the fairy bedroom for the children for now, until my employment situation is more certain and we know what we'll be able to afford."

". . . I may be able to help you out there, actually."

"Hen! We wouldn't want to take your money. You should be spending it on you."

"Ah, but darling, it isn't, in fact, all my money. Quite a lot of it is yours."

"I know I left my Winnie-the-Pooh piggy bank behind when I left home, but there can't have been *that* much in it."

"No, Davey-darling. It's from the sale of the house. When I sold it, I got far more than I needed for the cottage, so I put the money into trust for you until you're twenty-five. But we can break that, if you need it sooner, although your birthday's only a few months away in any case."

"You never told me all that."

"It never seemed to be a good idea, before. You'd only have spent it on something unsuitable. Or some*one*." She laughed, and David could picture her lovely face crinkling up into what he felt strongly should be described as a happiness of wrinkles. "And you seemed to be having such fun trying to find yourself a sugar daddy."

"I was not! I just prefer a certain maturity in a partner."

"So I've seen. *But* up until now, you've always preferred a certain minimum bank balance."

"That was a coincidence."

"No, darling, it was a trend. I'm not at all displeased to see you bucking it now. Money isn't everything."

"So you're happy I'm with Rory?" David couldn't help grasping for confirmation that they had her blessing.

"I'm sure, once I get to know him properly, I shall like him very much, and I can't wait to meet the children."

"You'll adore Leo."

"Not Lucy?"

"I suspect it'll be more a relationship of mutual respect, there."

"Well, forewarned is forearmed. I'll come prepared to spoil them rotten. It *is* a grandmother's prerogative, you know. Now, I'll get the solicitors to write to you with details of the fund, and you can draw on it when you want."

David considered. While it would be rather nice to have everything handed to him on a plate . . . "Thank you, but I'd like to try and make it on my own two feet for now, Henny-Penny. Although it *is* good to know the money's there, should we need it."

"Just don't make compromises you don't have to. Oh, and you should make sure you get a piano. I've missed hearing you play. In fact, that will be my housewarming present to you, when you move."

"Hen, you're a darling. Now, I have to go, as I can hear the sweet voices of angelic children demanding stories with menaces."

Hen laughed. "You would almost think they were related to you, wouldn't you?"

They said their good-byes, and David skipped downstairs to read *Francesca the Football Fairy* to the children, his heart light.

Rory was lying in wait for him in the hallway. "You got a mo?" he asked shyly.

David sent a significant look at the living room door. "Possibly, although only *one* mo or Lucy will be out for my blood." Even as he said it, he slipped into Rory's warm, strong, perfect arms.

Rory pulled him close. "There was something I wanted to say earlier, and I never got the chance. I mean, you never know what's gonna happen in your life, and I don't want it to not get said . . . I know we've only known each other a short time, and I ain't expecting you to feel the same, but, well, I, uh . . ."

About to burst with happiness, David couldn't wait for him to finish. "I love you too."

Rory's face lit up like a Christmas tree. "You do? That's . . . that's just . . . Oh, sod it."

He squeezed David tight and kissed him.

David wasn't *certain*, but he had the strongest impression that, in the distance, fairy bells were ringing.

Explore more of *The Shamwell Tales* at:
riptidepublishing.com/titles/universe/shamwell-tales

Dear Reader,

Thank you for reading JL Merrow's *Spun!*

We know your time is precious and you have many, many entertainment options, so it means a lot that you've chosen to spend your time reading. We really hope you enjoyed it.

We'd be honored if you'd consider posting a review—good or bad—on sites like **Amazon, Barnes & Noble, Kobo, Goodreads, Twitter, Facebook, Tumblr,** and your blog or website. We'd also be honored if you told your friends and family about this book. Word of mouth is a book's lifeblood!

For more information on upcoming releases, author interviews, blog tours, contests, giveaways, and more, please sign up for our weekly, spam-free newsletter and visit us around the web:

> **Newsletter**: tinyurl.com/RiptideSignup
> **Twitter**: twitter.com/RiptideBooks
> **Facebook**: facebook.com/RiptidePublishing
> **Goodreads**: tinyurl.com/RiptideOnGoodreads
> **Tumblr**: riptidepublishing.tumblr.com

Thank you so much for Reading the Rainbow!

RiptidePublishing.com

ACKNOWLEDGEMENTS

With thanks to all who helped with this book: Kristin Matherly, Susan Sorrentino, Pender Mackie, Jennifer Bales, and of course my intrepid local postman!

ALSO BY JL MERROW

ABOUT THE AUTHOR

JL Merrow is that rare beast, an English person who refuses to drink tea. She read Natural Sciences at Cambridge, where she learned many things, chief amongst which was that she never wanted to see the inside of a lab ever again. Her one regret is that she never mastered the ability of punting one-handed whilst holding a glass of champagne.

She writes across genres, with a preference for contemporary gay romance and mysteries, and is frequently accused of humour. Her novel *Slam!* won the 2013 Rainbow Award for Best LGBT Romantic Comedy, and her novella *Muscling Through* and novel *Relief Valve* were both EPIC Awards finalists.

JL Merrow is a member of the Romantic Novelists' Association, International Thriller Writers, Verulam Writers and the UK GLBTQ Fiction Meet organising team.

Find JL Merrow on Twitter as @jlmerrow, and on Facebook at facebook.com/jl.merrow

For a full list of books available, see: jlmerrow.com or JL Merrow's Amazon author page: viewauthor.at/JLMerrow.

Enjoy more stories like
Spun!
at RiptidePublishing.com!

Sweet Young Thang
ISBN: 978-1-62649-033-8

Clickbait
ISBN: 978-1-62649-495-4

Earn Bonus Bucks!

Earn 1 Bonus Buck for each dollar you spend. Find out how at
RiptidePublishing.com/news/bonus-bucks.

Win Free Ebooks for a Year!

Pre-order coming soon titles directly through our site and you'll
receive one entry into a drawing for a chance to win free books for
a year! Get the details at RiptidePublishing.com/contests.

45957337R00181

Made in the USA
Columbia, SC
23 December 2018